COLLEEN SNYDER

DESPAIR

Colleen Snyder

Editor: Cynthia Hickey
Book Design by Forget Me Not Romances

Fiction and Literature: Inspirational
Christian Romantic Suspense

ISBN: 978-1-0881-6166-1

A BRIEF HISTORY OF NAMES

Collin Walker = Caitlin Winger = Cane

Born Caitlin Winger, at fourteen, she was abandoned to the streets. Posing as a boy for safety's sake, she took the name "Walker." She added the name "Collin" "because I got tired of people 'calling' me Walker." At eighteen, she had her name legally changed to Collin Walker.

Cane is the nickname **only** her twin brother calls her. It started with his inability to pronounce "Caitlin," which sounded more like "Ca-yun." From that came "Cane."

Erin Winger = A-One

His name was to be "Aaron" at birth. His father was so incensed at his being born second that he declared, "If he can't beat a girl out of the womb, he doesn't deserve a man's name." Robert Winger changed the spelling from Aaron to Erin.

Erin thought about changing his name but learned the name can be for either a male or a female. In Ireland, "Erin" means "the one of Ireland." In the end, he decided to keep his birth name, considering it a badge of honor that Robert Winger could not take from him.

A-One is the nickname **only** his twin sister calls him. It started with her inability to pronounce "Erin," which sounded more like "A-won." From that came "A-One."

TUESDAY

Erin stared at the computer screen. The family tree, traced by DNA, branched and flowered and twisted. He knew the limbs, the assortments of aunts, uncles, cousins. He'd become familiar with the offshoots of grand-uncles and great-great-greats. All on his father's side. But his mother's side…

There had only been the name. Pulled from the marriage license found buried deep in a pile of papers hidden in a box of legal tax records yet to be disposed of. Felicity Meadows. Daughter of Catherine Peters and David Meadows. People Erin had no memories of. His mother passed when he and his twin sister Collin—Caitlin, at the time—were five.

But the marker…

The marker which indicated a DNA match on the maternal side. Erin had clicked on the link out of curiosity, thinking it might lead to some cousins or remaining aunts or uncles on his mother's side.

But there it sat. A sibling. Three siblings. A half-sister. Two half-brothers on the maternal side. And the first birth date…seven years after he and Collin were born. *After?? How is that even possible?*

It had to be a mistake. Had to be. His mom died. He didn't remember a funeral. Five years old? Who remembers something like that? Who takes a five-year-old to their mother's funeral?

But the marker… The names…

Erin stared at the screen. Did he want to know? Did he really? Was he ready to find out how much more of his life had been built on a lie? How much more had been stolen from him and Collin? *Our mother? Mom? We have a mom?*

Two questions rattled in his brain. *Where?* And most important, *Why?*

* * *

Erin drove to the Farrell house and let himself in the back door. Quietly. In case the triplets were asleep.

Fat chance. One might be. Two at most. But all three together? No. Never happen. Erin slipped in through the kitchen, its counters a jumble of clean laundry waiting to be folded. Through the dining room, past the table loaded with boxes of diapers, empty (clean) bottles waiting to be filled. Finally, into the living room.

Right as always. Collin sat in her rocking chair, tiny Talitha draped across his sister's shoulder. Collin had dressed in jeans and sloppy t-shirt. But that was as far as the self-improvement had gone. Her hair had been shoved into a clip and moved out of the way of clasping baby hands. Caleb and Joshua, the masculine two-thirds of the triplets, lay asleep on a blanket on the floor. Collin rocked and hummed and tried to put the littlest Farrell back to sleep. Or to sleep. Didn't matter.

Erin slipped in and picked the infant up. He kept his voice low. "Give her to me. I have the touch."

Collin leaned into her brother's arm. "Yes, you do."

Erin snuggled the little girl close to his chest and danced slowly around the room, crooning. The two-month-old (by "brought-home" date, not "birth-date," as the two months in NICU didn't count as "real" days) yawned and cooed and closed her eyes. Erin transferred her quietly and successfully to the playpen. He patted her tummy to make sure she settled, stood up, and smiled at Collin. He held his hands out wide. "It's all in the moves, Cane. All in the moves."

She shook her head at him. Erin walked over and kissed the top of her head. "You look terrible."

"Thank you for the vote of confidence, A-One. This motherhood gig is exhausting."

"I believe it. Jeff asleep?"

"Yeah. He got up with them during the night, so I could sleep." She leaned back in her chair. "You think the Lord will ever let us get them on a schedule we can all live with?"

"Probably. In about five years."

"Thanks a lot. You're a bundle of good news this morning."

Erin walked into the kitchen. "You want coffee?"

"Pleeeeeeeeease."

Erin chuckled and made a fresh pot. He guessed the last one had been made by Jeff during the night. No coffee filter. *That's our Jeffrey.*

While he waited for the pot to finish, he straightened the countertops, put the dirty dishes in the dishwasher, folded a load of baby t-shirts sitting on the table, and generally made himself useful. As soon as the amber brew finished dripping, he filled two cups and carried them into the family room. He handed one to Collin and sat down across from her.

Collin sipped the brew and let out a satisfied but quiet aww of satisfaction. "No grounds. Thank you."

"Maybe you should rethink the prohibition on single-serve makers. At least until they're out of diapers."

"If I have to chew through too many more cups of coffee, I might." She leaned back in her chair. "Okay, baby brother, you're not here to rescue me from my children. What's going on?"

Erin stared into the cup. "I got a hit on Mom's side of the family."

Collin's eyes lit up. "Really? This soon? I thought it would take longer, somehow."

"Yeah, like never?" Erin considered his words. "It's…it's a ninety-nine percent match."

"Wow. That's good. Grandfather?"

"No." Erin held Collin's eyes. "Half-siblings."

Collin stared at him. Her eyes widened, narrowed, widened, dropped, finally looked up at him. "You're sure?"

"I'm sure the site is giving me those results. Two brothers and a sister. The oldest boy would have been born about seven years after we were. He'd be about twenty-two. Maybe twenty-three."

Collin stared at her babies. "You know what that means?"

"I know a whole lot of things it means. Which one are you thinking of?"

"Let's start with our mother may still be alive." Collin cocked her head to look at her brother.

"Right. That's the easy one." Erin sipped his drink.

Collin's eyes focused on something far away in her memory.

"Then comes how and when and where and why and what do we do about it?"

"That's pretty much what I came up with, yeah."

Collin took a long drink from her mug. "Wow."

"Yeah." Erin stared at the floor.

They both fell silent, listening to the triplets breathe.

Collin rocked. "The babies could have grandparents. Not ones in prison—real grandparents."

"And aunts and uncles who don't hate them for being yours and mine."

Collin cocked her head and looked at him. "Yours?"

"My blood. Not mine, mine. But related to me. You knew what I meant." Erin scowled at his twin.

Collin smiled. "I know. I wanted to lighten the moment."

"Did it, too." Erin laughed.

Collin's smile disappeared. "What do you want to do about this?"

"I want to contact them." Erin leaned forward in the recliner. "I want to know all the answers to all the questions. I'm half afraid of what we'll find, but after what we've already learned about our past..."

Collin shook her head. "Finding out your father and uncles murdered their father before we were born. And Grandmother put them up to it."

"And hid the evidence so you would find it when you inherited everything..."

Collin held up her hand. "Stop. We're not going to rehash the litany of wrongs the Winger side of the family has done to either of us. We've moved on."

"Right. But now, we have a mother and a new past to deal with. And we're back to square one." Erin rocked in his chair.

"Did it give you an address? Like what state, maybe?"

"They're here. In Ohio. I got that much from the site."

Collin's mouth dropped. "Here?" She closed her mouth, sat back, and rocked. After a moment, she whispered, "You think she knows us?"

"I don't know, Cane. But I'm going to find out."

"Find out what?" Jeff stumbled into the room, but quietly. "I smelled coffee. And it wasn't mine."

Erin chuckled. "Sit. I'll get it."

Jeff leaned over and kissed Collin. "Morning, milady."

"Morning, sir."

Erin carried the cup in for Jeff. "Here you go. No grounds."

"Thank you. You need to move in here, bro, and help us keep this place going." Jeff took a long drink. The man choked on the heat but swallowed it anyhow.

"Hard to impress a woman with a job title of 'Manny.'"

Collin's mouth crinkled. "I thought you were well beyond trying to impress Vy. She loves you as you are."

"Yeah, but I still have all those aunts and uncles to win over. I'm still a work in progress with them."

Jeff chuckled. "Which is why marrying you came easy, milady. No family approval to get. Except Erin, and he already liked me."

"Truth." Erin looked at Collin and raised his eyebrows. He motioned with his head toward Jeff. His sister nodded. Erin began, "We…uh…think we've found some relatives on the maternal side of our DNA."

"Really? That's good, right?" Jeff looked pleased.

"Could be. Except it's from our mom."

Jeff frowned at Erin sideways. "That's what maternal DNA is, bro. From your mom's side."

Erin shook his head. "No, I mean, it's our mom's DNA. She's alive. Maybe. And she's had three children from another marriage. We've got two brothers and a sister we didn't know existed. Maybe." He waited for Jeff to process the information.

Jeff's eyes moved from Erin to Collin to the babies back to Erin. "Wow."

"Your wife's words exactly. Except she said it backward."

Two sets of eyes rolled. Erin shrugged and smiled. "A little levity now and then."

Jeff sneered at him. "Very little." He addressed Collin. "Is this something you want to look into?"

Collin rocked in her chair. "I don't know. I haven't had time to consider it." She pointed to Erin. "What about you?"

"I'm torn. Part of me wants to meet the siblings. Part of me is afraid of the answers I'll get to my questions if we meet our mother. Part of me is afraid she won't want to meet us."

Collin smiled gently. "Any other parts of you have opinions?"

Erin stared at the ceiling, squinted. "Probably. But not right this moment."

Caleb wiggled on the floor, put his fist in his mouth, and began sucking on it. Jeff picked up the still-sleeping infant and placed him on his shoulder. "Shhh, little one. Don't wake up the others. It's not time yet." Jeff eyed Erin over the head of the baby. "What are you going to do?"

"I'll make first contact and see if they want to answer. That's how the game is played."

Collin nodded. "And keep me posted of what and who you find. I may not be ready to meet our mother, but yeah, more aunts and uncles for the babies would be fun."

"Except I'll have to invite them to the wedding. We were trying to keep this a small affair, under a thousand, you know?" He raised his hands in despair.

Collin laughed. "Yeah, I know. There's always someone you forgot to include who needs a last-minute invite."

Erin sighed. "I know. Vy keeps saying we should elope. I'd do it, but I'm afraid of her mom and dad. Especially her mom. She nails me with a look and asks, 'Are you taking care of my daughter the way she deserves?' To which the answer is no, but only because Vy deserves the world and everything in it. I might be able to make a small down payment on it, but it will never be nearly enough."

"You know she loves you. And you treat her with absolute respect."

"At least that part her dad agrees on. I wouldn't dare not respect her. All those sisters? Yikes!"

He checked his watch. "I need to go. I've got pre-marriage counseling in an hour, and I don't want to be late."

"Who's it with?"

"One of the pastors from her church. Brother Tim. He'll be the one performing the ceremony. If we ever get to that point."

"Joint counseling, or just you?"

"Joint to start. If he feels the need, we'll go to individual. I'm hoping he sees we're perfectly compatible and will agree there's not a reason under Heaven why we shouldn't get married and expect to live happily ever after."

Collin dropped her gaze to the floor. "Oh, Erin. You do need counseling. I'm not sure marriage counseling will solve it, though."

"Hey, that's another story. One Vy will tell me about, I'm sure." Erin rose, blew kisses to the babies so as not to disturb them, kissed Collin's forehead, bumped fists with Jeff, and showed himself out the door.

He checked his emails before he started the car. Six read, "You have a match!" in the subject line. *Great. Fantastic. Who thought this would be a good idea?*

Me, I know. Don't remind me. Oh, well. He'd look at them at home. And turn the phone on silent.

* * *

Erin waited for Vy in front of the Calvary Chapel building on West and Cedar. Vy had been attending the church there since she was a babe in arms, so the story went. It would be the venue for their wedding. *"All Johnson babies get married and buried here. Been that way for a hundred years."* Erin muttered, "Yes, Aunt Viola. Of course, Aunt Viola. Whatever you say, Aunt Viola."

Vy's namesake. And the self-appointed family matriarch. *At least she adores me. I don't think I'd have a chance with Vy if she didn't.* Erin chuckled to himself. *I love her, too. She's a great lady.*

Vy tapped on the window to the car. Erin looked up and smiled. His whole being smiled. He slipped out of the vehicle and reached his hand out for her. "Hello, beautiful."

Her skin, a glorious mahogany, glowed against the gold ring on her left hand. "Almost-afternoon yourself, sir. How are you?"

The couple held hands as they walked into the building. Erin brushed the snow off Vy's coat and hat. Her hair, as dark as her skin, cut in soft waves circling her face. "Ready for the interrogation."

She shoved him with her shoulder. "I hardly think it will be an interrogation, Mr. Winger."

"Not that it wouldn't be worth it, mind you. I'll go through anything to marry you."

Vy smiled with her eyes. "You keep saying that, sir, and I may take you up on it."

He squeezed her hand. "I hope so."

They waited outside of Brother Tim's office for ten minutes while he "got ready" for their appointment. Erin's nervousness increased. *What's to get ready? Firing squad?*

Finally, the door opened, and Tim waved them through. "Come

in, Vy. Come in, Mr. Winger, is it?"

Erin shook hands with the man. His hand actually disappeared into Brother Tim's. Six-foot something tall. Weight to match his height. His grip felt firm but not intimidating. Skin tone darker than Vy. Coal-black hair, with only a few stray reminders of age in evidence. He pointed to the chairs, one on either end of the desk. No couch. *Oh, rats. No getting hints from Vy. This could be difficult...*

Tim sat in his chair between the two. "How can I help you today?"

Erin deferred to Vy. "We're here for pre-marriage counseling, Brother Tim." She wrinkled her nose at him, her eyes smiling. "Why else does a young couple come to you?"

He raised his eyebrows. "You aren't the usual young couple I see. Most of them are much younger. Much younger." He looked at Erin. "How old are you, Mr. Winger?"

"Erin, please. I'm twenty-nine."

Brother Tim turned away from Erin. Almost dismissing him. "And Vy, I know how old you are. Seems like just yesterday we baptized you in the river at summer camp." His smile was broad, and his eyes sparkled.

Vy ducked her head. "It's been a bit longer than yesterday, Brother Tim. I'm twenty-six."

Tim drawled, "So you've been walking with Jesus fourteen years now, right?"

Vy clicked her tongue. "I wouldn't say all fourteen of them, Brother Tim. I admit some of those years were spent walking closer than others." Vy sat up straighter in her chair.

Tim waved off her protest. "But you were coming here even during those times. Which means you were hearing the Word of the Lord."

"I may have been hearing it, but I wouldn't say I always listened." Vy's eyes narrowed, if only slightly.

Tim laughed. "Which is true of all of us, Vy. Some days, we listen better than others. But your walk has always been exemplary. You've served in this church since you were sixteen. You assisted the children's department, taught Sunday school, and been faithful to come every Sunday. I've looked at your attendance. I wish all our people had your devotion to being here."

Erin felt a twitch in his gut. He breathed out. *Speak truth.*

Nothing but truth.

Tim turned to Erin. The smile left the big man's face and eyes. His look turned stern. "And you, Mr. Winger? You do know the Lord as your personal Savior, don't you?" It came out more like a threat than an inquiry.

Erin nodded. "Yes, sir. It will be four years in August since I accepted Him. I've walked as close as I can since then."

Tim's voice became cool. "There's none of us walk as close as we can, Mr. Winger. We all have room for improvement." The man behind the desk glared at Erin.

Erin lifted his chin. "And I'll be the first to admit I'm a work in progress, sir. I have a long way to go."

"Why such a late start, Mr. Winger?" Tim made some notes on the writing pad in front of him.

"Erin, please. I wasn't raised in a home that acknowledged Jesus as Lord. The only god my father recognizes is money. It wasn't until the Lord freed me from my father's influence that I met Him, accepted Him, and came to own Him as Lord and Savior."

Tim's eyebrows rose. "Four years ago. You were twenty-five and still living with your mommy and daddy? Were you in college, Mr. Winger?" The insult was clear. And deliberate.

Erin saw Vy's eyes darken. He smiled at her. "No, Brother Tim. Not in college. But living with my father, yes. My mother died when my sister and I were five. I had an accident which left me paralyzed from the waist down at fourteen. The Lord healed me after I turned twenty-five. He freed me from my wheelchair and from my father's abuse and control. It's a debt I will never be able to repay Him, but I'll spend my life trying."

Vy relaxed slightly. Tim snorted. A little snort. "I see. And this father who worships money. Where is he now? Will he have opportunity to interfere in your lives together going forward?"

"My father and his two brothers are in federal prison. Life without parole for murder. Among other things." *If he doesn't ask, I'm not going there. Let the other things stay 'things.'*

Tim's eyes narrowed. "So you had a rough upbringing. How—"

Erin interrupted. "No, Brother Tim."

Tim corrected sharply, "It's Pastor Tim for you, Mr. Winger." He glared hard at Erin.

Erin felt the check in his spirit. *Do not answer in like manner. The Lord will uphold you.* "Forgive me. Pastor Tim." Erin kept his face solemn. "My father's greed is the corporate kind. The Lord delivered me from his influence and from the vices my father worked to instill in me. I can say money does not own me. Power does not own me. Stupidity may still have a foothold, but Vy is working on chasing it out."

Erin smiled at Vy. She chuckled. "Yes, I am. But the Lord did a good job on you first, Erin. I have no complaints."

Tim harrumphed and tapped his desk. "We'll see what the personality tests reveal. "

Erin nodded. "They will show Vy is perfect in every way and deserves someone far better than me. Her only character flaw is she loves a person so far below her standing he can't conceive why she loves him."

Vy lifted her chin. "She loves him because he first loved the Lord. And he lay down his life to save mine more than once. And he's gentle and fun and forgiving and makes me smile. And I want to spend the rest of my life knowing him better."

Tim cleared his throat. "All very impressive. Both of you. Wonderful sentiments. Unfortunately, sentiment won't hold a marriage together." He folded his hands and lay them on his desk. And glared at Erin.

Erin held Tim in his gaze. "No, sir, it won't. Only commitment to the Lord and to each other will. Along with hard work to put the other first in all things. To think of the other as more important than ourselves. To ask every morning, 'What would Jesus want me to do?' and do it."

Vy leaned in and took Erin's hand. "Reading the Word together. Praying together. Devoting ourselves to His service. Working to make each other the very best version of ourselves we can be in the Lord." She smiled at Tim, but she put a challenge in it. "And we've been doing so every day since the Lord brought us together. Mostly in groups or over the internet. We are careful to keep ourselves from temptation. We want the Lord to honor our union."

Tim sat back. Almost as if bored. "Very interesting. I hear all the right words. But right words can quickly vanish when one partner is unequally yoked with another." Again, he glared at Erin.

Erin drew in a silent breath. "Are you referring to our races,

Pastor?"

"I'm referring to Vy having walked with the Lord all her life, and you, by your own admission, only knowing of Him for four." He leaned in his chair, tipping it back on its legs.

Erin held Tim's gaze. "I don't know 'of' Him, Pastor. I know Him. He is my Lord, my Savior, my King. I know Him. His Spirit lives in me. I live and move and have my being in Him alone. I don't know how many ways to say it, so you will believe it."

Tim shrugged. "I hear your words, Mr. Winger. If you love this woman as you say you do, you won't mind me asking you a question." His eyes bored deep into Erin. "What is the proof of your faith? Where is your fruit?"

Vy's eyes lit up. Erin held his hand up. "I'll answer. Because he's trying to make sure you are getting someone worthy of you. Someone you deserve."

Her gaze could have cut diamonds. "Pastor Tim. You have no cause to ask this man—"

"Vy. I'll answer." Erin turned back to Tim. "I attend church at the Fifth Street Mission, sir. I serve breakfast to the residents, drive the bus to pick up the locals who want to attend but can't reach us. During the week, I teach chess at the downtown rec center."

Erin drew a breath, getting his emotions under control. "I tutor personal finance classes at the mission when we have enough interested residents." He felt calm sweep in. "I attend Bible study at the Mission as well as at my sister and brother-in-law's home. I'm part of a discipleship group that meets at six a.m. on Tuesdays at the coffee shop on Wesley and Main in the Hilltop district. None of which proves anything. I can't prove my faith, Pastor. I can only live it out." Peace filled his soul.

Tim seemed unimpressed and turned his attention to other issues. "What do you do for a living, Mr. Winger?"

"I manage property for Farrell and Son Inc. as well as for One Way Builders."

"What exactly do you do, Mr. Winger?"

"When the company begins a new building project, I oversee the fine details of budgeting, material purchasing, labor acquisition, and the like. I make sure projects in progress continue to move forward and are completed in a timely and fiscally responsible manner."

"Have you ever worked with your hands, Mr. Winger?" Again,

the eyes boring into Erin.

Erin smiled. He would not be intimidated. "Not without hurting myself, no."

Tim scowled. "Do you have any concept of the value of hard work, Mr. Winger?"

Vy stood up. Her voice sharp, she glared at Tim. "That's enough. Pastor Tim, you have no right to ask these questions of him or anyone else. Erin is a fine, Godly man who loves the Lord and lives out his faith every day."

She drew in a deep breath and continued to snarl at Tim. "I'm honored he wants to marry me, and if this is the kind of attitude he will be facing in this church, we will find somewhere else to go." She turned to Erin. "I am leaving. I won't sit by and watch you be bullied—"

Erin reached out to take her hand. "It's okay, Vy."

"No, it is not okay. Not for one minute is it okay. This—"

Tim began to chuckle. The big man's eyes twinkled. He reached over and held his hand out to shake Erin's. "Wonderful to meet you, Erin. Welcome to the church."

Vy's eyes widened, narrowed, flashed from Erin to Tim and back. Tim pointed to the chair. "Sit down, Vy. The clearest proof of a man's heart is when he is under pressure or being attacked. Erin demonstrated the fruit of the Spirit in his choice not to answer back, not to retaliate in kind. He trusted himself to the Lord despite my insults. Only a man with a heart given wholly to the Lord would be able to do that."

Tim raised his eyebrows at Vy. "You, however, need to work on controlling your temper."

Erin chose discretion and didn't laugh. He swallowed most of his smile. Most of it. Vy sank back into her chair, but her eyes maintained the fire. "I see. Well, Pastor Tim, what other surprises do you have set up for us?"

"None. I think you both will do fine. If you remember all you declared to me today, remember who and what you are fighting for, you will have a long, happy life together. When do you wish to get married?"

* * *

Vy and Erin met at the Beanery Coffee shop after they finished with Pastor Tim. Vy seemed to have some leftover resentment of the way the session had gone. Erin held her hand as they were served their drinks.

"It's all good, Vy. Honest. You can't insult me anymore. My father did it enough the twenty-five years I lived with him. Tim's indictments were nothing I haven't heard before."

"I still think it's an underhanded way of assessing someone's spirituality."

Erin chuckled. "I thought he'd tell me I couldn't marry you because I haven't known the Lord as long…and since you have such a head start on me, I'd never catch up."

"I don't know about the head start. I certainly blew it there."

Erin squeezed her hand. "I got a hit on the ancestry tree this morning."

Vy withdrew her hand and cupped both around the mug. "Oh? Someone you didn't know?"

"My mom's side of the family." A car honked outside the window. Someone yelled in response. It wasn't 'hello' either. Sigh.

Vy leaned in. "Your mother's parents?"

"My mother." Erin watched Vy's face.

Vy sat back. She cocked her head. "But you told me—"

"My mom died when we were five. I thought she had, too. It's what we were told. According to the DNA matches, she might still be living and breathing and married and have kids. I've got two brothers and a sister I didn't know about, not to mention my mother being alive. And here in Ohio."

Vy's eyes widened. "Oh?"

Erin looked at the ceiling. "I don't know what to think." He caught Vy's gaze. "Do I go forward with making contact? Or leave it alone?"

Vy's eyes pierced his. "Which do you want to do, Erin? Which will give you the most peace?"

"I don't know. And yes, I'm praying about it."

She smiled. "When you have peace, you'll have your answer."

Erin lowered his head and shook it. "If you're so smart, why do you want to marry me?"

"Maybe my heart is smarter than my brain."

"I'll never doubt your heart, Vy. I love you."

"I love you, Erin."

SUNDAY EVENING

Erin paced around the parking lot of the restaurant, waiting. Mindful of the ice hidden under the piles of blackened snow. *You know this trick. You've done this trick a thousand times. Be late, and throw your adversary off their game. Control the situation. That's all they're doing. Trying to throw you off.*

And doing a fine job of it, too.

Vy rubbed her hands together to warm them and shrugged her shoulders tightly in her long coat. She pointed down the street. "Is that the car? A royal blue sedan?"

Erin looked where she indicated and relaxed. "With Buckeye plates. Yeah, that's them. I hope."

"They're only ten minutes late, Erin. You know how traffic is."

"Then they should have left sooner."

"Erin Winger…"

Erin dropped his shoulders. "Yes, ma'am. I'll straighten up." He drew in a deep breath. "This is hard, Vy."

She slipped her gloved hand in his. "You can do this, Erin. I have faith in you."

Erin pulled strength from Vy's presence. He smiled. "With you here, I can do anything."

The car pulled into the small lot, dodged the snow piles, and parked next to the exit. A man, a few years younger than Erin, slid out of the driver's side. He donned his South-Hand parka, ran around, and opened the passenger's door. A woman slid out. Erin studied her closely.

Not tall. Five-three, maybe? Blonde hair, eyes hidden behind sunglasses. Still in "shape" for a woman who had to be approaching, if not past, fifty. Nothing about her rang any bells. Why would it? There were no pictures of her anywhere. He and Cane had barely known her…

The woman pushed her glasses up on top of her head. She slipped into a brown wool coat and walked towards the door. Erin held out his hand to the younger man. "Erin Winger."

The young man broke into a wide grin and bear-hugged him. "Brother! I have really been looking forward to this. Ever since you wrote to me, I couldn't wait to meet you."

Erin introduced Vy. "Braydon, this is my fiancée, Vy Johnson."

Braydon didn't try to hug her but shook her hand. "Nice to meet you, Ms. Johnson."

Erin stood and waited. He didn't know what to do next. The woman smiled at him, her eyes sad. "Have I changed so much, son?"

Erin searched her face for some resemblance, some hint she and he were blood kin. He couldn't see it. Nothing of her reminded him of Collin, either. He returned the smile. "We were only five. Father didn't keep any pictures. I'm sorry."

The woman's eyes clouded with tears. "I tried to warn myself this would happen. But I wanted so much to believe you would look at me and call me 'Mom' and rush to hug me. I should have known better."

Erin dipped his head. "I'm sorry. Felicity Bennett, my fiancée, Vy Johnson."

Felicity nodded to Vy but did not extend her hand. "Ms. Johnson. A pleasure to meet you." The tone sounded cool. Very cool. Bordering on cold?

Braydon clapped his ungloved hands. "Listen, people, it's thirty degrees out here. Can we move this inside where it's warmer? I'm freezing."

Erin laughed. "Of course." He held the door for his mother, Vy, and Braydon. The staff at the podium took their names, and in short order, they were seated.

Braydon picked up the conversation. "So, big brother. What do you do for a living?"

"I manage some properties for my brother-in-law, Jeff Farrell."

Felicity unfolded her napkin and placed it in her lap. Erin waited for her to say something, but she merely smiled at him. Erin continued, "Collin—Caitlin—and Jeff were married over three years ago. They just had their first babies. Triplets. Two boys and a girl. I have pictures…"

Felicity held up her hand. "Maybe later."

Braydon laughed. "Oh, wow! A houseful of babies all at one time."

Erin nodded. "Yes, it is. I help out sometimes. I'll do full uncle duties when they get a little bigger."

Felicity smiled at Vy. "What do you do, Ms. Johnson?"

"I work in accounting, ma'am." Erin swallowed his smile. *Accounting? Is that what we're calling it? Okay, better than saying, 'I'm a Drug Enforcement Agent for the Federal Government.' Yeah, accounting works.*

Felicity's tone remained cool. Uninterested. "I see. How long have you and Erin been seeing each other?"

Vy glanced at Erin, then back to Felicity. "Well, we met five months ago."

Erin added, "And I've been seeing her ever since. Wore her down. Relentless."

Vy's eyes twinkled. "He's been an absolute gentleman. Don't let him kid you." She squeezed his hand.

Felicity's smile seemed a shade less authentic. "Five months? And you're planning on marrying already?" She directed her gaze to Erin. "I thought today's couples waited a year or more. Even moved in together first. Just to make sure they are a true fit, you know. Are you sure about this?" She gave a small snort. "Living together might have made a difference with Robert Winger and me if we had."

Erin shrugged. "But we wouldn't be sitting here having this conversation, would we?" He smiled to take any perceived sting out of the comeback. "Vy and I both love the Lord. We know if we stay committed to Him first, we can tackle anything else together."

He could not miss the ice in Felicity's eyes. She buried it quickly, but Erin saw it if no one else did. She covered it well, however. "How nice. I'm happy for you. Would you like to see pictures of your family?"

Erin nodded. *Your.* "Certainly."

The server came and took their orders. Felicity pulled out her phone and scrolled through some images, pulling specific ones up. "This is your sister, Monica. She's the youngest, just turned 18.

She'll be graduating high school in the spring. She wants to attend OSU, but tuition is so high, we're not sure we can afford for her to enroll this year."

The woman scrolled down through more pictures. "And this is your brother Terry. He's twenty. He's going to night school, trying to earn his way through the second year of college. He had a scholarship, but with working and all, his grades slipped and he lost it. He wants to get into law school."

Erin nodded. "Those are great-looking kids. And lofty goals." He addressed Braydon. "What about you?"

Braydon chuckled. "I'm the family slouch. I never went."

Felicity shook her head. "Not a slouch. Just no opportunity when you came out of high school. Your dad being injured, you went straight to work."

At the coal mines?

Stop. These are your siblings. Of course, she wants help for them.

But on the first meeting? I mean, really?

Go with it.

"What do you do, Braydon?"

"Fireman."

Erin grinned and crowed. "That, I can relate to. Jeff is a fireman. Loves it. Loves it."

Felicity looked at Erin in confusion. "Oh? I thought you said you managed properties for him."

Erin nodded. "I do. Jeff's first love will always be firefighting and helping people. He's still a volunteer paramedic. Of course, the babies have slowed down his volunteer hours. But he also works with his dad, and I help them both out. Family business. You want to see the pictures?"

Felicity again held up her hand. "In a bit. What about your own family business? Aren't you working with Robert anymore?"

Erin tapped the floor with his foot. Silently. *How does she not know?* "No. Robert and his brothers are in prison. It was kind of a big trial three, four years ago."

"Really? I must have missed it. I don't keep up with the news." She smiled at him, brushing off his revelation. "I have enough going on at home with my boys to keep me busy." She raised an eyebrow. "Tax evasion? Money laundering?"

Erin debated. "Murder." It came out flat, and he left it there. "What does Mr. Bennett do? Or did he do before he got injured on the job?"

"Oscar is an ironworker. He fell. Negligence on the company's part. We're still waiting on compensation from the lawsuit. But these things take a long time to go through all the hoops and courts. It's why Braydon went to work, to bring in some income while we're waiting."

Erin directed his attention to Braydon. "What unit are you with? Where are you working?" *Back to a reality I can handle.*

"We actually live about forty miles southeast of here. Little burg called Harcort."

"I've heard of it. Haven't been there but heard of it."

"You two will have to come down and meet the rest of the family. Maybe next weekend?" Braydon had an enthusiasm Erin could appreciate.

Erin looked at Vy. She shook her head. "I've got commitments. But if you're free, you should go."

Erin nodded to Braydon. "Sure. I'll see if I can bring Cane— Caitlin— and the kids. I think she's ready to get out of the house for a few hours."

Felicity held up her hand. She protested, "I'm not sure it's a good idea bringing all those little ones out. Especially in the cold like this. It would be quite an undertaking with three. Why don't you come alone, and we can make arrangements to meet with your sister another time?"

Erin's gut checked. *Why is she shunning Cane? She's her daughter. Those are her…* "I'll check with her. We'll bring a picnic lunch." He smiled. "The little ones aren't eating anything yet." *No, but they sure do poo… Never mind.*

Dinner arrived. The conversation turned to who had what, whose looked better, and who wanted to swap with who. After the plates were cleared from the table and a final beverage served, talk returned to more personal matters. Braydon asked Vy, "Do you have family in this area?"

She smiled. "Yes, I do. Mother and Father, as well as three sisters, are all around here. I have one older and two younger sisters." Erin noted she included Iris, her older sister, as "here." Not technically accurate, but Canada is close. Close enough.

Braydon laughed. "It's a good thing you found us, Erin. You're surrounded by women!"

Erin touched Vy's hand and smiled at her. "Well, I got the best one of the bunch. Don't tell Cane I said that."

Felicity eyed Erin, her head turned to the side. "That's twice now you've called your sister Cane. Why? Is it some code name?" She laughed.

Erin's soul melted. *She doesn't remember. Did she even know? Yeah. We started it as toddlers. She has to know.*

He explained. "I called her Cane when we were little. I couldn't say 'Caitlin.' It always came out 'Ca-yin.' From there, it became Cane." He held Felicity's gaze. "Robert hated it. Maybe it's why I still do it."

"I'm sure Robert and your sister were very close. She must have been crushed when he went to prison."

Erin mustered every dram of his self-control not to react to Felicity's statement. He swallowed some of his drink. "You'll have to discuss the matter with her. Mother and daughter… I'm sure you two will have lots to catch up on."

Felicity shrugged, passing him off. "She always stayed with Robert. You spent more time with me. But you don't remember, do you?"

Erin looked at the floor. "Not yet. I'm certain there are memories buried in there somewhere." He smiled. "They just need to come back."

He pushed his chair back from the table. "I have really enjoyed meeting you, and I hope we can meet again soon. I'll let you know about next Saturday."

Felicity's eyebrows rose. "Oh? Not Sunday?"

"I serve at church on Sundays."

"Well, it's only an hour, isn't it? How long can a service take?"

Erin swallowed everything he wanted to say. "It's an all-morning commitment, Mrs. Bennett."

She shrugged. "It's only one Sunday. I'm sure your god can do without you for one morning."

"He can. It's the people I serve who need me." He hesitated. "We might be able to come down later in the afternoon. The babies would have had their naps and would be up for a trip. I'll check with Ca…Caitlin."

"It really is okay if you come without her, you know. With all those infants, I'm sure it will be too hard to wrangle them all. Just come alone, Aaron. This time." Her smile. Her eyes.

Erin felt Vy squeeze his hand. "Okay. I'll be down around two. And I'll still bring a picnic." *She's calling me Aaron, not Erin. It's the ending...the 'on' instead of 'in'.*

"Just bring yourself, son. That's all we need."

Felicity stood. Everyone followed. Everyone exited. The Bennetts returned to the car and left. Erin held hands with Vy. "You have some process time?"

She shook her head. "I'm sorry, Erin. I do have to go. Early court appearance tomorrow. I'll call you when I get a break. Okay?"

"Yeah. If that's the best deal I'm going to get, I'll take it."

He kissed her on the cheek, and she reciprocated. He watched her drive off and muttered. "But I gotta process this with someone." He looked at his watch. Collin would be up... Of course, she would be. But there remained a question he needed to have answered. He drove home and pulled up the ancestry agreement for the DNA results.

Results were guaranteed to be accurate, and close family even more so. Unless these people had hijacked someone else's DNA, they really were his relatives. And Felicity, his mother.

It didn't add up. Why didn't Felicity want to see Cane? Guilt for not protecting her? But to say Cane and Robert were close? Never. Not once. Revisionist memories? It didn't make sense.

He hadn't imagined the fire in Felicity's eyes when he spoke of the Lord. There had been a definite issue there. One he needed to discover. Maybe it would be better to go alone on Sunday rather than have Cane go and be hurt. He would find out what was going on first. No sense both of them being disillusioned.

Erin went to his bedroom to change into something more "baby-friendly." His phone rang. Collin. He drew in a deep breath and answered. "Hey. Glad you called."

"How did it go?"

"Braydon is a kick. I think he and Jeff will get on great. Braydon is a firefighter in Harcort."

"It'll give them something to share. What else?"

"I saw pictures of the other two. Um, Terry is the middle boy. He's twenty. And Monica is the girl. She'll graduate high school in the spring. Braydon is the family bread-winner until Oscar, their father, gets a settlement from a worker's comp claim." Erin paced around the small room, avoiding boxes packed for moving. When he had a place to move to.

"Must be tough on them."

"The kids are putting themselves through college. Except Braydon. He called himself the family slouch. I like him."

"Anything else?"

"I got an invite to go down Sunday afternoon and meet the rest of the family. Vy has commitments, so it will just be me."

"Uh-huh." Silence. "What aren't you saying, A-One? You haven't mentioned Felicity once. What's going on?"

"She's...hard to read." *Not really. She made it pretty clear she didn't want anything to do with Cane.* "She seems to have some memories...we don't have." He sat down on the bed.

"I don't have any memories, Erin. How much different can they be?"

"Different. Very different. She said she thought you and Robert were always together."

"Oh." Silence. "Yeah, that would be different."

"Her eyes lit up when I talked about the Lord."

"That's good."

"Not the way I saw it. She also suggested Vy and I move in together to see if we really want to get married." He removed his shoes. No going out tonight. He placed them carefully in their specified place. No, he would not use a stick to measure their position.

"Uh-hum. Well, that is different."

Erin answered the question his sister didn't ask. "She didn't ask about you. I told her about the babies. Braydon got excited about it, but Felicity didn't. I talked about you coming down on Sunday, and she wasn't a fan of the idea. Wanted me to come down alone. This time, she said."

Silence. "Okay. I'll have to take some time to work through those issues."

"I wanted to drive over and talk with you about it instead of on the phone."

"It's late, A-One. I'm going to bed shortly, and Jeff will take over the parental duties. Let's make it tomorrow, okay? You can go over it from the beginning, and we can try to make sense of it all. Deal?"

"Deal. I'll see you in the morning, Cane. Love you."

"Love you too, A-One."

Erin slipped the phone on the charger, kneeled on the floor beside the bed. "Lord, I don't understand what You're showing us. I don't have to understand. I only need to know what You want me to do. Show me, and I'll do it. In Jesus's Name. Amen." He undressed, crawled into bed. "Nite, Vy."

MONDAY

Vy stared at her car in disbelief. Four tires slashed. Scrape marks up one side and down the other. Paint splashed on the hood.

Just because hers wasn't the only car damaged in the same manner did little to make her feel better. Four cars joined hers in the 'gonna need a tow' department. Who would do such a thing? Why?

The security cameras had paint splashed on them as well. No recording of the culprits unless the cameras caught the person or persons decorating the lenses. She pulled out her phone, dialed the non-emergency number to report the vandalism, and took pictures for the police and insurance companies. She called her office to let them know someone needed to cover her court appearance, and she would be late. Very late.

Since she would be waiting for the police, she decided to call Erin. Hopefully, he'd had time to work through whatever bothered him about the meeting with his new family members. She'd gone over it in her head, too, and felt uneasy about some of what had been said. Or not said. No sense wondering if they had caught the same vibes. She dialed.

His smiling voice answered. "My day just got one thousand percent better. Good morning, beautiful."

"Good morning, kind sir. How did your evening go?"

"Downhill after you left. But that's what always happens when you leave the room."

Vy chuckled. "You really do need to get out more, Erin."

"No, I just need to marry you and have you by my side all the time. How is your morning going?"

"I've had better." Vy debated whether to touch the paint to see how dry it might be. Nah, leave it to the police. No sense adding fingerprints. She leaned against a pole.

"What's wrong?"

"Nothing. Someone destroyed the outside of my car." She sent him the picture.

"Look's horrid. Who would do that?"

"Someone with a grudge against this place. Four others have the same damage."

"Security camera catch anything?"

"Maybe if they got it before someone painted them, too. We'll see when security checks the cameras."

"They didn't check them last night? What good is a security system if no one is monitoring it?"

Vy grinned at his indignation. "We've had that very discussion with the property management. No resolution, but we have had the conversation. This maybe gives our argument some weight." *This, and the insurance damages they're going to have to settle.*

"Do you need to borrow a car? We have extras, you know."

"I may take you up on it if the insurance doesn't offer me a loaner."

"Let me know what they say. I can come take you wherever you need to go this morning or until then."

She smiled. "I know you will. You would swoop in and solve all my problems if I'd let you. But I still need to—"

"Handle it on your own in case I'm not around. I know. You do quite well handling life without me."

"Tell me about dinner. What did you see?"

"You tell me first. I don't want to coach you. Honest answers, Vy."

"Okay. Your...Felicity seemed to be all about you and not Collin. Her stories and the ones you two have shared don't match at all." Vy hesitated. *Get it all out there.* "She seems to want you all to herself."

"Bingo. Exactly the vibe I got, too. And I don't understand it."

"Are you going to go down on Sunday?"

"Yeah, if only to try to sort out what's going on with her."

"You'll be careful, right?

"Me? Of course. Always."

Vy saw a yellow tow truck swinging around the corner. "My tow truck is here. I'll talk to you later this afternoon.'

"Love you, Vy."

"I love you, Mr. Winger."

* * *

Erin drove over to Collin and Jeff's, let himself in the back door, went straight to the kitchen, and made a fresh pot of coffee. No sense not being useful. He repeated the chores from yesterday, except he folded burp rags instead of t-shirts, poured three cups, and carried them into the family room.

Jeff and Collin were asleep in their respective rocking recliners. The triplets were in their crib, all three huddled on top of each other. Did he dare separate the pile in hopes of keeping the one who woke first from waking the others? How good was he at anatomy? He twisted his head from one side to the other, trying to decide which leg belonged to which body, which arm attached to which shoulder.

Jeff's voice whispered, "Touch one, and you die."

Erin grinned and stepped away from the crib. He matched his tone to Jeff's. "I thought I could separate them."

"No. Leave them like they are. They're quiet. That's all that counts." Jeff lifted the cup Erin had placed beside him. "Thanks, bro." He swallowed. "You really should consider moving in until your place gets finished. We could use the help."

"Yeah, but if I did, Leesa would get jealous, and there's no way to explain to her why she can't take care of the babies the way I do." Jeff's sister Leesa had Down syndrome.

"True. I could tell her the babies are looking after you. She'd buy that."

"No doubt."

Collin stirred. She reached out, picked up the mug without opening her eyes. "Coffeeeeeeeee."

Jeff got up slowly. "How about we adjourn to the kitchen? I'm sure someone will let us know when the mass is awake."

Collin rose still with her eyes closed. She held out an arm. "Someone lead me."

Jeff took hold of her arm, directed her steps into the kitchen area, seated her at the bar, and said, "Here. Drink."

Erin waited until Jeff and Collin looked reasonably awake before smiling. "Morning, people. Did we have a good night last night?"

Collin growled and bared her teeth. Jeff patted her back. "It's okay, milady. We will make it through this growth spurt. I promise." She growled at him, too.

Erin swallowed the smile. Safer. This could be him one day. "Want me to fix breakfast?"

Both Collin and Jeff shook their heads. Collin saluted him with her cup. "Thank you all the same. Tell me about last night."

Erin sat and recounted the dinner party with as much detail as he could muster. He avoided the inflections he saw or thought he saw so Collin could draw her own inferences. He finished, "So I'll go down on Sunday and meet the rest of the group. And know more then."

Collin stared into her cup. Jeff reached over and poured more into it. She looked up at Erin. "She really said Robert and I were usually together? And I would be crushed for him going to prison?"

"Yeah. I don't get that at all. Harcort may be small, but they get the news from Oakton. The trial was a big deal. I can't see her not knowing about it. Especially because she talked like she had followed Robert's business dealings. Saying I would be working with him."

Jeff offered, "Or maybe she assumed you would be."

Erin considered Jeff's words. "Which might make sense. What doesn't make sense is why she took off. She never offered one word of, 'oh, I'm so sorry for leaving you' or said anything about the separation."

Collin nodded. "That's the part which struck me as odd. No, 'I'm so glad to find you,' or 'I've missed you' or any of the million things you'd think she would say. But to ask has she changed much? How much is a five-year-old supposed to remember?"

Jeff drank from his cup. "I don't know. This whole thing is unreal."

Collin swirled her mug. "What did Vy think?"

"We haven't really talked about it. Too late last night, and this morning, someone vandalized hers and a bunch of other cars. Slashed tires, keyed, paint everywhere. The tow truck came while we were talking. We're going to connect this afternoon. And hope someone saw something."

Baby sounds drifted in from the other room. Little grunts.

Whispers of movement. Someone sucking their fist. Someone not happy. Before it could become a full-fledged chorus, all three adults rose and headed to the living room. Erin waited to be handed one of the triplets. Jeff picked up Talitha, the little girl. Collin caught Caleb and swooshed him to Erin.

Erin cradled the chubby baby in his arms. "Morning, chunk. How are you this fine day?" Before Caleb could express his dissatisfaction with the food service delivery, Erin had him on his shoulder and began patting his back. Mollified, the baby settled down to wait.

Collin nursed Joshua. Jeff fed Talitha a half-bottle of formula. Erin fed Caleb a full bottle. When Joshua finished, Collin nursed the little girl. Jeff changed Joshua. Caleb finished, Erin changed him. Talitha filled her belly, Collin changed her. All three infants were placed on their stomachs for tummy time, and the adults got to sigh.

Jeff and Erin headed back to the kitchen for refills. Collin took off for the bedroom and a shower. Jeff commented, "You know, dude, it really is easier when you're here. I'm serious. We need the help. We're asking. You're not obligated. But it will save you a few miles on the commute to meet up with Vy."

Erin nodded. "Yeah, I've been thinking about it." He shrugged. "Thought about it a lot. Thought it would be nice to be able to invite Vy over and sit someplace we don't have to pay for a meal or drink coffee every time we want to talk." Erin and Vy adhered strictly to the "Billy Graham 'No traveling/being with the other sex unaccompanied'" rule.

He grinned. "Only problem will be having Vy around babies so soon."

Jeff laughed. "Oh, I don't know. Having to care for these three will make a monk out of anyone."

"Possibly true, too. Yeah, I'll do it. At least until you five can manage on your own. Or Vy and I get married."

"Thanks, bro. You have no idea what it means to me."

Erin chuckled. "I think I do. Sleep at night. Naps during the day. And a little less chaos around here."

Collin came in from the back, showered and dressed. "Less chaos? How are you proposing to make that happen?"

Erin spread his hands wide. "I am here. I'm moving in until Vy and I get married."

Collin put her arms around her brother's neck, squeezed him. "Thank you, A-One. You're the best twin brother a girl could have."

"Of course I am. But I'm going to need Sunday afternoon off to go to Harcort."

"We'll manage."

Someone voiced an opinion they had been neglected long enough. A plaintive cry whimpered from the living room. A second voice took up the complaint. Jeff shook his head. "I believe we're being summoned."

Adult conversation had to be abandoned again, and the littlest Farrells got some desperately needed (to their minds, anyhow) cuddle time.

Two hours later, Erin headed into town to work on his projects, manage his properties, and generally do adult business. No call from Vy. He checked his phone hourly to make sure he didn't miss her.

But no calls came. Not the remainder of the morning. Not the afternoon. Not even in the evening when he moved his clothes over to Collin and Jeff's place. By eight p.m., he was concerned, but not overly so. He did leave a short message on her phone. "Missed your call. Available any time."

* * *

Tuesday morning, and still no call. Erin sighed as he gazed at his phone. *Lord, this is precisely what I've been afraid of. She'll disappear, and I'll have no idea where she is or when she'll be back. If she's on assignment, she wouldn't be able to tell me. Neither can the office nor her parents. We're all in the dark, hoping she's okay.*

Except You know. And I guess that's all that matters. You know, and You have her. Keep her, Father. Keep her safe, please? Thanks.

Erin spent the day with Jeff and Collin. He didn't have any pressing appointments, and the babies needed fresh air. Cold air, as January can be bitter. But the babies were getting "stir crazy" and wanted to go out. So decreed Collin, and so they went out.

By the time the triplets had been fed, changed, dressed, undressed, changed again (Caleb), dressed, bundled into car seats, unbundled, slipped into strollers, undressed, changed, dressed...

The experimental outing lasted two hours. Collin came home exhausted and declared, "Never again. Not until they're old enough to buckle their own seatbelts. Who came up with this idea?"

She glared at Jeff and Erin. "And do not tell me I did. As you value your lives, you will not remind me I asked to do this."

Jeff put his arms around her. "It will be fine, milady. I promise. We'll survive. They'll survive. All will be well."

Erin slipped his phone out. No call. He put it back in his pocket, hoping no one noticed.

Collin did. "Still no word from Vy?"

"No." He didn't even try to keep the disappointment from his voice. "My biggest fear has always been this. She's gone, and I have no clue where or for how long."

He caught his sister's gaze. "But God has her, I know. I want Him to share, okay?"

Her smile reflected his sadness. "Understood, A-One. I'm praying for you and her."

"It's all I got."

Jeff lay his hand on Erin's shoulder. "Heard." He squeezed the shoulder.

* * *

Wednesday. No Vy.

Thursday. No Vy.

Friday. No Vy.

Saturday. No Vy.

Sunday morning. No Vy. Erin pushed his nightmares aside and focused on serving the people of the mission. Breakfast of pancakes, sausage or bacon, scrambled eggs, orange juice. Get 'em started out right, anyhow. He drove the bus to pick up the less mobile members who wanted to come to church. He worshipped in the services. He drove the bus to return people home. By twelve-thirty p.m., he had finished his service to the Lord.

And still no word from Vy.

Erin gathered his attitude and behavior and drove the distance to Harcort, Ohio. He followed the GPS to an unassuming street. It took him to an unassuming neighborhood. Which took him to the Bennett house, third house on the left. "You have reached your destination."

The driveway had been shoveled, but the recent snow still piled on top of the cars. Sidewalk had been cleared, but only as far as the next house. *Every man for himself? Hmm.*

Erin checked his phone one last time before getting out of the car and walking to the door. He knocked.

A girl in her mid-to-late-teens opened the door. Blue jeans, stylish tears in the knees. Pullover hoodie with a Buckeye in the center. "Can I help you?"

"I'm Erin Winger."

She groaned. "Another brother. All I need." She laughed and extended her hand. "I'm Monica."

Erin nodded. "Graduating in the spring. Wants to go to The Ohio State University."

"Ah. He pays attention. I'll take a brother like you." She motioned for him to enter and yelled, "Aaron's here."

Again, he heard it in the pronunciation. The difference in the spelling of his name. "Aaron" had been the original spelling. "Erin" served as his father's punishment for Erin not being first out of the womb. He'd thought about changing it. But it became a badge of honor, a sign of rebellion.

Still, he could tell when people said it one way or another. And Monica had definitely said, "Aaron." He tucked the item away in his head and went in.

Monica took his coat, led him through the house downstairs to the basement/family room. A pool table took up half the space. A TV screen hung mounted on the wall opposite the pool table. Metal folding chairs were placed against the walls, angled to watch either the pool game or the TV. NFL football—the Cleveland Browns—looked to be the game of the week.

Felicity rose as Erin came down the steps. Braydon looked up from the pool game and shouted, "Erin! Come on in, bro. This is Terry." He pointed with his cue stick to the younger man across the table from him.

Younger, but taller and heavier. Maybe not linebacker, but tight-end? Running back. Curly blonde hair. Erin waved. Terry waved back, turned to continue studying his next shot. Felicity came to Erin's side and gave him a tentative hug. "Welcome, son. I'm glad you made it." She took his arm and led him to the one recliner in the room.

Its occupant didn't rise but reached out his hand. "So. We finally get to meet the man behind the myth."

"Mr. Bennett." Erin shook the man's hand. Not the hands of an ironworker. Less physical. But he hadn't worked in three years, so guess it made sense.

"Oscar." The man settled back in his chair and turned to watch the TV again.

"Oscar. I'm pleased to meet you, sir." *Late fifties, maybe. I see where Terry gets his girth. The height has to be a throw-back somewhere.* Erin noted the braces on the man's legs. "Felicity said you had an accident at work."

"Yeah. Fell from a scaffold. Workman's Comp tried to settle with us, but we got a lawyer who's going after the big bucks. Enough to put all three kids through college and set Felicity and me up for the rest of our lives." His eyes never left the screen.

"How long has the suit been going on?"

Oscar glanced at his wife, then back to the television. "Braydon had just graduated from high school, hadn't he?"

"Yes, dear. It's why he didn't go to college. He needed to find a job to help with expenses here."

Erin nodded. "I see. I hope it all works out for you."

Oscar grunted. "Yeah." *It's the Browns, man. They'll lose. They always lose.*

Felicity pulled on his arm. "Come on over here. I've got lunch for you."

"You didn't need to fix anything." Erin struggled with what to call her. *Felicity? Mrs. Bennett? I'm not calling her Mom. Or Mother.*

She smiled. "Nothing but the best for my boys."

She led him to a folding table set up with a lunch buffet. There were cold cuts, sandwich buns, fixings, jelled salads, potato salad, chips, salsa, and an arrangement of cookies. Felicity handed him a sturdy paper plate and insisted, "Eat." She called over his head, "Come on, boys, it's time." She squeezed his arm and said, "I'll fix a plate for your step-father."

Erin felt his gut flip. He smiled at her. "Thank you." Braydon and Terry joined him at the table, reaching and forking items, generally making it a free-for-all. Erin noticed Monica waited on the outside. He motioned her up to the table. "There's room. Come on."

She shook her head. "Not until the men are done. Then the women get to fill their plates. Mom's rules."

Erin stared at Felicity and nearly dropped his jaw. *Where did that come from?* He finished filling his plate and found a chair to sit in. His brothers piled food high on their plates, returned to the pool table, and set them down.

Oscar yelled, "No food on the pool table! You know the rules. Use a tray."

Erin watched the man drop the footrest of the recliner, bending his knees and standing. Erin peered closely and noticed the braces weren't fastened tight. In fact, they weren't doing anything at all except being window dressing. Oscar accepted the plate Felicity handed him, walked to the buffet table, and added extras his wife had forgotten. He returned to the recliner and sat.

Erin dropped his gaze before Oscar could notice him watching. *We fake an injury, keep the kids out of school, all so we can cheat some company out of millions. And they show me...why?*

Because Felicity assumes I am Robert Winger's son and will applaud the fraud? Why else be this transparent?

Felicity came and sat beside him. "It really is good to see you. I tried to keep up with what you were doing. I saw Robert's companies were doing really well. Life must have been easy for you." She smiled. "You being in the wheelchair must have made negotiations a breeze. Did Robert come up with the idea?"

Erin swallowed hard. And prayed harder. *Guard my words, Lord. Guard my mouth. Don't let me say what I want to say. Let me honor You.* He cleared his throat. "Uh, no. The chair wasn't for show. I broke my neck at fourteen and became paralyzed from the waist down. I only got healed of it four years ago. The Lord moved a bone pressing on the nerves, and I got feeling back. Took a lot of rehab, but with the Lord's help, I finally worked my way out of the chair. I can stand on my own two feet now." He ducked his head. "Mostly. I'm having some issues again, but only now and then. I'm grateful to be standing."

He watched Felicity's eyes. His mention of the Lord triggered the same angry flaring of her eyes. But she smiled anyway. "Amazing. Whose fault was the accident? I'm sure Robert sued them for every last dime."

"No fault. Caitlin threw the ball. I went up for it, came down on my neck. Just an accident."

"Hmm. I see. Obviously, he did nothing to her about it."

Erin stared at Felicity and let his expression show his confusion. "Why would you say that? He hated her."

Felicity laughed. "Oh, Aaron. Your father is a master manipulator, I agree. But hate Caitlin? The golden child? The one who would inherit all the money? He did everything for the girl. Everything. Nothing else mattered but precious Caitlin. Think about it."

Felicity leaned in and lay her hand on Erin's arm. "How much attention did she get growing up? Finest schools, finest clothes. I bet she had a wardrobe the envy of most Hollywood costume designers. What kind of car did she drive to school? Hmm? What did he give you?"

Erin felt a numbness inside. He chose his words carefully. "Robert threw her out of the house, onto the streets of Oakton, because of that accident. He told her I had died and let her believe she'd killed me. He hated her. Abused her. Had Patrick drive her to Oakton at three in the morning and put her out in the slums."

Erin caught his breath and his composure. "He told me she'd run off because she didn't want to be bothered with a brother in a wheelchair. Twelve years she thought I was dead. Twelve years, I thought she didn't care about me. The Lord brought us together. We can't make up for the lost time, but we're making every day count now."

He lifted his chin. "Please don't tell me how much Robert loved her or anyone else. There is no love in him, except for money."

Felicity never lost the smile. She patted his arm. "They really did a number on you, didn't they? To make you believe a story like that? Robert must have—"

Erin rose. "I'm sorry. I won't stay and listen to this. I—"

Felicity caught his arm. "No, Aaron. Stay. I won't talk about Robert or your sister again. I promise. We'll talk about you. Where are you living? What vacations have you had? Tell me about your girlfriends. I know you must have plenty of them. What made you choose Vy, of all people?"

Lord, do I stay or go? The check in his soul said stay, so he sat back down. "I moved in with Caitlin and Jeff this week to help them out with the triplets. Life does go easier with three adults."

Felicity's eyes flared. "She has you taking care of the children?"

"I'm helping. Hel-ping. Not taking care of them. Jeff and Collin are giving me a place to stay until my new house gets finished, and Vy and I get married and move in together." The tug at his heart opened the door to fear and loss. He let the Lord close it with His assurances of peace.

Erin continued, "I chose Vy because she is intelligent, beautiful, she laughs at my jokes, and she loves the Lord. She saved my life, I saved hers, and we complement each other. I've never met another woman like her. I'm grateful she agreed to marry me."

"But you looked around first, right? I'm sure there are lots of women who would be happy to have a catch like you."

Erin nodded. "I looked around enough to know Vy is the woman I want to spend the rest of the life the Lord gives me with." He stopped, ran the sentence through his head again, nodded. "Yeah. Sounded off, but that's what I meant."

Felicity shrugged. "And you say she works in accounting? Sort of menial for a woman her age."

"Not where she does it." Erin left out the DEA part.

Felicity sniffed. "Whatever. Still not a field with much advancement. Did she go to college?"

"Yes. Graduated with a degree in Accounting, so she's working in her field." He smiled. "Which is better than me, who never went and have no idea what field I'm in."

Felicity didn't smile at the joke. She continued to press. "How did you meet her? Clubbing? Online dating site?"

Erin dissembled. "We had a…situation…where our jobs overlapped. We ended up working together to solve it. I was impressed with her, and for some reason, she liked how I worked, too. We dated briefly—*very briefly*— then got engaged and plan to marry in the fall. Or late summer. We're not sure yet."

"Oh, so you haven't set a date?" Felicity's face lit up.

"We're still trying to make the stars align." He chuckled. "Schedules. Hers, mine, the church, the venue for the reception, the bride's attendants, the groom's attendants. Everyone has a say in it. I'm ready to throw away all the schedules, throw a dart at the calendar, and wherever it lands is when we get married."

"Maybe you should just put it off. If it's that much work, why bother? No woman is worth that kind of hassle." Felicity's face reflected the disdain in her words.

Erin smiled. "She is."

"Well." Felicity looked around the room. "At least now you can have one of your brothers as your best man. It should be family, right? I'm sure Braydon will be thrilled. Maybe you can talk to him about it today. I doubt he'll have any serious plans for then."

Erin shrugged. "We'll see. Lots of details to be worked out."

"I suppose her family is making all the rules about who and where." Again, the disdain bordering on disgust.

"No, Vy and I are. We're adults. It's our wedding. Her parents are quite happy to let us plan things the way we want." *Except for Aunt Viola and the Calvary Church. We can live with her quirk.*

"I'm surprised your sister hasn't taken charge." Again, the sneer.

"She's got her hands full with the triplets." Erin chuckled. "Especially Caleb. He's the chunk of the group."

"Hmm. I can't imagine anything would stop her."

Erin finished the food on his plate. "I'll take this to the trash."

"Don't you want more?" Her voice almost pleaded.

"No, I'm fine. Really. I want to watch Braydon and Terry play. See who knows the most about trigonometry."

He drifted toward the trash can, saw Monica holding her empty plate, and smiled. "You done with your plate? I'll take it for you."

Monica eyed him. "You'd take my plate for me? Why?"

"Because it's empty, I'm on my way to the trash can and thought I'd save you a trip. If you're done with it."

Monica smiled. "I like you. You're different. Thank you. I appreciate it." She handed her plate to Erin. She glared at her brothers and called, "Aaron took my plate for me. He's a gentleman."

Catcalls answered her. But she smiled with satisfaction at Erin. "Thank you."

Erin shook his head. "Not a big deal. You're welcome." *Apparently, it's a big deal in this house.*

He moved over to the pool table, maintaining a safe distance from pool cues needing the space he occupied. "Who's ahead?"

Terry banked a shot too sharply and had the ball careen off the side impotently. He grumbled, "He is. He always is."

Braydon smiled. "It's all in the eye, Terry. All in the eye. You gotta know the angles." He placed a shot which bounced off two sides, came behind the six-ball, and knocked it expertly into the corner pocket. "And the pressure. The physics of force and weight and mass and gravity…all those important things."

Terry chipped, "Says the slouch."

Braydon only shrugged and sank another ball. "I loved science."

Erin nodded. "Nice. If you could go, what would you major in?"

"Science. Engineering. I love numbers. Enjoy making them work for me." He sank another ball. Expertly. Effortlessly.

"Looks like you'd be good at it."

Braydon lowered his voice. "If the stupid lawsuit ever comes through, I'll go. But I'm not holding my breath." He lowered his voice further for Erin alone to hear. "You can't cheat and think you'll get away with it. They think they're such great scam artists."

Terry seemed of the same opinion. "It's like being stuck in limbo. We can't do this, we can't do that. Can't go on vacation. Can't take trips for fun. Gotta maintain the image he can't work, and we're suffering because of it. We're suffering, alright. From their greed."

He whiffed a shot. "But it's Mom and Dad. What we gonna do, right?"

Erin hated himself but offered, "Move out?"

Braydon shook his head. His face darkened. "Can't. Not yet. Gotta protect Monica. Once she graduates, and we can move her out as well, maybe. Not until then."

Erin squelched the urge to whip around and stare at Felicity and Oscar. "Protect her?"

"Monica can't do anything right. If someone says something nice about her, Mom comes unglued. She's pathological. Seriously. Dad says she's in therapy, but we haven't seen any difference. We're not leaving Monica behind."

Erin continued to focus on the players. Safer than staring at Felicity. "Was there a trigger? Something happen? Or has she always been off?"

"Ever since Monica came along." Terry looked to Braydon for confirmation.

Braydon nodded. "Yeah. She had severe post-partum depression, so Dad says. Which turned into hatred of the one who caused it. Mainly Monica. Or that's Dad's explanation of it."

Erin ground his teeth. "Except she seems to be the same with Collin. Doesn't want to have anything to do with her or the babies."

Braydon shrugged. "I can't explain it. I just know it's there, it's bad, and we're not leaving Monica here by herself."

Terry motioned with his chin. "Mom's coming."

Felicity smiled at the group as she joined them at the pool table. "Are you boys getting to know each other? It's nice having all my boys in one place." She put her hand on Erin's shoulder. "I knew one day I'd have all my children in one room together."

Erin smiled. *It needs to be said.* "Except you're still missing one. Caitlin isn't here."

Felicity shrugged. "She has her own family now, so she doesn't count. I'm sure she's very happy where she is."

He made sure not to react. Visibly. "She's happier than she's ever been. It's good to see her getting the good stuff finally."

Felicity's eyes flashed. Her voice sounded frigid. "I'm sure your sister has had more than her share of the 'good stuff' in her lifetime." She rubbed his shoulder. "It's you who's missed out, I'm sure."

Erin shut the line down. "Past history. All is well. The Lord brought us through. He gets all the credit." He watched Feliticy's eyes for the anger, and she did not disappoint. *What is it, Lord? What does she have against You?*

Braydon caught Erin's eye. The younger man nodded almost imperceptibly. He called out, "Monica, you're up next. Terry's done."

Felicity held up her hand. "No, you should let Aaron play. Monica can wait."

Erin waved both hands in surrender. "No. I like to watch my opponents first. See how they think. Monica can play, and I'll get a better feel for how she and Braydon compete."

Felicity's voice darkened. "She cheats. It's the only way she can beat anyone."

Braydon waved his sister over. "She's not very good at it, is she? She still loses."

Felicity's eyes would have torched Braydon into tiny embers if she could. She turned and walked away, careful to avoid touching Monica as the teen passed her. Braydon handed his sister a cue stick. He grinned at her. "Show him the real stuff, sis. No pulling punches. I'll shield you."

Monica glanced from Braydon to Erin and back again. "Really?"

"Yeah. She won't do anything with Erin here. Or, better yet, run the table and scratch the eight-ball. Either way, show him what you got."

Erin stepped back to watch Monica proceed to do exactly what her brother told her to do. Ball after ball sank. Erin grinned at Braydon. "You teach her all that?"

Braydon nodded once. "She's got real talent. She's got talent in lots of areas if she would be allowed to develop them."

"Like..." Erin left it open-ended.

"She's a wiz at math. She's writing college-level essays and papers." He shrugged. "I admit, she wrote one or two of mine in high school..." Braydon grinned. "And she's death on a basketball court."

Erin grinned. "It's in the blood, I tell you." He held Braydon's gaze. "You're proud of her, aren't you?"

Braydon's eyes narrowed. "Yes. I'll do anything to protect her. While I can."

Erin touched fists with Braydon. "Good man."

Monica scratched on the eight-ball. "Oh, well. It was a good run while it lasted." She smiled at Erin, touched fists with her brother, returned to her place, and sat down.

* * *

Erin stayed a respectable three hours, then went over to Felicity. "I've got to head back. Want to get home before dark and the storm hits."

"What storm?"

"Forecasters are calling for three inches of snow tonight. I want to get back to Oakton before someone declares a level-three emergency, and I'm not allowed to be on the roads."

She smiled. "You could stay here the night."

"No. Thank you, but no. I've got work in the morning." *And I won't mention helping Collin and Jeff.* "It's been fun to meet everyone. We'll have to do it again when the weather is better, and you can come to the house in Oakton. Vy will be there, and Caitlin, Jeff, and the babies will be able to meet all their new uncles and aunt."

Felicity's eyes belied her words. "That will be nice."

Erin made the rounds, high-fived, and fist-bumped the appropriate people. He wanted to hug Monica but decided against it. He caught her eye, nodded, and moved on to say goodbye to Oscar and Felicity. Oscar waved rather than rise. Erin waved back.

Felicity followed him up the steps to the front door. She hugged him close and hard and warm. "I am so glad you came, Aaron. I knew. I knew you would find me and come back to me. I knew it."

Erin returned the hug but at half the intensity. "I'm glad I got to meet your new family. Looks like you're very happy." *Saying something on the way out the door is a cheap shot and a coward's way out. But…*

Felicity handed him his coat. He slipped into it. "Next time, maybe we can talk about what happened."

She tilted her head to look at him. "What happened? About what?"

Erin dropped his gaze to the floor. "About why you left. Where you went. Why we were told you were dead. Those questions."

Felicity drew in a deep breath. "Does it matter? We're here, now. Let the past be dead and gone. I don't think about it."

Erin lifted his head. "It would fill in the gaps for us. Caitlin and me. It's important to us."

Felicity tossed her head. "I'm sure your sister has other concerns." She smiled. "When will you come down again?"

"I'll look at my schedule and at the weather forecast. Though I think it's your turn to come up and see my place."

"You said you're living with your sister. You don't have a place."

"You can come see Caitlin's place. And your grandchildren."

Felicity shrugged. "One of these days." She hugged Erin again. "Be careful, son. I'm so proud of you. I love you."

"Bye." Erin walked out the door, got in his car, closed out the world around him. He waved through the window, turned the car on, and drove away. He cleared the corner, cleared a second corner, stopped. Erin shook out his whole body, trying to work out the anger, disappointment, frustration, and any and all other emotions.

He let out a nonsensical, "Blaaaaaaahhh." He felt better. Erin checked his phone. Vy had messaged. Short, sweet, *Love you.* That was all he needed to hear.

Erin smiled all the way home.

COLLEEN SNYDER

WEDNESDAY

Three days passed before Vy could come over to the Farrell house and make a foursome for discussion. They sat in the living room. Collin sat on the floor, keeping an eye on all her offspring. Vy (with Talitha) and Erin (with Joshua) sat on the couch while Jeff held Caleb. Erin had Joshua on his shoulder, patting the baby's back. Whether Joshua liked it or not, it gave Erin a way to ease the tension he felt talking about the weekend visit to Felicity's.

When he'd finished giving the blow-by-blow of the afternoon, he sat back. He waited for comments, questions, discussion…anything.

Collin glanced at the floor. "How much of Robert Winger's influence do you think played a part in her…disdain…for women?"

Erin shook his head. "We can blame him for a lot of things, but I'm not sure we can lay this at his feet. Not thirty-some years and a whole separate family later."

Collin eyed Erin. "You were still under his sway—"

"Granted. But I lived with him twenty-four/seven. I never saw anything but what he let me see, and only through his eyes. She'd been away and with other people for years. Plenty of time to learn something new."

Vy offered, "I love your brothers' attitudes." Her eyes sparkled. "They seem to be following a family tradition."

Erin shrugged. "They're good kids. Trying to navigate life the best they can. Unless I'm being played and can't see the forest for the trees."

Jeff chuckled. "I think you're a good judge of character. You liked me, didn't you?"

"Hard not to." Erin lowered Joshua to his lap. He caught the infant's feet and bicycled them. Joshua giggled and laughed. Erin looked at Collin. "The important question is where do we go with this? I'm not comfortable with Felicity's attitude, but I don't want to abandon Braydon and the others."

Vy settled Talitha on her lap as well. She held the infant's hands and gently exercised them. "You say the older boys are waiting until Monica graduates, then planning a mass move-out. With what resources? If everything they have is being spent on family expenses, what do they have for deposits, down payments, and the like? Moving out isn't cheap."

Erin shook his head. "I don't know. We didn't discuss plans. We didn't discuss much which could be considered 'important.' Most of it was banter."

Collin tapped her finger on the rocking chair. "What do you think would happen if you invited the whole family for a visit? Knowing Felicity doesn't want to see me, do you think she would pass and let the siblings come?"

Erin stared at the carpet. "What and talk escape plans? And if they don't have one? Propose one? Front them the money?" He looked at Collin. "I don't like it. I don't want anyone in this family thinking we can be suckered into a sob story, and the money will start flowing." His face stayed even, but his spirit darkened.

Collin frowned at him. "That's not quite what I had in mind."

"I'm sure it isn't, but with the Winger bloodline, it's the first thought I have." *Wise as serpents...and I've got a fifteen-foot python in my background. You're working on me, Lord, I know. But there are still these triggers...*

Collin raised an eyebrow. "How many years does it take to quit being a Winger?"

"More than I've been out of his house."

Collin dropped her head. "Okay, I'll give you that one."

Vy glanced from Erin to Collin and back again. "Why not front them the money? In a way where they don't know it is coming from you? Tell them you know of an apartment complex or a housing area where they can get a place to live for a couple of months. They need to show proof of employment...good faith efforts. You'll know whether they're serious or not."

She turned Talitha onto her tummy. "My father used to do it with my sister when she would come home and swear she wanted to clean up her act. He'd refer her someplace she didn't know he paid for, and she'd move in. She'd stay clean for a few months, then bail on him. He didn't have to be the 'bad guy' and tell her to move out, but she did end up back on the street."

Erin thought he knew the answer but asked anyhow. "How did your mom take it when it happened?" He shifted Joshua to a sitting position, leaning the baby against his chest.

"Hard. Always hard. But she never once fought my dad over doing what needed to be done. They were in total agreement on it. They still had children at home to protect. It was tough love at its toughest." Vy rubbed Talitha's back. "They had faith the Lord would take care of her, one way or another."

Jeff put Caleb on the floor on a blanket. "My folks did the same thing with me. I know it tore them up. But it finally got me turned around."

Vy cocked her head. "I didn't know that about you. What happened? Drugs?"

"Alcohol. Beer mostly. But the vice doesn't matter. It's the behaviors and the mindset."

Erin held up one hand. "Can we get back to Braydon and company?"

Collin smiled at him. "Patience, grasshopper." He sneered at her. She rolled Caleb to his back so he could see more of the world than the carpet. "I say invite the family up. See what happens. If only the boys and Monica come, we learn their plans and see where we can help. If the whole family comes, we'll play it by ear. Sound fair?"

Erin turned to Vy. She nodded and asked, "Why am I even voting on this?"

"Because you love me and what concerns me concerns you." He reached over and kissed her lightly. "Right?"

Her eyes smiled. "Right."

Collin looked up at Jeff. "Ah, young love."

Jeff reached down and kissed his wife. "Old love, too."

Erin settled Joshua more firmly in his lap and made the call. He invited the entire Bennett family up the following weekend. He made it clear he wanted the boys to look at tuxes and Monica to help Vy and Collin look at dresses. Felicity could join either party, but they assumed Oscar would stay with the boys.

Felicity's voice came across cool. "You don't need Monica. She won't be any help."

"That's okay. Vy wants to get to know her new sister. It'll be fun. For them, anyhow. It would be torture for me, but that's why I'm having Braydon and Terry come, so I don't have to go with the girls."

"I think Oscar would rather stay home. If he does, Monica will have to stay to take care of him. We can't have him left alone. The insurance might get wind of it and use it against us."

"So let me pay a healthcare worker to come in for the morning or the day. Vy really wants Monica to come up."

"You'll have to explain to your Ms. Johnson we can't have everything we want. I'll come up with the boys. Monica will stay behind." The curt tone brooked no argument.

Erin frowned at the phone. Vy leaned in and whispered in his ear. He nodded. "Okay, Vy says she can go dress shopping another time. She will drive down to your house and meet Monica and Oscar while Braydon, Terry, and you come up here. Does that work?"

"No. Having another woman in the house does not work. I'm surprised you'd suggest it, Aaron."

"But she wouldn't be alone with Oscar. Monica would be there."

"No. I prefer she not come down. Not this time."

"What if we just come down there instead of you coming up here? We can—"

"I prefer it is just you who comes down right now, son. Monica can meet Vy later."

The frost in her voice chilled Erin. He swallowed, counted to ten, breathed out. "I'm sorry you feel the way you do, Felicity. Vy is part of my life now and will be from now on."

Felicity laughed. "Oh, Aaron. I'm sorry you misunderstood me! Of course, I want to get to know Vy. I know she's important to you. This isn't a good time, what with Oscar and the lawsuit. That's all I'm saying. We'll be the best of friends, I assure you. I don't understand why you got so defensive."

Erin rolled his eyes. Vy hugged him, laughing silently. Felicity's voice became concerned. "I'd worry about being in a relationship where I constantly had to defend my partner. It's not healthy, son. You might need to think about it some more."

Erin narrowed his eyes. Felicity couldn't see it, of course. But she should hear it in his voice. "I have thought about it. Long and hard. And if I spend my life defending Vy's honor, I'll have spent it well."

Silence. "She would be more important than your family and friends? If everyone around you said the relationship wasn't right, you'd throw everything away for her? That's not right, Aaron."

"If everyone I knew told me, I would probably listen. I'd still make up my own mind, but I might listen." He glared at the phone. "But happily, most of the people around me are supportive and agree with my choice. If anything, they wonder why Vy would choose me. That's the real mystery."

"Yes, well, perhaps you need a better class of friends. Ones who are better judges of character."

Vy leaned back and mouthed, "Ooooo!"

Erin rolled his eyes. "So none of us are getting together this weekend, right?"

"No. Braydon, Terry, and I are available to come. We can all go looking at tuxes."

"Fine. You can come here, meet Collin and Jeff and the babies, then Vy, you, me, Braydon, and Terry can all go looking together."

"If this trip is to spend time with your brothers, I don't see how bringing your girlfriend helps."

"It helps because you two can get to know one another while I bond with the boys."

"Why are you deliberately making this difficult?"

The anger in her voice twisted Erin's gut. He swallowed his immediate response, choosing instead to remain calm. "I'm not. I'm trying to clarify who it is you have a problem with. Is it Vy, Collin, Jeff, the babies, or some combination of all of them? Because I really want you to be part of my family like you want me to be part of yours. It can't go just one way, Felicity."

"'Love me, love my dog.' Is that what you're saying?"

Vy lay her hand on his arm, squeezed it, and shook her head. Erin let the fire die before he answered. But he did choose his words discriminately. "You picked a pretty crude analogy, but yes. Love me, love my family. All of my family."

"So, I'm not allowed to have disagreements with anyone?"

"Of course, you are. We have disagreements all the time. But we still love each other." He paused, inhaled, exhaled. "This is a bad idea. We'll do this another time. I'm sorry I brought it up. Bye."

He stayed silent for several moments. He looked around. "Thoughts?"

Jeff asked, "You think it's all women she has a problem with or just the three in the family?"

Erin scowled. "I don't know, and I'm not sure it matters. I'm ready to close the whole chapter."

"And leave your brothers and sister to fend for themselves?" Vy's voice stayed gentle but firm.

Disgust washed through him. "At this point, yeah, I am."

Vy cocked her head and stared at him. She said nothing.

Erin sagged. "Okay, I know. Bad attitude. Tell me how to negotiate this."

Joshua began to fuss. Collin stood, crossed the room, picked up her son. "It's okay, little one. Uncle Erin is having a bad moment. He'll be better soon." She nuzzled the baby and returned to sit back on the floor, Joshua sitting in her lap.

Vy motioned to the phone. "You have Braydon's information, don't you? Can you contact him without his mother being involved?"

"Go behind Felicity's back?"

"More like around her. Braydon is an adult and can make his own decisions. An email might get you more information on their plans and give you some insight on what to do next." She smiled. "Just a thought."

Erin leaned over and kissed her again. "And that's another thing I love about you. You're always thinking. I should leave all the thinking to you."

Jeff huffed. "I thought you already had."

Erin looked for a pillow to throw. Jeff picked up Caleb and held him in front of him. Erin groaned. "Low, man. Pretty low. Hiding behind your son."

"He doesn't seem to mind."

"Wait until he's older. He might have an objection."

Collin turned to Vy. "What about your car? Did you ever find out who vandalized it?"

"No. Whoever did it spray-painted the security cameras before they trashed the cars. The police have interviewed all of us who had damage, trying to see if there is a link or not. So far, not."

"Does that mean maybe one of you is the target, and the others were collateral damage?"

Vy shrugged. "Or they trashed the others to hide their real target. We'll have to see what happens."

Erin pursed his lips. "Is there any way for you to let your family—meaning me—know when you're out on assignment? And haven't just disappeared or been kidnapped or snatched by aliens." Jeff rolled his eyes. Erin glared at him. "It happens. A lot more often than anyone will admit." He turned back to Vy. "Without putting you in danger?"

Vy picked up Talitha and lay her on the blanket with her brother. She returned to her seat. "There is a way, but it would have to look like any other text I'd send." She chewed her lip. "If I text you 'love u2,' that means I'm going out. I can't tell you for how long because we don't always know. But you'll know I'm legitimately gone."

She smiled. "Since we throw 'love u' around, it won't look suspicious."

Erin nodded. "Yeah, no one looking at my phone will think that's out of the ordinary. Especially now."

His phone rang. Felicity. Erin hesitated before answering. "I'm here."

"I'm sorry you got upset, Aaron. I didn't mean for that to happen. I want us to be one big happy family, too. I just need extra time where your sister and your girlfriend are concerned."

"Why? Make me understand what's different between seeing me and seeing Caitlin."

There came silence on the phone for several moments. "It's hard to explain, son. I'd rather tell you in person. Braydon, Terry, and I will come up and meet just you at the tuxedo store. After we're done there, you and I can talk."

"Where will Braydon and Terry be?"

"They can cool their heels someplace else. They're used to it. With all the medical appointments and insurance agents and lawyer meetings, they've gotten good at disappearing for an hour or so."

Erin cocked his head. Felicity couldn't see it, of course, but it expressed his confusion. "Why do they go with you?"

"I can't get your father in and out of the car without their help, you know. Or you don't know, do you?"

Erin cleared his throat. "Oscar is not my father, Felicity. Robert

Winger, bad as he might be, is still my father. Always will be."

"I'm sorry, Aaron. I misspoke. Your stepfather. With the braces and the back support, and the canes, it's too much for me. So Braydon and Terry have to come help."

"And Monica gets left at home?"

"Yes." It came out flat and sharp and cold.

"You'll have to explain that to me, too."

"Explain what?"

"What you have against Monica. She's a good kid."

"The fact you feel like you have to defend her proves otherwise. She's trying to poison my relationship with you already."

Erin drew in a deep breath. "What time do you three want to come up?"

"Will eleven a.m. work for you?"

"I'll make it work. I'll send you the directions to the store after I get confirmation from them. Talk to you later."

"I love you, son."

Erin disconnected the call. He closed his eyes and shook his head.

    * * *

Vy left the Farrell's and drove to her apartment. The tenor of the phone call with Felicity ate at her. It ate at her all the way home. Only when she closed the door to her apartment did she stop to analyze the mood. *Why? What bugs me most? The line about Monica trying to poison her relationship with Erin is a good candidate. Everything she said bothers me.*

Lord, this is not the way I want to feel. I'm angry, I'm disgusted, I'm offended... I don't want this to wash over into my love for Erin. Help me. Help him. Please.

Her phone rang. Vy stared at the number. Unfamiliar, she let it go to voicemail. The resulting ping said they had left a message.

Vy punched up the message.

"Hi. This is Felicity, Aaron's mother. I'd love to get together and talk to you, woman to woman. I am meeting my son on Saturday afternoon. Would you have time to meet me before then? And not tell Aaron? I want to surprise him with it later. Could we meet at Shady's for breakfast, about nine a.m.? Please give me a call back and let me know. We have so much to discuss. I look forward to hearing from you."

Vy stared at the phone. Her gut twisted. *Don't tell Aaron? Not a chance. Erin and I swore not to play those games.* Vy muttered, "But if I do tell him, she'll back out. I know she will. How do I handle this? How? How how how?"

Vy paced around her room. "If I don't tell him before, but tell him after…she denies the conversation ever happened. Hmmm…"

Think, Vy. Think. You're a DEA agent. You do this stuff for a living. How do you say yes, tell him, and not compromise your integrity?

Vy kicked it around her head. A slow smile spread across her face. *Bingo. Exactly.* She picked up the phone, hit the redial, and left a message for Felicity. "I'd love to meet you, Mrs. Bennett. Nine at Shady's will be fine. I'll see you then."

She disconnected the call, hit "forward" on her phone. "I didn't tell him a thing." Saturday should prove very enlightening for them both. She hoped.

COLLEEN SNYDER

SATURDAY

Erin waited for Felicity and his brothers to show up. He'd like to say he waited "patiently," but that would be an overstatement. So would saying he waited "anxiously." He waited. Period.

And greeted the trio twenty minutes late. Felicity sailed in and hugged him before he could say anything. Braydon and Terry kept non-committal faces. Perhaps accustomed to their mother's tardiness? She kissed him on the cheek. "Now, don't blame your brothers. I'm the one who ran late. I had an errand, and it took me longer than I thought. But we're here now, so that's all that matters."

Erin held the door and let Felicity in first. Braydon ducked his head as he went past. "Sorry, man."

Erin shrugged. "It's okay. We'll live." Terry tapped knuckles with Erin as he went into the store. Erin sighed.

Erin had no intention of choosing a tux for the wedding without Vy in attendance. But getting the measurements, looking at styles, looking at prices (!!), all served as the bait—the way to get time to actually talk to Felicity and get answers. It seemed kind of fun, in a narcissistic way, to dress in the tuxes. Braydon 'cleaned up' well, as did Terry.

Felicity ooed and ahhed over the selections. When all three men came out at once, she clapped her hands. Her voice choked. "My boys. All my boys. Together at once. I knew it. This is perfect. Perfect."

Erin raised an eyebrow. "It will be when we get all the others with us. Don't forget about Patrick." Felicity's eyes went from joy to ice in record time. Erin ignored the mood shift. "We'll have Gareth and Garth, our cousins, plus Jeff in the wedding party.

Harmon and Vy's father will be included, and anyone else on her side she wants to add."

Felicity kept her voice light, but Erin could read tension. "How many girls does Vy plan on having?"

"We're still in the talking phase. I know she has three sisters, except one may or may not be around at the time. She has some close friends. Her mom. Her grandmother, three aunts, two great aunts… I think that's all. I may be missing some. But the men will have plenty of people to escort."

Felicity's eyes narrowed. Her jaw tightened. "She doesn't have any male relatives who can assist her side of the family to their seats?"

Erin smiled. "No. And that's fine because we're not going to sit by families. No 'his side' and 'her side.' We're going to mix it up."

"I'm sure it will be delightful for you."

Sarcasm becomes you, doesn't it, Felicity? Second nature. Lord, guard my tongue. Erin thanked the store owner and manager, tipped the sales staff, then waved the Bennetts out the door. He looked at his watch. "There's a place around the corner where you and I can get a cup of coffee and have a talk. I think we'll survive if we walk." He looked at Braydon and Terry. "You think you can stay out of trouble for an hour? The mall is down two blocks."

Braydon's face broke into a grin. "Great! We can go window shopping. For women."

Terry shoved his brother. "You're favorite pastime."

"Nothing wrong with looking."

Felicity nailed her sons with a glare that would melt ice and the container it sat in. "You will not speak to anyone, do you hear me? No collecting phone numbers. You both have responsibilities in Harcort."

Terry sighed. "We know, Mom. We know."

Braydon took the keys and grabbed his brother around the shoulders. "Let's go. We're wasting time."

Felicity glared at them until the car turned the corner. She huffed. "I don't like letting them loose. They'll get into trouble. I know they will."

Erin offered Felicity his arm for the walk down the street to the shop. Security against sudden patches of ice. They sat inside, shucked their heavy outer coats, ordered, and sampled their drinks.

Erin ran his finger around the top of his mug. *Get to it.* "Why did you leave? When we were little."

"What do you remember?"

"You were there, then you weren't. Father said you died. I don't recall a funeral. We were five. What memories could we have?"

Felicity twisted her cup around. "Robert only wanted me to have the heir he needed. Once he had Caitlin, nothing else mattered. He had no use for you or me. He complained about everything you did. You couldn't do anything as good as your sister. She could do no wrong, ever. You? He never had time for you. Never spent a moment longer than he had to with you."

Felicity sipped at her cup. "It hurt me to watch you be left out, to be so heartbroken because your father had no time for you. No love for you. It was always Caitlin. Caitlin did this. Caitlin did that." Venom filled her tongue. "The little—"

Erin held up his hand. "You haven't answered the question. Why did you leave?"

"I couldn't stay. Not and watch you be ignored and cut out of your rightful place."

Erin's gut froze. "My 'rightful place?' What do you mean?"

"You should have been first. You were first. But the doctors screwed up the delivery and brought her out before you. I tried to make them put the order right on the certificates, but they wouldn't do it."

"Why did you leave?" Erin refused to be derailed.

"Robert wanted me gone. He didn't want anyone to see how much he adored his precious little girl. He said he could find a use for you. A son could come in handy sometimes. But Caitlin would be the only one who mattered."

"Robert wanted you gone. So you left? Just like that?"

"No. He promised me you would be taken care of. He would make sure you had all the things you needed. Good schools. Clothes. A home. Caitlin would—"

"Stop with Caitlin! Answer the question. Why did you leave? If Robert wanted you gone and didn't care about me, why would you leave me with him?" Anger and anguish wrapped around his tongue, making his words harsher than he wanted.

Felicity stared at her cup. "I couldn't take care of you. I had no money. No place to go. No one to take care of me. I had nothing.

How could I take care of you? It nearly killed me to leave you, but I had to, for your sake."

"Robert said, 'There's the door,' and you left? Just like that?"

Felicity lifted her cup, looked him in the eyes. "Just like that."

Erin let the information swirl around his brain for several moments. "And you hate Caitlin because she was his favorite, right? Even though she was only five and couldn't do anything about it if she wanted to?"

"She didn't want to do anything about it. She loved being the princess. She—"

"She was five years old. He was the adult. She is your daughter."

"She is his daughter. He created her. He can have her."

Erin sat back. He stared at Felicity, his heart pounding. *Where? Where did this hate come from? And what do I do about it?* He dropped his eyes. "What do you have against Vy?"

"I have nothing against Vy. Except she isn't the right woman for you."

"How do you know? You've talked with me three times. You've seen her with me once. What makes you think she's not right for me?"

"Mothers know these things. I can see it in her eyes. The way she looks at you. How she walks. How she addresses you. Says your name. She's not right, Aaron. I know it. You'd know it if you'd be honest with yourself."

"I've never been more honest than knowing I want to spend my life with Vy Johnson. She loves the Lord. She loves me. Anything else we can work out."

"Are you sure? Are you totally sure you can work out 'everything'?"

Erin held his mother's eyes. "With the Lord, yes. We can work out anything."

Felicity shook her head. "Your reliance on an imaginary god is pathetic, Aaron. You don't need anything but yourself. You're my son. I gave you all you need." The fire in her eyes flashed again. "I suppose Vy taught you to need a god, didn't she?"

Okay, this needed to end now. He'd find a way to contact Braydon. But this was beyond help. "No. Vy didn't teach me to need a 'god.' I recognized my need on my own. Years before I met Vy." *There's too much I want to throw at her. Lord, close my mouth.*

Please. "What do you have against God?"

Vy all but snarled. "I had him shoved down my throat for years. My father used to be a preacher. Such a saint on Sunday but beat the snot out of me on Monday. My mother didn't do a thing to protect me. Never lifted a finger to help. He could beat me bloody, and she'd tell me, 'If you did what you were told, he wouldn't have to punish you. He loves you.' Love like that I didn't need. My brothers shielded me the best they could, but God? He did nothing. Don't talk to me about God. There isn't one. I know better."

"Where are your brothers now?" *The DNA match didn't mention them. Maybe they didn't sign up. Lucky them.*

"I don't know. I don't care. They abandoned me when I left Robert Winger. They were counting on me sharing Robert's wealth with them. Once the cash cow got cut off, they had no use for me."

Remember, she skews everything. Leave it alone. Focus on now. Erin downed the remainder of his coffee. "I'm sorry you feel the way you do. Caitlin is my sister. I love her. I owe her. Vy is my fiancée. I love her. And we are going to be married. Jesus is my Lord and Savior. Nothing will change that. And I make no apologies."

He nodded to her. "I don't expect you to accept my choices. You don't have to like my choices. I ask you to respect the people I love and treat them with courtesy."

Felicity glared at him. "And if I don't?"

"We have nothing to build a relationship on."

"So we're back to the 'love me, love my dogs' condition. What if I hate dogs? Does this mean we can't have a relationship away from them? You can't come to my house where there are no dogs, where I'm comfortable and happy? It has to be your way or no way?"

"Isn't that what you're saying? We can be together but only at your place, with your people."

"It's different. You accept my people. I don't accept yours."

Give it up. It's over. Erin pushed his chair back from the table. "We're done. I'm sorry you've made the choices you have. I wish you and your family well."

Felicity's eyes flared. "That's it? I'm your mother. You can't dismiss me like I'm some underling employee. You owe me."

Erin stood. "I owe you nothing! You abandoned us when we were five. By your own admission, walked out on us. You said you followed us, but you never made one attempt to contact us. Your daughter was abandoned on the streets of Oakton to die, but you claim none of it ever happened."

He breathed deep. "You say he never abused her, but I've seen the x-rays and the scars from all the broken bones she suffered as a child. I lived alone with Robert for twelve years and heard nothing but how much he hated her. I broke my neck...and you say that never happened, either."

He couldn't stop. "You hate the very ones who saved me and gave me my life back. No, we can't build a relationship." He threw money on the table to cover the bill. "I'll walk you back."

"Aaron, wait. Sit down, please." Felicity lay her hand on his. "Please. Give me one minute to explain myself."

Erin breathed heavy. He closed his eyes. *Lord, make it clear. Otherwise, I'm outta here.* He opened his eyes, stared at Felicity, nodded, then sat down.

Felicity patted his hand, then pushed the money back to him. Erin pocketed it. "Thank you." Erin waited. Felicity dropped her gaze to the table. "You have to understand, son. It hasn't been easy for me, either. I had to rebuild my whole life apart from your father. I had to scrape and claw and fight to make it. I resented your sister for pushing me out, for taking my place. It's something I'm not proud of. But I'm trying to deal with it. Having you in my life will make it better, I know. Will you give me a chance?"

"If we can do joint counseling. The three of us."

Felicity shook her head. "I don't need counseling, Aaron."

He interrupted her. "Let's start there. My name is Erin. With an 'in.' Not 'Aaron.' Robert Winger changed the spelling. I resented it at first, but I came to see it as a badge of honor."

She shrugged. "What difference does it make?"

"Because one is my name, and the other isn't. It's the first link of 'respect' I'm talking about. Of you respecting who I am."

She sighed slightly. "If it will make you happy, I'll try."

Take it. "Counseling will help all three of us. Believe it or not, there are still some scars about you leaving. Disappearing."

"And I'll make them up to you, son. I will. If you give me a chance."

"It's not something you 'make up for.' And your feelings about Caitlin need to be resolved. She's your daughter. My sister. Mother to your grandchildren. You have no reason to hate her."

Felicity's eyes burned. So did her voice. "Don't tell me what reasons I have or don't have. You don't know—"

Erin stood. Felicity grabbed his hand. "Okay, okay. I'll consider doing counseling. By myself. I don't need her to be there."

"But you do need to meet her. And the babies. Your grandchildren. My niece and nephews. They are part of the family. They have done nothing to deserve being shunned or hated."

"I'll meet the babies."

"Hard to meet them without their mother."

"You're pushing too hard. I can't make all these changes at once. And you have to give me something in return."

"Like what?" Erin cocked his head. "I've been to your house. I met the family. I like the family. I had the boys come up here. What more do you want?"

"I want you to call me 'Mom.' And Braydon and Terry, your brothers."

"I have no problem calling Braydon and Terry my brothers. I have no problem calling Monica my sister, either." He saw the fire in Felicity's eyes. "And there's another thing you need to explain. What has Monica done to deserve your anger? Her brothers love her, she's a good kid, and she's working hard in school. What is your problem with her?"

"You don't need to know. Except she is evil and twists everything she touches."

Erin went still inside. He'd heard this before. From Caitlin. Echoing Robert Winger's accusations about her. *I'm wicked and evil and soil everything I touch.*

He held Felicity's gaze. "Have you ever been in counseling, Felicity?"

"Mom. You're supposed to call me Mom."

"Not yet, I won't. Not until you can call Caitlin your daughter."

"I won't. I can't. I'll respect her as a person, but no further."

"And you'll respect Vy?"

"If I have to."

"She's done nothing to you. Why would you hate her off the bat?"

"She's not right for you. You deserve better. You're the last Winger, the last of Robert's line. You have an image and a standard to uphold."

Erin stared at her, then burst out laughing. "Image? Standard? Of what? Of three men who murdered their father, at their mother's insistence, because he wanted to give away the family fortune after he came to Christ? That image? Or the image of three men who conspired to murder my sister because Fenton Mudd left the whole inheritance to her?"

Erin tapped the table with his fist. "I'm supposed to uphold the standard of the man who used me my whole life, who twisted my existence to satisfy his need for power? Ah, no. I have no desire to replicate anything of the name Winger. Let Garth and Gareth carry on the family tree. But I don't see them wanting to follow their father's footsteps, either."

"Then to uphold mine. Aren't I important to you? Doesn't my heritage matter?"

Erin narrowed his gaze. "What heritage, Felicity? The one where you walked away from your children? The one where you're trying to cheat the insurance company? Or the heritage where you hate your daughters? I'm supposed to preserve that? I don't think so. Vy and I are starting a new line, a new family. One which will have a proper heritage of love and respect."

"She's black. No black woman deserves to belong in our family. Ever."

Erin nodded. "Now it comes out. The prejudice."

Felicity glared at him. "No son of mine marries a black woman."

Erin smiled. "Well, this has been enlightening. I'm sorry, ma'am. We're done." He stood, took the bill to the cashier. "Anything she orders after this is on her."

The cashier refused the payment. "This one's on me. You deserve the Nobel Peace prize for keeping your cool. You're a better man than I'll ever be."

He tapped knuckles with Erin. Erin shook his head, walked out the door, back to his car, and drove to the office.

He held it all in. The anger, the disgust, the frustration, the pity, the hurt...and a thousand other emotions wanting to come to the surface. He would let none through. Not until he could filter them through the Lord. And for that, he needed time.

But focused time. And this wasn't it. He needed to work, to get his mind on something other than the meeting with Felicity. He pulled out the oldest, most complicated invoice he could find. There was a conflict in the billing of the hours. Or so the property owner claimed. It would be the perfect project to work on. He set his alarm for three hours. If it took longer, he'd extend the time. Or not. Depending on the quietness in his soul.

SATURDAY AFTERNOON

Vy waited until two to call Erin. They agreed not to talk about their individual meetings with Felicity until both occurred. And they both were able to take some "processing" time. She hoped he'd had all the time he needed.

Her phone rang. She looked at the number. "Hi, Mom. What's going on?"

"Nothing special. Thought maybe you could bring your Mr. Winger over for dinner this evening. Great Aunt Ruth is coming in town and is looking forward to meeting him."

Vy smiled. "You mean checking him out, right?"

"Your aunt does like to express her opinion on important matters."

"Like who marries who in this family?"

Mom laughed. "Well, she has been known to state her preference. No one actually listens to her, but she does get to state it."

"Sure, Mom. I'll see if Erin is free. We both met with his biological mother today. I'm about to call him to compare notes."

"Oh? How did it go?"

Vy smiled. "I'll let you know tonight. I want to talk to him about it first."

"Of course you do. Just because your mother wants to know something is no reason to…"

Vy laughed. "I love you, Mom. And I'll tell you all about it tonight."

"Love you, girl."

"Love you, Mom." Vy hung up, shaking her head. "Mom." She

dialed Erin's phone.

He picked up. "Hello, beautiful."

"You can't know that over the phone."

"Oh, yes, I can. You're beautiful inside and out, whether I see you or not."

"You sound happy. Did the afternoon go well?"

"No. It didn't. Want to meet at Jeff and Collin's so we can talk?"

"You need a baby to hold so you don't throw something?"

"Now, how did you guess?"

"Irrational conjecture."

"Educated conjecture more like it."

"How soon?"

"I called Collin about five minutes before you called me. She said for you to come on over, and if we watch the babies, she'll fix dinner later. How does that sound?"

"It would sound wonderful, except Mom wants us to come there for dinner. Aunt Ruth is in town and wants to meet you."

"What time?"

"Dinner is usually at six. Does that give us enough time to talk about meeting with Felicity?"

"It does. Short and not so sweet."

"I'm sorry, Erin."

"I know. I love you, Vy. I'll see you at Collin's."

"I love you, Erin."

She hung up. "I guess he answered the question. I wonder how bad it got?" She pulled on a sweater, thought better of it, and put on an older sweatshirt. Less worry about bodily fluids. She would change into the clean shirt before she left the Farrell's. Vy shook her head. Practice. Call it all practice.

The roads were frosty but not slick as she crossed town to the Farrell's house. The Farrell house with all the littles in it. Temps were supposed to drop during the night, but the forecast didn't mention ice. The loaner car's tires would hold.

She pulled into the circle drive, parked, and walked in unannounced. One time at the Farrell's and you had refrigerator privileges. Twice a visitor, you got access to the whole kitchen. Third time, you're family, so why are you knocking and waking up the babies?

The family sat assembled in the living room. The triplets were on their bellies, wiggling and rolling and generally being their infant selves. Erin kissed Vy as she came in. Jeff hugged her. "Collin's in the kitchen."

Vy poked her head in to say hi. "What are you doing, and do you need help?"

Collin laughed. "I'm deciding on dinner. 'Chopped Kitchen' style. You know, whatever is in the pantry? Get a drink and sit."

Vy grabbed a soda and joined Erin on the couch. He took her hand, looked at Jeff. "I know we spend a lot of time discussing my issues here. It won't be this way forever, I promise."

Jeff shrugged. "Eh. Your issues, my issues. We're family."

Erin nodded. "And this concerns Cane, too. I figured she deserves to hear it, such as it is."

A voice from the kitchen hollered, "Wait until I get in there. Give me five minutes."

Erin flopped down on his stomach with his nieces and nephews. "How's it going down here, hmm? Everything okay? No complaints about the housekeeping? Vacuuming getting done?"

Caleb lifted his head and smiled at her fiancé. The baby babbled and cooed. Erin babbled back. Vy smiled. *He's going to be a great father.* Collin came into the room, drying her hands on her jeans. "Okay, now you can start."

Erin rolled to his feet. "I'd rather talk to Caleb." He returned to sit beside Vy and she squeezed his hand. Erin breathed deep then sighed. Vy's eyes narrowed. *How bad did it get with Felicity? I've never seen him this…troubled? Bothered? Down. Lord, lift him.*

Erin squeezed Vy's hand in return. "Why don't you start?" He looked at Collin. "Felicity left Vy a message to meet with her."

Collin raised an eyebrow. "Oh?"

Vy nodded. "Yes. This morning at nine at Shady's. She arrived early, but so did I. She wanted to tell me I'm a delightful person, but even I know I'm not right for Erin. I struck her as too sophisticated, too intelligent for him. I would get bored. She knew her son, and he would never be able to keep up with me. All in the sense of wanting the best for both of us, you understand. I should look for someone 'more like me.' I thanked her, told her I had carefully considered my choices and would be very happy to spend my life trying to keep up with her son. I had seen him under pressure and knew him to be a man of God."

Erin interrupted her narrative. "What did she say?"

Vy's eyes narrowed. "She had a few things to say about God. It amazed her an intelligent woman like me would resort to a fairytale for strength and support. Her son would never share such a weakness. He might say he did, to be with me, but he'd never live it. No, I should really look for someone else. And if I had your interests at heart, I would tell you we're done, and I'd walk away."

Erin shook his head. "I'm sorry you had to listen to her. It won't happen again."

Vy cocked her head. "Oh? How do you know?"

Erin lowered his head but looked at his sister. "Because I won't be associating with Felicity again. Without going through the whole exchange, she is a woman who doesn't share our values. And has no desire to."

Vy held Erin's eyes. "Just because she doesn't share our values doesn't mean—"

"In this case, it does. Felicity wants me. No one else. She refuses to have anything to do with anyone else in this room. Including the triplets." Vy ached for Erin. As much as he tried to display an air of confidence and composure, Vy sensed the fragility of his mood. She could feel him shaking inside.

Vy lay her head on his shoulder. "We have the Lord. We have each other. We have our families. We are complete."

Erin lay his head on top of hers. She read the pain. He chuckled but without mirth. "I didn't realize how much I wanted it to work out." He lifted his head. "I'm going to keep in touch with Braydon as much as possible. But Felicity is done."

Collin kept her voice gentle. "What did she say about leaving? Did she give you that much?"

Erin stared at his sister. "Robert Winger wanted her gone, so she left. Period."

"And I caused that how?"

Erin faltered. "You really need to hear this? All of it?"

"I don't want you carrying this alone, A-One. Tell me."

He lowered his eyes. "She blames you for all of it. In her version of reality, Robert only wanted you, not me. He paid all the attention to you. You were never abandoned. I never broke my neck. She has only contempt for her daughters and the Lord but obsesses over her sons."

He squeezed Vy's hand. "She is deeply prejudiced against people of color. I asked her if she could respect you, Collin, the Lord, my choices… She said no. There really wasn't anything more to say. So I left."

Collin reached out and picked up Caleb. She handed him to Erin. "Uncle Erin needs a hug."

Erin cradled the squirming infant on his shoulder. Collin picked up Joshua. "Uncle Erin needs two hugs." She deposited the second child on his other shoulder. She gathered up Talitha and handed her to Vy. "Auntie Vy needs a hug, too."

Vy hugged the littlest Farrell. She closed her eyes, and the tears burned. *I don't know who I'm crying for most. Everyone. Lord, forgive her. Turn her heart. And comfort Erin. And Collin. This has to be hard. But thank You, Erin made the right choice. For all of us.*

She kissed the infant on her shoulder. "Auntie Vy and Uncle Erin need to go. We've been commanded to appear before Aunt Ruth." She shook her head. "This day just keeps getting better."

Erin handed Caleb, then Joshua, to Jeff and Collin. "Hey, it'll get better. We're eating your mom's cooking. And your parents love me."

Vy smiled. "Truth. Very well, I agree. Things are looking up." She kissed Collin, hugged Jeff, and together she and Erin walked out.

He opened her car door. "Watch the ice. And the snow. And the other drivers. And—"

Vy laughed. "We're five miles from my parents' house, Mr. Winger. I think I can make the crossing without a problem. Even in this loaner."

"Fine." He leaned in and kissed her. "Meet you there."

Vy pulled out.

* * *

Erin pulled in behind Vy at the house. *I hope Aunt Ruth is as accepting as the rest of the family. I don't know how much more rejection I can handle in one day.*

She waited for him, and they went into the house together. Erin smelled pot roast and smiled. "Love it. Your mom makes the best pot roast in the state of Ohio."

Martha Johnson called from the kitchen, "You need to sample a few more pot roasts, Mr. Winger."

Vy's mom came out wearing a comfortable lounge suit and an apron. Like Vy, Martha presented slender and tall. Not as dark as Vy, but with the same sparkling brown eyes. Her hair, pulled back in a tight bun, showed more gray than black. She walked over and gave Vy a hug and a kiss, then hugged Erin. "Dinner will be half an hour. Waiting for Ruth to get here. She hates to drive these roads after dark."

"Why does she?"

Martha smiled. "She's too stubborn not to. I told her we'd meet tomorrow after church, but Aunt Ruth refused. Too busy. The woman is eighty-five. I hope I have half her energy when I get to that age."

I'll be happy to get to that age.

Vy offered, "Can I help with anything?"

Martha shook her head. "No, it's all ready. Just staying warm. Table's set, so go find your father and get comfortable."

"What's he doing?"

"He's studying the last chess game you and he played, trying to see where he went wrong."

Vy chuckled. "You didn't tell him I'm taking lessons from Erin, did you?"

"Now, why would I do that?" Martha raised her voice a few decibels. "I say it's 'bout time the man got brought down a peg or two. By his daughter, no less."

"Martha!" George Johnson yelled from his office. "I heard you. Send my daughter in here. I've got some questions to ask her."

Vy grinned at Erin, her eyes twinkling. "Coming, Father."

Erin and Vy entered the office. Wall-to-wall books and bookcases, but neat. Organized. A man after Erin's own heart. *Well, maybe not as organized, but that's a good thing.*

The chessboard showed pieces in play. Vy put on her most innocent air. "You called, Father?"

"Don't 'Father' me, young woman. I see your gambit. Took me a day or two, but I have you now." He turned to Erin and smiled. "Welcome, son. Good to see you again. Been what, a week?

Erin glanced at the ceiling. "I believe you're correct, sir. It might have been a week ago."

George raised his eyebrows. "You keep showing up here eating my food, drinking my tea, you're going to have to marry one of my daughters. I've got four you can choose from."

Erin held up Vy's hand. "I'll take this one, sir. With your permission."

George narrowed his eyes and glared from Vy to Erin and back to Vy. "You sure you want this one? She's hard-headed at times."

Erin nodded. "I believe I can handle it, sir. I'll simply turn her over to the Lord and let Him deal with her."

George nodded. "Wise man. Wise man. Daughter, you need to hold on to this one."

Vy laughed. "Oh, I am, Dad, I am." She hugged her father. "Aunt Ruth call?"

"Before she left. She'll be here in a few more minutes. Your mother told her we'd eat at six. Which means Ruth won't be here until six-thirty, but we give grace here."

Erin took a seat on a barstool to watch the contestants. George had indeed figured Vy's gambit. The question now: could he figure a way out?

Twenty minutes later, the front door opened. Erin heard the calls of, "Aunt Ruth! Welcome! How were the roads?"

Vy looked up from the board. "Call it a draw?"

"I should say so. You've either been sandbagging, or you're studying on your own. Either way, this is more fun than I've had in a while." George looked at Erin. "When do you and I get to play?"

Erin smiled. "After the wedding."

George eyed him sideways. "Oh?"

"Yeah. If you beat me now, you'll think I'm not worthy of Vy. If I beat you, you'll withhold her hand in revenge. After the wedding, it won't matter."

George chuckled. "A man who figures all the angles. I like this one, daughter." The three joined the small crowd which had formed in the kitchen. Ruth, her Westie, Melvin, two of Vy's sisters, and a boyfriend all gathered around the kitchen island.

Aunt Ruth hugged Vy. "Girl, look at you! When did you grow up? You were just a little thing last time I saw you. Now, look at you. All tall and skinny like your mama…someone needs to feed you more. You'll never catch a man without some meat on those bones."

Vy laughed. "It hasn't been so long, Aunt Ruth. Only a year, maybe? I haven't changed."

"No, you're still as beautiful as you ever were. You found a man yet?"

Vy wrapped her arm in Erin's. "That's why you came, isn't it, Aunt Ruth? To meet my man?" She smiled at Ruth.

Ruth eyed Erin up and down. He sensed a hesitancy, a lack of approval, a—*Say it. She doesn't like me*—in the woman's gaze. He held out his hand to her. "Ms. Stone. I'm glad to get to know you."

"I don't believe you, young man. I don't believe you at all." Her tone was frostier than the air outside, and the temperature already sat well below freezing. She turned away from Erin. "George! Where is my nephew?"

George stepped up to hug and kiss the woman. "Welcome, Aunt Ruth."

"Since when did you let your daughters start dating men who aren't husband material? I thought the only reason to date is to find a man to marry."

George smiled. "Vy and Erin are going to be married in the fall, Aunt Ruth."

Ruth pulled herself up to her full five-foot-four height. "Oh? And with whose approval?"

George kept smiling. "Mine, Aunt Ruth. Erin asked for her hand, I threw in the rest of her, and they will be married when the church can find the space. Your sister Viola has already made it clear Vy will be married at Calvary Church. Vy and Erin agreed, and it will be a wonderful match."

The reference to her sister Viola's name caused Ruth's face to crinkle as if she'd sucked on something bitter. "For who? George, I thought I raised you better than this."

George never lost his smile. "You did, Aunt Ruth. You raised me to teach my daughters to love the Lord, to put Him first, then to follow their hearts when it came to who to love. Vy has done just that. Erin is a fine man in the Lord, and we're blessed to have him joining our family."

Erin made as if to step up, but Vy waved him off with her eyes. *Oookay...I guess I'll watch.*

Ruth continued to stare at Erin, her eyes narrow and on fire. "Joining our family, you say?"

"That's what I said, Aunt Ruth. He's joining our family. Not stealing Vy away, not hustling her off somewhere. Joining our family." George's face creased in amusement.

She side-eyed Erin. "We'll see."

Vy stepped forward. "Yes, Aunt Ruth, we will. You will always be welcome at our home."

Ruth raised her eyebrows. For the first time, she addressed Erin. "You agree there? I'm always welcome?"

"You'll be as welcome as George and Martha and everyone else in this family, Ms. Stone." *Now is not the time for jokes about except the honeymoon, right?*

Riiiight.

Ruth huffed. She turned away from Erin and smiled at Martha. "So good to see you, Martha. Whatever you're cooking, it smells like it's burning. Maybe I should help you in the kitchen."

"No need, Aunt Ruth. I turned the stove off to let it rest. I'll have it on the table in five minutes."

Ruth huffed again. She looked at Vy's sister and pointed to the boyfriend. "Who is this?"

"This is Reggie, Aunt Ruth. He's a friend."

"Doesn't look like much." She eyed him up and down. "Looks like a shabby streetwalker who's after a free meal."

George put his arm around Ruth's shoulders. "Come on, Aunt Ruth. Let's go sit down, and you can tell me all about the trip down. Which did you find worse, the roads or the drivers?"

Vy squeezed Erin's hand. She leaned in to murmur in his ear. "She disapproves of everyone and everything. We love her anyhow."

Erin nodded. "Glad it wasn't just me. Too much rejection in one day is bad for my self-esteem." He chuckled. "Or would be if I had any."

Vy kissed him on the cheek. "You did very well."

"How do I win her over?"

"You don't. She'll accept you at the wedding when she sees there is no hope of changing my mind."

"Ah, I see. Or I will."

Before they could all get seated, George's phone rang. He picked it up. "Yes, Pastor Wells." His face drew into a frown. A concerned frown. "Is everyone out? Any idea… Absolutely. We will start the prayers here. Call me if you hear anything else."

All eyes turned to the patriarch. "The church is on fire."

Erin looked around at frozen expressions of horror. George continued. "Pastor Wells says they've called up a second unit to keep the neighborhood from going up as well. Evening service got out an hour ago, so there wasn't anyone in the building. Pastor Wells said he would call with any updates."

Coincidence. It's only a coincidence.

Erin asked, "Is there anything we can do besides pray?"

"Not right now. We'll have to wait."

Martha glanced at George. "Well, let's get to praying."

The group joined hands, and George led. When he finished, Martha waved to the table. "Still got food to eat. Everyone sit."

News about the fire didn't keep the discussions from getting warm. Ruth did indeed have an opinion—a negative one—about everyone and everything. While Erin thought the food excellent, Ruth badgered Martha about the amount of salt, the lack of seasonings, the tenderness of the beef... Anything she could find. Martha responded to each insult by smiling and saying, "Thank you, Ruth. I'll remember for next time."

Erin saw the twinkle in Vy's eye. He gave her a side-long look. Vy lowered her voice so only he could hear. "She'll remember it, alright. She'll forgive, but she will remember."

He lowered his eyes to keep the smile from showing. So, Martha had an ornery streak in her as well. He'd suspected it, but this proved it. He could only imagine what kind of retribution might be served the next time...

Dinner finished, the group retired to the living room. More chatter, more laughter. A good family feel. *Lord, let my home be this way. Everyone welcome, everyone accepted, everyone loved. Help me make it so.*

By eight-thirty, the party began to break up. Ruth decided it was too late to drive home. Fortunate for her, she'd left some items at the Johnson house on her last visit so she could spend the night with minimal problems. Melvin, her Westie, would sleep with her in the guest suite. Good thing she decided to bring him along, hmmm.

Erin slipped into his parka. With Ruth keeping a jaundiced eye on them the entire time, he and Vy said respectable goodbyes at the front door. He kissed her cheek. Vy held his hand. Erin bowed his head. "Lord, keep Your eyes on this family. Make us walk like

You."

Vy squeezed his hand. "Amen."

Another kiss and Erin walked outside. The frigid air chased away any sleepiness he might have been feeling. He scraped the frost off his windshield then drove back to the Farrell's house. Erin slipped in as quietly as he could and snuck to his room. He listened for any cries or whimpers, which meant he'd been detected, but there were none. *Success!*

Erin kneeled by his bed, prayed, climbed in bed. Sleep. Just for a little while. Until a baby cried. But for now, sleep.

SUNDAY

Six a.m. Sunday, Erin received a short note from Braydon: *Will call. Mom had the phone.* He shook his head. *My fear. What kind of crazy did I unleash on the kids?* He had a hard time relieving himself of any responsibility for what Felicity might do. He really couldn't see any other choice. But still…

Erin dressed (quietly) and slipped into the kitchen. The coffee pot was clean. How did that happen? No one made any last night. Maybe…maybe…maybe they slept through the night? Really?

Collin wandered into the kitchen. She sat at the bar and stared at the pot. "No coffee?"

"I wondered so myself. You think maybe they slept through the night?"

"No one got me up." She looked at the time. "And they should have been awake an hour ago." Collin moved to the nursery, Erin behind her.

All three infants were huddled together, peacefully sleeping. Collin sighed and rested her head against the wall. "They're so sweet when they're asleep."

Jeff peaked around the corner. "Did someone forget to get me up for my shift?"

"No, the Lord worked a miracle, and we all got to sleep. Let's be grateful and not blow it." Erin caught both Jeff's and Collin's arms and pulled them out of the doorway. "Kitchen. Quietly. Now!"

The three adults tip-toed back to the kitchen. Erin made the first carafe, Collin got out some cups, and Jeff watched. Erin poured, they toasted one another, and got the first sips in.

Still no noise from the nursery.

Collin shook her head. "This isn't right. It's not."

Jeff dropped his head. "Let me guess. You're going to go in there and wake them up to see if they're okay, right?"

"No. Not until I finish this cup. Then, I'll go in and wake one of them up. Someone needs to eat. Soon."

Erin swallowed his drink. "Whose turn is it?"

"At this point, I don't care. Bring Talitha if you can get her. She needs to eat more to keep up with her brothers."

"One baby girl coming right up."

Erin snuck into the room. The baby tangle had loosened enough for him to carefully unravel Talitha out from under her brothers without waking them. The littlest Farrell wiggled and stretched and made sucking noises loud enough to wake the dead. Except her brothers slept through it. Erin changed her quickly and brought her to Collin, who had taken up her baby-feeding position in the living room.

Collin took Talitha, got her settled eating. She glanced at Erin. "What are you going to do after church today?"

"Probably go see what it will take to rebuild the Calvary Chapel and surrounding area."

Jeff's head snapped around. "That was Vy's Calvary Church? I didn't know. Everyone got out, right? I didn't hear anything about casualties."

Erin nodded. "Yes, her church. No, no casualties. The neighborhood may have sustained some damage, but I'll know more after I go down. I want to see what kind of help we can offer. Without being pushy or annoying."

Collin smiled. "I understand. But you're always diplomatic."

"I can be." *When I'm dealing with rational people.*

Erin poured a cup of warmth into his travel mug, kissed Talitha and Collin, bumped fists with Jeff, and walked into the garage. He keyed the opener...

...to be greeted by vandalism, the like of which he'd not seen before. Whole buckets of paint had been thrown against the house, the trees, the sidewalks. Three or four colors had been indiscriminately splattered on the roof. Words too wrong to even acknowledge were painted across the driveway. The buckets themselves joined the carnage, overturned on the mailbox. Erin glanced up and down the street to see if they were the only ones who had been hit.

The houses on either side had been damaged as well, but not as severely. No curses or foul words. Paint had been restricted to one color and thrown primarily on the yard. And no damage to the mailboxes.

Erin sighed, pulled out his phone, and dialed the non-emergency police number. He got put on hold as he walked back inside.

Jeff looked up. "What'd you forget?"

Erin shook his head. "Come outside a moment."

Jeff's eyes narrowed. He grabbed his parka, threw it over his pajamas, pulled on his slippers, and stepped out into the garage. Erin watched Jeff's eyes burn as soon as he saw the wreckage out front.

Erin murmured, "Sorry, man. As soon as the police come, I'll get a crew out here to clean it up."

Jeff stared at Erin. "Why are you sorry?"

"Because this may be my fault."

Jeff dropped a firm hand on Erin's shoulder. "Unless you bought the paint and gave it to her, or threw it yourself, don't take this on, bro. You didn't make her crazy." He surveyed the damage. "We don't know it was her. Pretty good idea, but we have no proof. Even mentioning her may sound petty."

"Maybe. But not mentioning her isn't exactly being honest when the police ask, 'Do you have any idea who might want to do this?' Just saying, you know."

"I know. We'll see what they say. If they get here. I'm going back in before I freeze. You can head out, and I'll take care of the report." Jeff huddled his arms around his chest in front of his chest and blew on his hands.

"You sure?"

"Yeah. Check in with Vy and make sure she's okay. And her family."

"It will be my next call."

"Make it your first one from now on." Jeff scowled at Erin.

"I hear you." Jeff headed inside. Erin speed-dialed Vy.

Her voice sounded terse. "I hope your morning is going better than mine."

"Um…no, not really. Tell me about yours." He slid into his car to continue to church.

"Just got off the phone with the parents. They were vandalized last night. Paint everywhere. Someone wrote a few misspelled words."

"Any other neighbors get bothered?"

"Ones on either side, but not as bad. Why?"

"Because Jeff and Collin got hit last night, too. And the neighbors north and south..." He hesitated, rolled his eyes skyward, thought hard, nodded. "Yeah. North and south. But only just so. Jeff has a call to the police."

"So does Dad. You think this is Felicity's doing?"

"Of course I do. Do I have any proof? No." Erin turned the corner, leaving the wreckage behind. "Unless the police can find something to tie her to all this, all we have is a woman scorned. Don't think it will hold up in court."

"Trust me, it won't." Erin grimaced. *She would know.*

"What are you going to do?" He waited for her to answer.

"I'll go in to work on Monday and see if we have any loose agents who can do some digging around." Vy's tone carried some heat.

Erin's eyebrows rose. "They'll arrange that?"

"When it comes to our families being bothered, you better believe we do that. You don't mess with an agent's family. Ever." There was a finality to the promise which made Erin smile.

"I'll file the information away for future reference." He hesitated. "Vy...be careful. Please. I love you."

"I love you, too, Erin. I promise I'll be very careful. And I'll text you if anything else happens."

"Hit my speed dial, text zzzzzzz if you're in trouble." He turned the corner to the freeway.

"Is this another one of you and your sister's tricks?"

Not this one. "No. I just thought it up for you. Please? Humor me."

"I will if you will."

"I promise." *Our first covenant and Felicity caused it. Not sure she'd approve.*

"So do I. Love you, Erin Winger."

"Love you, Vy Johnson."

He put his phone back in his pocket. "Lord, I don't know what all this is about. I don't have to know, right? All I have to do is follow Your will. Make it plain, Dad. Make it very plain. Please."

Erin fulfilled his duties at the mission then drove to the Calvary church. He walked around and looked at what remained of the building. Damage had been limited somewhat by the installation of a sprinkler system some five years ago. The kitchen, where the fire started, suffered the most carnage. *It needed to be refurbished anyhow.* The sanctuary showed mainly water damage. The hymnals and Bibles in the seatbacks would need to be replaced, as would the carpet. Most of the pews would dry.

Brother Tim surveyed the mess when Erin caught up to him. "Brother Tim!"

The man stepped over a pile of fire-damaged cookware. "Erin! What brings you down here?"

"I want to see what I can do to help." Erin dropped his eyes. "I…uh…I may know who is behind this. And I feel like it's partly my fault."

Tim's eyes bored holes into Erin's. "Care to explain?"

Erin did. Short form. "But I don't have proof."

Tim nudged the broken crockery around with his size 13 shoe. "That's a lot to confess to, Brother Erin. Especially since you didn't make her crazy or light the match she held."

Erin rolled his eyes. "Won't anyone let me take responsibility for this?"

Tim chuckled. "Probably not. Well…one person may. But I wouldn't trust her judgment. So no. Not your fault. Vy told me what happened between Ms. Bennett and the two of you. I can see she is a sick, sick woman who needs help. But it's up to the police to decide. We will pray for her."

Erin nodded. "Right. In the meantime, can I help here? I know you have insurance, but we can help make sure you get honest repairs, and at a fair price. And faster than a few weeks or months. " Erin thought hard. "I know a place nearby where you can meet until you get repaired or rebuilt. And I know some people who can provide transport for those who need it. It'll help out some. If you want."

Tim nudged the pile again. "I'll check with the pastoral team and the elder board. We should be able to have an answer by tomorrow. If I can get ahold of everyone." He sighed. "And we don't need to have a congregational vote." The man shook his head. "Someone will complain no matter what color we choose for carpeting. We lose more congregants that way."

Erin huffed. "So I've heard. People."

"I have your number. I'll give you a call." Tim clapped Erin on the shoulder.

"Thanks, Brother Tim. We can work through the Mission if it makes it any easier for people to accept the help."

Tim's face grew stern. "This body of believers needs to come into the present and realize all God's children don't worship alike, sing alike, or look alike. But we all love the Lord the same."

Erin laughed. "I hear you. Thanks again."

He spent the rest of the day making calls from the office (fewer distractions) to crews for clean-up, restoration, getting the neighbors squared away, and generally doing damage control and repair. Late in the afternoon, his phone pinged.

Braydon texted, *Can you talk?*

Call away.

The phone rang. "Talk to me, Braydon. What's going on?" Erin leaned back in his office chair.

"Life got real interesting after Mom got back yesterday. What did you say to her?"

Erin rolled his eyes. "I'm sorry, man. She won't respect anyone I love. She's prejudiced against Vy, she refuses to have anything to do with Collin or the babies. I don't know how to have any kind of relationship with that. I walked out on her. Probably shouldn't have, but I was furious. I'm sorry for causing trouble for you." Erin sat up straight. Whatever Braydon wanted to tell him, it probably wouldn't be good.

Braydon actually chuckled. "I figured it might be something like that. Not going to tell you what she said about it. I'm sorry it didn't work out."

"So am I. I still want to see you and Terry and Monica. Any chance you can get away from there?"

"Um…we're moving out. All of us. Basically got tossed out for defending you as a good person."

"What? Why?" Erin wished this had been a video call. He wanted to see Braydon's expression.

"Someone called the insurance company and reported Oscar for fraud. An investigator came out while we were gone. Found Oscar in the backyard shoveling snow. Yeah, it went downhill from there.

She accused you of calling the insurance adjuster out of spite. I said you wouldn't be that petty. She told me to pack my things and get out."

"I'm sorry, man. I am." Erin tossed the pen he held. *Stupid.*

"Terry backed me, and she told him to leave, too. Monica said she wouldn't stay, and Mom happily threw her out, as well."

"Where are you living?" Erin's eyes narrowed. *This is my fault.*

"In the car right now."

"All three of you? That's insane." Erin nearly exploded. "It's winter! You can't live in a car." *I caused this. I need to fix it.*

Braydon explained, "I rented a storage unit for our stuff, and we moved everything in there. Took us a few trips, but we got it all out. What she allowed us to take, anyhow." Erin's teeth ground together. "Mostly personal stuff. No furniture. Clothes…well, clothes we bought ourselves, books, music, electronics and the like. She'll be shutting this phone down tomorrow, she said. I put applications in at several apartment places. But with no credit history, it's going to be tough to get approved. Paying the bills will be tight until Terry gets a full-time job. But it's better than being at the house with all the ranting and screaming going on. And we're together, so we've got each other. We'll make it. I know we will."

Erin's thoughts raced. "You're wanting to stay in Harcort?"

"Or as close as we can. Monica needs to finish up school. I don't want her dropping out."

Seconded. Thirded. Never mind. "Understood. Listen, I may know of a place nearby. I can put in a word for you, and maybe it will help. Let me call them, okay?" *As soon as I find one.*

"Hey, man, that would be great. I'd appreciate it." Braydon's voice sounded relieved and grateful.

"I'll call you back." Erin stopped. "Are you where you can take calls?"

"Yeah. I'm in my car. Call any time."

"Give me five." Erin hung up, thought hard, thought harder, pulled up maps on his phone, looked at all the possibilities, and placed a call. *Thank you, Vy, for the suggestion. You really are the brains in this bunch.* It took longer than five minutes, but when he had finished, he had a two-bedroom furnished apartment (with a pool…or skating rink, depending on the season) ready for occupancy. Washer and dryer included. All Braydon had to do was sign the agreement.

Erin called his brother back. "Okay, here's the deal. There's a place on the west side. It's close to the school so Monica can walk if you can't take her because of work schedules. Two bedrooms, furnished, ready for you to move in. Rent is reasonable."

Erin scribbled on the notepad in front of him. "I took care of deposits, got the electricity and water started, and the cable is free. The rent is all yours, though. But you should be able to manage it. Get moved in and let me know you're safe, okay?"

"Man, you didn't have to do this. We can make a way—"

"God just did, okay? I'm paying it forward for something Someone did for me. Pay it forward when you can."

"Thanks, Erin. You don't know what this means."

Erin lifted his eyes Heavenward. "Yeah, maybe I do. My sister lived on the street for a couple years. I don't want anyone else in my family to have to."

"I don't know what to say. "

"Say you'll get your anatomy over to the rental office, sign the papers, and get off the street, okay? Call me when the three of you are safe."

"Thanks, Erin. I'll call you later."

"Do it." Erin hung up. He looked at the ceiling. "Thanks, Brother Golding. You took Cane off the street. I took the rest of them off. Maybe they can take someone else."

He finished up his work, drove back to the Farrell's house. A clean-up crew had been hard at work removing the paint, cleaning up the front of the house, and making it at least look liveable again. Repainting would have to wait until spring when the temperatures stayed above fifty. Until then, they would make do.

Jeff filled him in. "The police came out, took pictures and our statements. I didn't implicate Felicity but did mention the 'falling out' you two had. They will see if they can make a connection to the church arson, too."

"And the vandalism at Vy's parent's house."

"They got hit, too?"

"Yeah. Pretty much the same theme as here."

"Busy night." Jeff shook his head in disgust.

"Vy said she'd see if she could swing some professional help with investigating the matter."

"Oh?" Jeff's eyebrows rose.

"Yeah. In her words, 'you don't mess with an agent's family.' Her company takes a very dim view of things like that."

"Which could help."

"Let's hope so." Erin didn't mention getting his brothers and sister situated. He didn't need the smirks, and *I told you so* looks.

The rest of the evening stayed quiet if you ignore babies crying, babies laughing, adults laughing at babies laughing, and generally, life being lived. And enjoyed.

Six p.m. Braydon called. "We got in. This place is great, Erin. I can't thank you enough. We'll pay you back somehow."

"Pay it forward. I had some time to think, and I know of some scholarship programs. You and Terry and Monica, when it's her time, should look into them. I'll send you the info. Full rides. Check them out. See if they work with your schedule. I know Jeff went to school and worked for the Fire Department. Took him a while, but he's a slow study."

Jeff launched a pillow across the room at Erin. Erin ducked. *Note to self: insult Jeff only when holding a baby.*

Braydon didn't speak for several moments. "You don't know us. Why are you doing all this?"

"I said, Someone did it for me. Did more for than that for me. We can talk about it later. But for now, just know I'm paying forward a debt I can't ever repay. Accept the help and be glad of it. Make the most of it." Erin chuckled. "You three be good students. I may choose to take classes myself one of these days, and I want to be able to say I'm related to you. And not have a teacher throw me out for the connection."

Braydon laughed. "Yeah, I get it. Poor Monica had to follow me and Terry. I'm surprised she didn't try to go under a false name."

Erin chuckled. "I won't tell you the trouble Cane and I got into being in the same grades. Teachers earn their pay, I know."

"Okay. Thanks, brother. Send me the information on those 'scholarships,' and we'll see what we can swing. I appreciate it all."

"Like I said, pay it forward when you can. Keep me posted on how you're doing. And you're always welcome over at the house. I'll send you the address. Just don't knock. You'll wake up a baby, someone will cry, things will get ugly."

Braydon laughed again. "You got it. Thanks, man." He

hesitated. "It may sound stupid, but I love you, man."

"Never stupid. Love you all, too. Go enjoy your new place."

"Oh, we are. Trust me. We are!"

Erin disconnected the call. He looked across the room at Collin. She had a Cheshire cat grin on her face. Erin's eyes narrowed. "What?"

"What happened to, 'I don't want anyone in this family thinking the money is just going to start flowing' huh?"

Erin scoffed. "Those weren't my words. And besides, this is different."

Collin challenged. "How? How is it different?"

Erin thought a moment, thought a moment longer. "I could explain it, but you'd never understand it. We'll just leave it there." Erin dashed forward and snatched a small child before Collin could launch anything at him.

She growled. "You two stop using my children as human shields!"

Jeff looked at Erin. Erin looked at Jeff. "Us? Never."

And so the silliness continued.

Until about eight p.m. Jeff went to get a couple hours sleep before the midnight shift. Collin and Erin sat in the living room, folding clothes. Erin's phone rang. Felicity. *This should be a real joy.* "Hello, Felicity."

Venom spit through the phone. "You..." Felicity added some rather uncomplimentary descriptions of Erin he refused to acknowledge.

He let the cursing go on for several moments before interrupting. "If you have something you want to say to me, say it. Otherwise, I'll consider this conversation pointless and hang up."

"You snake. Son of your father, you are. It wasn't enough for you to call the insurance on Oscar. Now you're buying off my sons? How despicable can you be? You think I'm going to take this? And do nothing about it?"

"You mean besides trash Jeff and Collin's place, set fire to the church, and vandalize the Johnson's house?"

"You think that equals what you did to me? We welcomed you into our home. Treated you like family. And this is the way you reward us?" Felicity did everything but scream.

Erin kept his tone even to match his temper. Or maybe his

temper to match his tone. Either way, he remained calm. "I did not turn Oscar into the insurance agency. I did not attempt to buy your children. I offered them help after you threw them out on the street."

"You had no right to interfere. I put them on the street so they would realize how much they owe us. How much we've done for them. They owe us everything."

"They're adults. They can make their own choices. Even Monica is eighteen."

"Age means nothing. We are their parents. We decide when they leave. If they leave. They live where we tell them. We brought them into the world. We make the rules."

Erin swallowed all the retorts and insults he wanted to hurl. When his base nature had been corralled, he chose something less caustic to say. "I am sorry to hear you say all that, Felicity. That's not what parenting is about. You have good kids. They deserve a chance at life. I'm glad I could help."

The cursing started again. Felicity shrieked at him. He didn't try to interpret the words or the intent. He let her rant. Until she took a breath. "Felicity, we're done. Goodbye."

Before he could hang up, she seethed, "You'll regret this! I will make sure of it! You think you can destroy my family and get away with it? Watch your back! I will get even."

The line went dead.

Erin put the phone in his pocket. "So much fun."

Collin smiled. "Let me guess. Our mother is unhappy with how we are assisting her children?"

"What was your first clue?"

"She is one unbalanced woman. I'm glad she didn't want to see me. Who knows what she might have done?"

"Yeah, I know." He kissed her on top of the head. "I'm gladder you didn't turn out like her."

"'Gladder'?"

"Go with it. It's late."

She wrinkled her nose at him. "Goodnight, A-One."

MONDAY

Monday morning, Erin got up to find Jeff sitting in the kitchen at the bar, staring at the calendar on his phone. From the look on his brother-in-law's face, something didn't make sense. Erin tried to look over Jeff's shoulder but couldn't. "What are you staring at?"

"I have some notes which say 'invoices,' but I have no clue what they're supposed to mean." He looked up at Erin. "I've been home too long. I need to get to the office."

Erin grinned. "Don't let Cane hear you say that. She might bury you in the office."

"But who would run the dishwasher?"

"True. Okay, tell you what. You go in for a few hours this morning, and I'll cover for you. You come home, and we'll surprise Cane by letting her out for an hour or two. Without the babies. Should make the deal sweeter."

"What deal?" Collin drifted in from the back, unaccompanied by baby of either distinction.

Collin kissed Jeff in passing. "Morning."

"Morning. How much sleep did you get?"

"About four hours. Which is a huge win in my book. How about you?" She pointed to Erin.

Erin shrugged. "I got lots of 'we time' with them."

Collin patted her brother's arm. "I'm sorry." She eyed Jeff. "You?"

"I got a couple hours more than you did. They seem to sleep most in the evenings."

Erin grumbled, "Not when it's my shift."

Collin smiled at him. "They love their Uncle A-One." She cocked her head. "What deal were you talking about?"

Jeff pointed to Erin. Erin nodded. "We thought we could get some office work done this morning, then you could go out by yourself for as long as you want. As long as you promise to come back."

Collin glanced from her brother to her husband. "You two thought that up? All on your own?" Both men nodded. "Aww, you're so sweet. And I'm taking you up on it. Holding you to it. Who's going in?"

Erin pointed to Jeff. "Last time I went in, I saw a group of invoices which need your 'okey-dokey.' I'm sure our contractors would like to be paid."

"Probably."

The smile on Collin's face told Erin all he needed to know. Time away would be a good thing for her. Jeff needed time away, too. Erin? Eh... *I'm fine. I'm practicing. That's what I call it. Practice.*

Jeff motioned to the back of the house. "Keep them safe, bro."

"I will. Don't be gone long."

"I won't."

Collin kissed him on his way out the door. "Love you."

"Love you, too."

He left.

Erin looked around to determine what needed the most help. Unload and load the dishwasher. Clean the sink. Bake cooki... *Bake cookies? Where did that come from? I am getting too domestic here. There are limits!*

Collin poured herself a large glass of juice, downed it in one long swallow. She sighed, refilled the glass, kissed Erin on the head as she passed him, and went to the living room to sit with her feet up.

Erin chuckled. *Wonder how long it will last? I should set a timer.* He found a load of clothes (onesies mostly) in the dryer and another load (blankets) in the washer. He shifted them around, brought the basket into the living room. *Give Cane someone to talk to she can understand without trying to interpret. Too much.* He started folding. "How are you doing, Cane? Honestly."

Collin dropped her head back on the chair. "Honestly? I don't know what I would do without you and Jeff here. With you, it's tolerable. With Jeff, it's a dumpster fire, contained but still out of control. Alone?" She shook her head. "I'd never make it. I'd be a weeping puddle on the carpet. Motherhood is not for cowards or the unprepared. Whoever thinks it's easy needs to come here at feeding time."

Erin grinned. "So I'd noticed. But you're handling it. You are. You haven't killed Jeff or me or eaten your young, so you're winning in my book."

"Mine too. Especially the part about eating my young. It would not do for me to be an animal in the wild."

He chuckled. "Give yourself some credit. The kids are clean, fed, happy, growing. The house is still standing, meals are being made, laundry is done, dishes are washed… You've got this."

She shook her head. "No, you got this. You're doing the housework. You and Jeff. And I do know who's doing most of it."

"Eh, it's practice."

Collin chuckled. "You won't need a lot of training when you and Vy get married. She should be very happy."

"I hope."

Erin's phone pinged. He looked at the number. Vy.

But the message…the message. His heart stopped. The world stilled. Light vanished.

Zzzzzzzzzz.

* * *

Vy picked up a call at her desk. "Rather? What do you need?" Rather was the guard in the parking garage.

"Sorry to bother you, Ms. Johnson. But someone hit your car, and you need to come down and talk to them about it."

Vy closed her eyes. *It's a loaner! How do you crash into a loaner?* She sighed. "I'll be right down." She looked at the still-closed office door of her supervisor, Agent Duves. She'd have to catch him later. She grumbled under her breath, grabbed her backpack and coat, and walked to the garage.

The culprit drove a deep blue mini-van. Current model. A young woman stood in front of the van, wringing her hands and pacing. The van and Vy's car sat at angles to one another. The front right bumper of the vehicle had made contact with Vy's left back bumper. Approaching the two vehicles, it didn't look too severe. The terror on the young woman's face, however, said this could be bad. Very bad. Very, very bad.

She began crying and shaking as soon as Vy reached her. "I am so sorry! I'm sorry. My dad is going to kill me! It's the second accident this week, and it wasn't my fault, I swear it wasn't. A car tried to get past me, and I had to pull over to miss him, and I hit your car instead, and I'm so sorry."

Vy walked around the back to look at the damage. There didn't appear to be much, if any. She looked up at the distraught woman. "It's okay. I don't think it did any real harm." She pulled out her phone to take pictures.

"No, I crushed the trunk, I know I did. I'm going to get in so much trouble."

Vy stepped between the two cars. "Here. Back the car up just a little bit, and we'll see. I don't think it's too serious."

The woman ran around to the driver's side of the van. As she did, Vy turned her back to the blue car.

Motion behind her startled her. The van door slid open. A man grabbed at Vy. Vy tried to duck under his grasp, keying her phone at the same time. A second man jumped out, grabbed her, while the first man slapped a gag over her mouth. Vy kicked and fought and gouged and strained. Her captors threw her on the floor, slamming her head against the running boards.

Vy saw stars. She fought to stay conscious, to stay awake and alert to her surroundings. Someone wrapped a blindfold around her eyes and pulled it tight. Her feet were bound, her hands tied behind her. She listened to the rumble of the motor. Listened for any conversation. Road noises. Anything. Something to tell her the who, what, why of it all.

At the same time, she made her appeal. *Lord, help me! Please!*

Assurance all would be well tried to seep into her brain. But her position on the floor, and the suddenness and brutality of the attack, made her believe it was wishful thinking on her part, not any reassurance from the Lord. It would have to come later. When she could see some hope of escape.

No one spoke. No one moved her, either. They were content to leave her sprawled on the floor, chewing on the strip of fabric tied between her teeth. The gag cut the corners of her mouth. She gnawed at it anyhow.

Her shoulder ached from the awkward way she'd landed on it.

Her arms began to tingle, losing circulation. If she could roll over on her stomach, she could relieve the pressure on her arms. She could also get knocked around for moving.

Live dangerously. Vy arched her back, tried to angle her way to her front. One of her attackers recognized her attempt to shift and grabbed her arms, pulling them up and behind her, leaving her face down in the padded carpet. *Thanks. I think.*

Vy continued to chew on the gag. If she could get it wet enough, she would leave DNA on the carpet. Maybe it would help. At least for a conviction.

Think positive. She tried keeping time. Counting the seconds. But she kept losing track of exactly how many minutes had gone by. Slushing took the place of the smooth highway vibrations. The occasional pothole jarred her body. The engine whine didn't change, which meant they were going the same speed. Same speed, different road. Highway versus freeway.

The highway became a country road. Stops. Starts. Turns. More potholes. More slushing noises. The snow hadn't been cleared.

Gravel replaced the blacktop. Vy could feel the incline as the van climbed a hill, felt the shift in her awareness as the vehicle went down the other side. Then up again. The car stopped. The engine continued to run.

The door slid open. Grunts. Two men(?) grabbed her arms, one on each side. They dragged her out of the van and dropped her on the wet, slushy gravel.

Two words. "Pay up."

A pause. The van door closed. The vehicle turned around and pulled out. Away.

A pair of arms pulled her to her feet. Someone threw her over someone's shoulder like a bag of grain. The person grunted only slightly and started walking. Vy listened to the sound of the boots on the ground. Not the crunch of gravel. The sucking slosh of dirt and mud.

Hard going as well. Twice she felt her captor nearly lose his balance as a foot slipped or a boot stuck. Again, she had no sense of time. Being. Only being.

Until it stopped. They set her down, leaned her against something solid. She rubbed her hands against the texture. Wood. Rough wood. Boards. Paint peeling. Vy heard a door open. They dragged her inside, over a solid board. Not a proper doorjamb. Shed, maybe? Outbuilding?

Picked up again. Carried inside and set down on the distinctive crinkle of a tarp. *Blue? Silver?* Leaned against two walls at angles to each other. A corner.

"Sit." The voice hissed, deliberately masked. *You hide a voice if you plan on letting the victim go. Otherwise, you don't worry about being recognized.*

I might actually get out of this alive.

But why kidnap me in the first place? Ransom from Erin? Possible. Taking quite the chance he cares enough. He does, but still...

Vy sat, leaving her knees in front of her with her hands still clasped behind her. She sniffed cautiously. The area had an odor...an odor of meat. Pork. Cow. Bacon?

Smokehouse? Am I in a smokehouse? She hadn't bumped against anything, nor had her captor ducked to avoid hitting his head. So, an empty smokehouse. Abandoned? Small, anyhow.

The tarp would indicate the floor could be dirt. Hard, too. Frozen. One tarp would not keep the freezing temps from sucking all the warmth out of her. Maybe she'd been hasty in her "get out of this alive" assessment.

She would not panic. She would not freak. She would pray. She would trust herself to the Lord. And she would get out of this one way or another.

She leaned against the rough-hewn lumber and waited for what came next. She heard sounds of her captor rustling around. What could they be doing? Vy listened, heard the distinctive crack of a match, smelled the sulfur. Something went "woosh," and she felt warmth in front of her. A fire? Were they going to incinerate her? *Lord! Please!*

Her captor walked across the floor, closed the door behind him. The fire grew no closer, but the heat warmed her. *Thank You, Lord. Be with Erin, please. Help him. Help me. Please.*

* * *

Zzzzzzzzz.

Erin closed his eyes. *Lord, no. Please. Please. No. No. Not Vy. Save her. Please!*

He came back to himself to Collin's insistent, "What's wrong? What happened? Who is it?"

He found his voice. "Vy. She's in trouble." *Who do I call? Police? Her boss? Her boss.* He punched in the number for Vy's supervisor.

"DEA, Agent Wyatt Duves. What's up, Erin?"

He fought for control. "Vy is in trouble. I…we…" Erin shook himself to get the words out. "We created a code. She activated it. She's in trouble."

"I'll get back to you."

Erin set his phone on the table. Collin's voice sounded careful. "What code? What did you have?"

"If something went wrong, bad wrong, she would speed dial me, then hit z. That's what she did."

He waited, staring at the phone. "Come on. Come on. Let me be wrong. Please let me be wrong."

Wyatt called back. "We're activating protocols now. She wasn't on assignment, and she's not answering her phone. We'll sweep the area."

Erin closed his eyes. "Thank you."

"What tipped you off? Why the code?"

"Uh…long story short, I think there's a mentally unstable woman with a grudge against me taking it out on those around me. No solid proof. Vy went into the office to see if she could get some help chasing down the possible culprit."

"I'm not worried about proof. Give me the name and any information you have on this person."

Erin filled Agent Duves in on all the particulars of Felicity's address, phone number, and any other information he could come up with. "That's what I've got."

"Vy filled us in on the vandalism at her folk's place and possibly the church. She mentioned the Farrell's, but I didn't make the connection. I'll add it to the sheet."

"Thanks." Erin couldn't control his voice from shaking.

"We're on it, Erin. If you think of anything or hear anything, let us know."

"I will."

"Hang in there, man."

Erin pocketed the phone. Collin moved beside him, lay her hand on his arm. "Lord, You know where Vy is. Nothing touches her You don't allow. Please. Keep her safe. Bring her back. Give her people comfort and hope and peace. But bring her back, please. We want Your will, yes. But we want her back, too. In Jesus's Name. Amen."

Erin forced himself to pick up another onesie and carefully fold it. Collin held his eyes. "What do you need to do, A-One?"

"Stay here. Do what I said I'd do. Not go running off trying to find her and get in the way of the official investigation."

Collin nodded. "I hear you."

He stared at the basket of baby clothes. "Will you call the prayer chain? I should call her parents."

Collin squeezed his arm. "I will. And yes, they should hear it from you."

Erin pulled his phone back out. He swallowed hard. He punched in the number.

George answered, his smooth baritone pleasant as always. "Mr. Erin Winger. A pleasure to hear from you."

"It won't be." Erin had to steady his voice. He pulled himself under tight control. "Something has happened to Vy. I don't know what, yet, but her office is looking into it. We…Vy and I…made up a code to tell if one of us was in trouble. She keyed it a few minutes ago."

He breathed out, breathed in, breathed out. "I don't know anything more. I had to call you."

"Our Lord has Vy. She is in the Lord's hands, and nothing touches her He doesn't allow. We will storm the gates of Heaven, Erin. Call when you hear anything. Anything at all."

"I will."

"And Erin, does this have to do with the paint on our house the other morning?"

"I believe it does, sir. What the police believe is up to them."

"I'll trust your gut on this."

Erin hesitated. "I'm…I'm sorry, sir."

George's voice thundered. "This better be the only time I hear those words from your mouth, Mr. Winger. None of this is your fault. Do not apologize for something over which you had no control. Do you hear me, Mr. Winger?"

"Yes, sir. I do, sir."

"Good. I'll let you know if we hear anything. Hang in there,

Erin."

Erin hung up.

The baby monitor picked up sounds from the nursery. Grunts. Complaints. Small talk. Collin and Erin went in. Talitha still slept, so they left her alone. Collin handed Caleb to Erin and picked up Joshua. The babies were stripped, diapered, dressed, and moved to the living room in assembly-line fashion. Collin sat on the floor with Joshua, holding the baby in a sitting position.

Erin did the same with Caleb, to have the boy roll over on his side like a child's wobble toy. "Not ready for that yet, huh, Caleb?"

Collin chuckled. "I think he's too round on the bottom to stay—"

Glass shattered. Smoke began to fill the room, billowing out from a canister. Erin ordered, "Get the boys out of here! Out back. Go!"

Collin scooped up the blanket the boys were on and dragged them out of the room. Erin tried to pick up the canister and throw it out, burning his hands in the process. Before he could toss it, a second canister flew into the room. This one exploded into flames. Erin dashed for the nursery.

Talitha. All that mattered. He caught up the screaming infant, hugged her to his chest, and ran towards the back door. Another canister smashed through the bedroom window. Flames barred his way. He reversed course, headed deeper into the house, to the main bedroom with the sliding glass door to the side yard.

Yet another sound of breaking glass, and another firestorm greeted him. Erin pulled on the door. Smoke clouded his vision, filled his lungs, confused his thinking. *Lord! I have to get her out of here! Help me!*

The door opened, and someone made a grab for Talitha. Spurred by some internal warning, Erin fought against whoever. Someone pounded his head against the wall. Erin lashed out with his foot, trying to disable the attacker. A metal bar crashed against his ribs. Erin shielded Talitha, turning his body to absorb the blow. More strikes flew at him. Erin ducked to the floor, came up behind the attacker, and raced to clean air. He stumbled, fell, got to his feet, and yelled as he escaped. "Help! Help!"

The attacker came at him. Erin felt the blow against his skull. He crumbled to the ground, still shielding Talitha. He grabbed at the attacker's legs, trying to bring them down. There came a second blow to his head. Darkness delayed one moment, giving him time for one final bellow, one last plea. "Talitha! No!"

And blackness closed around him.

MONDAY AFTERNOON

Vy rubbed her face against the ground, hoping to dislodge the rags binding her. It might be useless, but it was something. When she grew weak from scratching her face, she would work at her wrists and feet. She would get free. Somehow, God willing, she would get free.

She instinctively knew there would be no Erin to save her this time. No "hole in the roof" rescue. This would be all her and the Lord, or nothing and no one.

She heard a door open. She perked her head to listen for any clues so she could nail the kidnapper when she got free. And she would get free. She had a wedding to plan. *Right, Lord? You told me Erin would be my husband. Can't have a husband if I don't get free. You never change, and never change Your Mind. I will be free!*

Someone lay something beside her. A voice, disguised but definitely female, hissed, "Hold this." The door closed.

Vy wriggled and contorted her figure to touch the object. It moved. The smell… Smoke. Yes. But something more. More like…

The sound of a pitiful cry tore through her soul. An infant's cry, with the warble at the end to twist the gut of any female within hearing range. *Oh, my Lord…is this one of the Farrell triplets? Dear Father, how? Why? Please! Help us. Help this little one! Help Collin and Jeff, Lord. Please.*

Would the Farrells even be alive? Collin would fight to the death for her children, Vy knew. So would Jeff. And Erin. If they could… *Oh, Father…please! Please!* There were no words. She cried out all her anguish and fear and pain and heartache and mourning…but without words. The Holy Spirit would interpret all of it, she knew.

Vy continued to pour out her heart, all the while scraping her chin, her hands, her feet against the dirt. She would emerge raw, but she would emerge. She arched her body to nestle the child with her own, to provide some warmth and protection from the frozen ground.

Muffled voices came from outside the walls of her prison. Angry voices. Or one angry voice. Vy strained to hear any words she could.

"..diot! Waste of...told not to kill... Can't get revenge if...hospital...cracked skull...pay him back...dies, you'll die...his place... Now...wait to see if...take more time..."

The voices moved away. Vy tucked the words in her mind. Was this the same female who had shoved the baby at her? Maybe the words would make sense later. Now, she had here and now. And a child. And escape.

Time passed. Vy arched her back to bring her head close to the infant. She could only hope they were head-to-head. She leaned in and hummed, willing the child to hear, to take some comfort, some solace in the sound. It seemed to work for a while. But music would not replace food, nor would it change a soiled diaper. Would the baby be cared for at all? *Please. At least that much.*

The door opened. The door closed. The female voice. Still whispered. Still concealed. "I'm not a monster. When the time comes, this one will die quickly. You will not."

The sound of a baby eating greedily. The female voice crooning. Someone patting a baby's back. A satisfied belch. Rustling around. The child placed beside her again. Wood added to the fire. The door opened. The door closed.

Paul sang praise songs during his captivity. I can't sing, but I can hum. And I will. While I work to escape.

Time passed. The baby cried. The baby slept. The baby cried. The door opened. The baby ate. The door closed. The baby slept. The baby cried. The door opened. The baby cried. The door closed. The baby cried. The baby slept. The baby cried. The baby ate. The baby cried.

The crying became constant. Every minute not actively being fed or falling asleep after wailing for hours, the baby bawled.

The door opened. Someone kneeled beside her. "What is wrong with her? What does she need?"

This voice was different. Male. Distorted to hide his identity, but male. And filled with frustration and concern.

Hands roughly removed the mask around Vy's eyes. Dim light filled the room. A figure in a gorilla mask kneeled beside Vy. Its voice strained above a whisper, in a tone not its own. "What does the baby need? It's dry. It's been fed. I've covered it up. I can't make it stop crying."

The figure moved behind her. "I'm going to remove the gag. But if you scream or yell, I will kill the baby. Do you understand?" The infant's cries were piercing in their desperation.

Vy nodded. She doubted the threat but wasn't willing to take the chance of being wrong.

The gag fell from her mouth. Vy took several unimpeded breaths. "Thank you."

"What does the baby need?"

"Her mother. To be held and cuddled and played with and loved."

"I can't. I can't take her back."

"Would you if you could?"

The answer came in a shot. "Yes. I hate this. This is not my idea. I don't want to do any of this." The baby screamed.

"Are you being forced?"

"Can you help the baby?"

"Untie my hands."

"You promise you won't try to go anywhere? You won't try to hit me and escape?"

Who is this person? Who are they afraid of? "I promise."

Vy's hands were loosened. She rubbed the wrists, raw and bleeding. Her captor saw them. A whispered, "I'm sorry."

"Hand me the baby."

The infant's misery made Vy want to cry. She cradled the little one in her arms, holding her to her chest and rocking back and forth. She hummed and crooned and sang and rocked until the little girl settled, snuffling as she stopped crying.

It was Talitha. Vy lay her head on the infant's and continued to hum. Talitha yawned, closed her eyes, and fell asleep. Vy peered at her captor. "She'll start up again the next time she isn't held. Babies need physical contact. They need to be cuddled and to know they are safe and loved. They'll die without stimulation. She needs to be held."

"How long?"

"An hour, two hours."

"A day?"

"No. Every time she's fed. You want to keep this child alive and healthy, you need to hold her."

"I can't. I don't have the time. Can you do it?"

"If my hands aren't tied."

Her captor fell silent. Vy sensed she needed to cooperate, to learn more about where they were, who this man could be. Trying to bring down whoever it might be would work in the short run. But not if escape and return to freedom were the ultimate goal. She waited.

"I'll leave you untied for now. When I come back, I'll have to tie you up again, and the baby will have to cry. I'm sorry. I can't do better than that. Not yet."

The door opened. The figure stopped, turned around. "I am trying to figure out how to save you and the baby. I am. I need time. I just need a little time." The door closed.

Vy leaned back against the wall. She hugged Talitha. "Oh, little one. We need Jesus to help us. We do." She lifted her eyes to the ceiling. "Father, please. Help us. All of us. In Your Son's Name. Amen." She rocked in time to the baby's breathing.

She strained to hear anything coming from outside. The dim light which oozed through the breaches in the smokehouse walls gave her the impression it might be midday, maybe. If there were people around, they should be moving, making noise. Doing something to be heard.

But only birdcalls reflected back to her ears. The ever-present crows cawing. Wrens with their "teakettle teakettle teakettle." The Eastern Kingbird. "Kit kit kit kitter kitter." The Flycatcher with its "pet-sé pet-sé." *Pizza. Lord, I am hungry. Will they feed me, too?*

Last of all, the Vireo. "Pick up the beer, check." No beer. Water would be good. Anything to drink. *If he wants to save me, he has to bring me water and food. He has to.*

Silence and the sound of tree limbs creaking against one another answered her. Vy lay Talitha on the tarp long enough so she could untie her feet, stand up, pick up Talitha, then move to the door.

Locked? It had no handle. Only a hole with a pull-rope. Did she dare? Would she be breaking faith with her captor by looking outside? Would she lose the progress she had made?

Vy pulled the rope. The door opened. Light poured in, and Vy had to shield her eyes. She made sure to cover Talitha's as well, though the baby slept well. The DEA agent peered out and around. She took care not to step over the threshold onto the snow. Footprints would betray her excursion.

And the snow lay "deep and crisp and even," as the song said. She could see one path leading to a gravel road twining around through pine trees, disappearing as it wound down the hill.

The shack seemed to be perched on top of an island in the trees. No houses. No buildings. No power lines. No cell towers. Nothing to suggest Vy could walk away from the shack and find help. If she were alone, she would take her life in her hands and go. But with Talitha, she couldn't take the chance of the two of them being lost and freezing to death. *We will get free. We will. This isn't the way it's going to happen. But we will get free. I promise, Talitha. We will.*

Vy walked back to her place on the wall, retied her feet, picked up Talitha, and rocked with the baby. God would provide. He promised. She crooned, "Jesus loves me, this I know, For the Bible tells me so…"

THURSDAY

Erin heard screaming. A desperate, hopeless, anguish-filled shriek of despair. It repeated over and over and over… It filled the air around him. Accusations tore at him.

"How could you?? The baby is gone! How could you? You should be dead. Die! It's the only way to make up for losing the baby! How could you? The baby is gone!"

Whose voice is screaming? Collin's? Has to be. She hates me for losing Talitha.

Does she? Is she blaming you and wanting you to die?

Jeff. He hates me. He'd say I should have tried harder. I shouldn't be alive.

Would he?

Someone blames me. Someone knows I shouldn't be allowed to live. Someone is screaming at me.

Are they?

Someone should be. Talitha is gone.

I'm screaming at myself. I lost her. I should die.

Will it bring her back?

It might.

Will it?

No. But I don't want to live. I don't want to face Cane. And Jeff.

Why don't you want to face them?

Because they'll forgive me. I don't want to be forgiven.

You've been forgiven before. I forgave you.

She's a baby. I failed her.

Would she want you to die?

No! No one wants me to die except me!

Then live. And be forgiven.
* * *

Three days since Vy and Talitha disappeared. Collin and Jeff held hands in the hospital room. They listened to the beep…beep…beep of the monitors, and they prayed. Tears fell, one size fits all. They lay their heads on each other's shoulders, and they wept. And they prayed. Collin's voice cracked with the effort. "Please, Lord. Please. Wake him up. Tell him we forgive him. There's nothing to forgive. I know. Make him know, too. Tell him it's okay. We love him. We want him back. Please. Bring him back."

Jeff's voice croaked as well. "God, You're the Only One Who can get through to him. He needs to live. He needs to want to live. Tell him it's not his fault. No one is blaming him. No one. We…" Jeff's voice faltered. He cleared it. "We love him. Kick his rear and tell him to come back to us. We need him. Please. Your will, Lord. We know. But please, let it be Your will. Bring Erin back. Bring Talitha back. Bring Vy back. Please."

Collin reached out and touched her brother's face. "I know you can hear me, A-One. It wasn't your fault. You did everything you could. Please, please know it. We know it. We know you tried. No one could do more. There were two of them, bubby. That's why you couldn't hold on to her. The police said no one could do more than you did. You tried. It's all you could do. And it's enough. We love you. Please, come back to us."

Erin's eyes flickered. Collin held her breath. More flickering. Collin touched his face. "A-One? You in there, bubby? Can you hear me? Talk to me."

The eyes closed. Tears flooded from both. Collin leaned in and lay on his chest, not putting her weight on the fractured ribs but letting him know she was there. "I'm here, Erin. I'm here. It's okay. It's okay, bubby."

His voice. A broken whisper, nothing more. "Talitha. Talitha. I…I…tried…"

Jeff approached him from the other side. "We know, bud. We know. You did everything you could. We'll get her back. I know we will. But we need you, too. Got it? We need you."

Erin's hand moved. Jeff grabbed it, mindful of the burns and bandages. "I got you, bud. I got you."

Collin caressed his other hand. "We've got you. You're gonna be all right. You will. We'll get Talitha back, and we'll get Vy back. It'll all be okay, you'll see. You'll see."

A whisper. "Vy? Vy? Vy is gone?" More tears. Fading consciousness. "Vy. Talitha."

Collin lifted her chin to the ceiling, closed her eyes. *Make it all right, Lord. Please. Please.*

Erin's phone pinged. She didn't bother to read the message. It had been the same each day since the kidnapping. *Is he alive?*

She typed one word. *Yes.*

It was all she could say.

* * *

Three more days passed. Doctors moved Erin from ICU to a regular room. Collin stayed with him, bringing the boys with her. Private room, equipped with a crib for the babies. Every day the same: nurses. Wound check. Rehab. Occupational, physical. Emotional. Collin reminded him none of this was his fault. They would get Vy and Talitha back. They would.

Visits from pastors. Prayers. George and Martha came. Harmon and Lacey came. Braydon came. Terry and Monica came. The FBI came and stayed. Life moved forward. Erin fought to get strong enough to leave the hospital. Fought the therapists. Fought the doctors. Fought the internal demons which screamed at him for his failure. Collin watched it all. Watched and prayed and supported and fought with him. And every afternoon, answered the text which asked, *Is he alive?*

Yes.

Is he home?

No.

FBI agent Ireland Pope sat with Collin, monitoring Erin's phone and the queries from a texter with no number. She shook her head. "Takes some skill to text and not leave an identifying number. Our people are tracking it down, though. We'll have it nailed before tonight, I guarantee you."

Collin stared at the floor. She held Caleb, trying to draw a semblance of calm and strength from his pudgy body. For him. She needed to keep it together for him. "I hope you're right. I know there aren't many clues."

Agent Pope lay a hand on Collin's arm. "We'll get them back, ma'am. We're very good at what we do, and we will get them back."

Collin's eyes burned. They hadn't stopped burning since the smoke canister filled the house with toxic fumes. The fumes were gone, their effects long washed out by the tears that would not stop. No amount of faith replaced the emptiness that had been Talitha. She met the agent's eyes. "But what do they want? Why?"

Agent Pope squeezed Collin's arm. "We don't know. Not yet." She glanced over to see if Erin could hear. Collin knew from the sound of his breathing he slept. Pope lowered her voice. "Possibly your brother. Maybe you, but since they keep asking about him, our guess is him. Revenge over something, most likely."

A green-gowned and masked orderly walked into the room. "Is the patient ready for transport to X-ray?

Collin glanced at him sideways. "X-ray? Dr. Rich didn't say anything about X-rays."

The orderly looked at the board with the patient vitals. "Oh, I'm sorry. I got the wrong room. Never mind. Sorry I bothered you."

He ducked out. Agent Pope and Collin exchanged narrow-eyed glances. Pope keyed her radio. "Someone check out a male orderly, 5'10", dark hair, mask, and lanyard around his neck. Silver wristwatch. Black shoes. Laces. Said he needed to transport a patient to X-ray."

Collin listened, amazed. If Agent Pope had added, "rose tattoo on right bicep," she wouldn't have been surprised. She didn't, but Collin wouldn't have been surprised.

Five minutes passed. Agent Pope touched her earpiece. Collin heard faintly, "Unable to locate anyone of his description. Radiology says they didn't call for transport."

Collin's eyes flared. Pope radioed back, "Watch the exits for a suspect of his description. Someone came in here."

"We can't stop every visitor who leaves here with that description. It would be half the men in the place. Especially since he's probably changed clothes by now. We need more to go on."

"Send up the security footage of everyone leaving from ten minutes ago. And anyone up to ten minutes from now. We'll look at it here and see if we spot him."

"As soon as we can."

Agent Pope nodded to Collin. "We'll catch him. Or at least get a look at him. Then we'll have something to go on."

Collin moved to stand beside the crib, holding Caleb tighter and sliding Joshua closer to her side. "What did he want?"

"My guess is to verify your texts, see if your brother is still here."

"Why? Why take the risk?"

"Maybe someone is getting impatient. Let's see what the security footage shows."

Agent Pope opened her laptop and turned it so Collin could see as well. "Let me know if you see anyone who looks like the guy."

Footage from the front doors revealed nothing and no one suspicious. Ditto the back entrance. Two side entrances were also negative. But the maternity exit…

Collin pointed at a man approaching the camera. "There. I'd swear that's him."

Agent Pope stopped the playback. She wrote down the time signature, restarted the stream. Three more men passed. Collin scrutinized each one. Not the man. No.

A fourth man looked close, but Collin shook her head. "No. Not him. He's close, but not right. He doesn't look the same build."

Pope nodded. "Let's look at him again, though." She ran the sequence back. Collin peered closer but still shook her head. "Not him. I'm sure of it."

The agent wrote down the time signature as well but said nothing. Another five minutes of recording, and Collin looked at Agent Pope. "It had to be the one man. The one I pointed out. I'm sure of it."

"I agree. You've got a good eye."

"Survival technique. Be aware. So what happens now?"

"We have our people isolate the frame, send it to the files, and see if we get a match. If he's in the system, we'll know. We'll also have it printed off old-school and carry it around the area, showing it to people. See if anyone recognizes him. We'll find him, Mrs. Farrell. We will."

Collin's defenses melted. She put Caleb in the crib beside his brother. "Then what? Do you bring him in?"

"No. Not yet. Not until we know where the hostages…where Ms. Johnson and Talitha are." Pope's eyes smiled. "It's a break. We'll take it."

Collin nodded. "Right. We'll take it." *Lord, please. For all of us. Please. Let this lead to Vy and Talitha. Please. I want my baby back. I want Vy back for Erin. And for Vy. I'm sorry... I'm not thinking straight, and the words aren't coming out right. But You know what I mean. Please. It's all I can say. Please. In Your Son's Name. Amen.*

SUNDAY

Vy heard the crunch of footsteps on the gravel. Time for Talitha's bottle. Clockwork. Usually, she could count on it being the man in the gorilla mask, and Vy got to hold and cuddle Talitha. The man would wait until Vy sang Talitha to sleep, usually a verse or two of "Jesus Loves Me." He would retie Vy's bonds, leaving the baby nestled in her lap. Always he made sure the fire in the stove burned hot and warm. Always.

But when the female captor came, Talitha got fed, set back in place, and left to cry. Vy would rock and hum and do everything she could to comfort the little girl. Sometimes it worked, and Talitha would drift off to sleep. Sometimes it didn't, and the baby would have to cry herself to sleep.

Those were the times Vy cried as well. And scraped at her hands and cheeks and feet. And prayed. And prayed.

Tonight, the heavier footsteps were interrupted by the noise of tires spinning gravel up the hill. The person on foot stopped and waited until the truck came to a rest. Vy heard the car door open.

"She says we have to keep waiting. Dude's still in the hospital. She insists he has to be home before we can do anything." The deliverer of the news spit and cursed. *This guy's voice is different. So, two males and a female? And these orders are not to your liking, hmm?*

"She have any idea how long? I'm going to need more supplies." The voice of her gorilla man.

"You'll have to get them yourself. I'm not buying any more diapers. You go through them too fast. Let the brat sit in her mess."

The response came back angry and cold and furious. "I'll make you sit in her mess! She's a baby. She deserves better. And we were told to keep her alive and well. That's what we're doing. You want me to tell her you're refusing to do what you're told?"

"I'm not refusing. You're going overboard. I'll get the diapers, but I'm not changing them."

"Fine. Stay away from the building. I'll take care of the hostages. Get a bigger case this time. And make sure they're for a newborn. Last bunch you got were too big. She's little."

"She's not a newborn. She's older than that."

"Yeah, but she's a preemie. She needs little diapers. Just get what I tell you."

How does he know she's a preemie? How long have they been watching? Planning? Lord, help me understand what this is about.

"Fine. But I'm getting tired of all this. How many people does this make? Three? Four? She kidnaps them for spite, and we never see a dime of any reward."

"She says it's not about the money. It's about revenge. They killed Dad. All of them. She wants them to suffer, to feel what she feels."

"Yeah, well, this one could be different. This one could be our big payday. This bunch has money, and lots of it."

Gorilla man's voice filled with anger. "Go do what I told you. Now."

The door slammed shut, the vehicle roared down the hill, and the silence returned.

The door creaked open. The man in the gorilla mask stepped over the threshold. "I got food."

He untied Vy's hands, handed her a bottle of water and a container with two chicken strips. He motioned towards the food. "She says to stop feeding you. She wants you to look thin in the pictures she's going to send."

"Pictures? What pictures?"

"I don't know. Those're the instructions I got. I'll sneak in food when I can, but try to look hungry when you hear her come in."

"I promise I will." *Easy promise to keep when I'm only being fed every other day. Of course, you don't know, do you? You think she's been feeding me as well as the baby. What game is this? Is it Erin who's still in the hospital? How long has it been?*

Vy had given up trying to keep a record. The ground stayed too frozen to make marks, and the walls peeled no matter how much or little pressure she put on them. The nights were dark and cold. The days were gray and dull. Neither mattered. Time had ceased to move. There were feeding times, there were quiet times, and there were crying times. How many of each went without telling.

She prayed without ceasing. When it's all you have, it's what you do. And she did. And found her comfort and rest in the middle of the fear and anxiety. God had her. There could be no safer spot. She believed it, or she didn't. And right now, she had to believe it or surrender to the despair threatening to swallow what light she had. *"Jesus loves me…"*

THURSDAY

Day Ten... Erin checked himself out against the doctor's orders. Work crews from One Way Builders had much of the damage to the Farrell house repaired. Carpets had been replaced, walls painted, glass windows installed. Everything like nothing had happened... Except the hole which had been Talitha remained unfilled.

Collin adjusted Erin's wheelchair to have the best line-of-sight view without having to turn his head. Layers of bandages still swathed his skull. Burns on his hands still hampered his dexterity. Vision remained limited to a precious few feet directly in front of him. Anything further out blurred into nothingness. It would get better. He knew it. Time. He needed to give it time.

Except there isn't any. Vy is gone. Talitha is gone. We have to get them back. We have to. God, please, bring them back.

Despair threatened to wash over him. He shouldn't be here, he knew. He should be in rehab somewhere. Still in the hospital recovering, even. But he couldn't. Yes, God could work without him. But Erin couldn't rest apart from the search. He had to know.

The official task force to bring Vy and Talitha home consisted of FBI Agent Scott Nicks, the city police, and DEA Agent Wyatt Duves. FBI Agent Ireland Pope was assigned to the family for protection and to help with any communications from the kidnappers. The not-so-official task force consisted of retired City Homicide Detective Jim Russo, retired DEA Agent Mason Ewent, George and Martha Johnson, Lacey and Harmon Farrell, Jeff and Collin Farrell, and Erin Winger. Jim Russo gave his report. "All the official city, county, and state channels are doing the best they can.

Infant kidnappings get lots of press and lots of pressure to be solved. Word is they've got every man and woman they can spare out combing the streets."

DEA Agent Duves leaned in. "Same with the search for Vy. We get real testy when one of our own disappears."

Mason nodded. "All the unofficial channels are being monitored as well. Anyone who might know anything has been alerted to call it in."

George and Martha held hands on the couch. George had started the meeting in prayer. Erin knew his future father-in-law would continue to pray throughout.

Jeff squeezed Collin's hand. "Do we need to raise the reward level?"

All eyes turned to FBI Agent Scott Nicks. "No. 100K is incentive enough for snitches to come out of the woodwork. More, and there will be as many false clues as real ones. Someone who might have been searching will have to be sorting them. Better this way."

Erin held up his hand. The others would have to strain to hear him. "I put in a call to Felicity. She hasn't answered yet."

Collin squeezed his shoulder. "Good."

Jim Russo motioned to Erin with his chin. "The email you gave me for Braydon helped. Felicity still blames you for ratting out the insurance fraud scheme. I get the feeling he knows who did, but he's not sharing. He also said he doubts his mom had anything to do with the kidnappings. She has enough hate, true, but not enough money to buy thugs like came after you or Vy."

Mason shook his head. "Um, I have other information that might shed a different light on things." He turned to Collin. "And I apologize in advance. Digging back through your old financial records, I found where Robert Winger made a payment to her of 500K. Written the month you say she disappeared from your lives." He lowered his eyes. "We also found monthly payments of ten thousand up until the time she married Oscar Bennett."

Erin heard the sarcasm in his sister's voice. "Well, well. So Robert said leave, and she left, huh? Any bets on who initiated the transaction?"

No one seemed inclined to want to jump on the wager. Erin raised his hand to be heard. "Is it possible to track the finances?"

Agent Duves cleared his throat. "We're waiting for a judge's signature on the court order. Should have it by this afternoon."

Russo eyed Erin. "I still think we need to cast a wider net. Felicity Bennett can't be the only enemy the children of Robert Winger might have."

Anger surged in Erin's gut. He glared at the former detective. But memories of Jim's help in the past and his particular insights into people and situations stopped Erin from shouting. Figuratively. He started to nod, thought better of it, and whispered, "Where do you want to start?"

Jim relaxed. Erin realized the man anticipated Erin's possible negative reaction and braced for it. "With your permission, I'd like to interview Robert Winger. I'd like to tell him what's happening and see if he can give me any clues."

Collin tapped Erin's arm. "You don't need our permission to talk to anyone in our past or present. We're way past caring about who you dredge up. If you want to talk to my first-grade teacher, go for it. I don't care about anything but getting Talitha and Vy back."

He would hate himself for it later, but it had to be said. "Don't expect much. She hated me."

Collin groaned. "She did not. She liked you. She didn't like when she called on one of us and both of us would answer at the same time with the same answer."

Erin offered his defense. "She was hard of hearing. We turned up the volume for her."

Mason laughed. "Good to see your sense of humor is still in there."

Erin lowered his eyes. "Vy liked it."

George's voice rose strong. "She will like it again. They are coming back to us. Both of them."

Erin drew in a breath, raised his eyes. "Right." *Lord? Right?*

His phone pinged. Collin picked it up to read the text to him. *Which one do you choose?*

Erin cocked his head. "What?"

"That's what it says. 'Which one do you choose?' It's from the same person who kept texting, asking if you were alive. I thought you knew them."

The FBI agent held out his hand. "Let me see." Collin handed the phone to him. He keyed in several digits, a few letters, a Roman numeral, or two... Erin had no clue what the man did. But after a moment, he read, "614-555-5752. Anyone you know?"

"No." Erin looked at Collin. She shook her head. Jeff followed suit. George and Martha shook their heads as well. Harmon and Lacey made it unanimous.

The agent did some more typing. "It's a Shop and Go on the south side. Been closed for six months." He punched in some numbers on his own phone. "Probably someone bounced their number to it. Harder to backtrack, but we'll see where it leads."

Collin asked the first question on Erin's heart. "What does it mean?"

He voiced the second. "Do I answer?"

Russo rapped the table in front of him. "We know the game now."

Jeff looked lost. "Game? What game?"

Erin pointed to the phone. "Choose one."

Agent Duves's voice came down hard. "Make you choose, but kill both, right?"

"Am I the only one who has to choose?"

Russo nodded. "Unless anyone else gets a text. Right now, you appear to be the target."

Duves agreed. "You have the most invested in both. Your niece, your fiancée. It's up to you to decide. That's the game they want you to play. To make you suffer over the decision."

Mason added darkly, "But there's no real choice."

Erin held his hand out for his phone. Agent Nicks gave it to him. Erin tried to force his fingers to type the answer but couldn't. In frustration, he handed it to Collin. "Tell them this: Prove they're alive."

Collin typed in Erin's response. Agent Nicks held out his hand. "Give the phone to me again. I want to link it to the office. Anything that comes across will bounce to the lab and be analyzed. Maybe we can get a location."

Collin handed the phone back. The man typed, linked, and handed it back. "That should do it. Now whatever they send will come to us, and we can work with it."

The agent's eyes sparked. The corners of his mouth twitched up. "It's the break we needed."

No text came. Erin waited. Pain in his head threatened to put him out. He swallowed hard, closed his eyes, focused on nothing. He breathed slowly. In. Out. In. Out.

No text. Ten minutes.

Fifteen minutes. No text.

Thirty minutes. No text.

Jim Russo looked at his watch. "If I leave now, I can get to the DA's office and get permission to go see Robert Winger. We can at least start tracking some of the leads down."

Nicks cleared his throat. "Mr. Russo." He made the emphasis on the "mister" very distinct. "As a private citizen, you can talk to anyone you wish. We would prefer you coordinate with us first, so we can keep all our ducks lined up."

Jim smiled but without mirth. "I did my job for a lot of years, Agent Nicks. I never failed to coordinate with any other agency which had skin in the game. The stakes are too high for me to go rogue on anything. I will give you a complete list of the questions I intend to ask Robert Winger before I go. If he deviates from the agenda, I'll be sure to let you know."

Nicks held up a hand. "I didn't mean—"

"I know you didn't. Just want you to know I'm playing by all the rules." Jim pointed across the room where Jeff held one of the boys. "The chunky baby over there? He's my godson."

Erin sighed. Exaggerated. "No, it's the *other* one who's your godson."

Mason crossed his arms over his chest. "Yeah. Caleb's mine. Joshua's yours."

Jim looked over to Collin. "I pointed to Joshua, didn't I?"

She shook her head. "Comedians. All of you." She kissed Jim on the cheek. "And I love you for it." Jim smiled at her. Collin showed him out.

Forty-five minutes. No text.

Agent Duves stood. "I'll see about the court order and get our accounting people looking at the financials."

Jeff showed Duves and Mason out together.

Sixty minutes. No text. Harmon and Lacey left. Agent Nicks departed as well, leaving Agent Pope to watch over and defend the family.

Collin nursed Caleb, then Joshua. Jeff lay on the floor with the boys for tummy time. Joshua rolled front to back for the first time.

George held Caleb, bouncing the boy on his knee. Martha cuddled Joshua, playing patty-cake with him. Erin saw the pain mingled with the joy in Collin's eyes. Shining with tears. Laughing as drops washed down her cheeks.

Two hours. No text. George and Martha left. So did Lacey and Harmon. Jeff prayed them out. FBI Agent Pope settled in for the evening shift.

Collin brought Erin his pain med. "Take it, A-One. You need to sleep. I know you." She kissed the top of his mummified head.

Erin lifted his head. He swallowed the medication. Jeff wheeled him to his room and helped him get into bed. Erin let the powerful drug do its work. But he caught Jeff's hand before his brother-in-law could leave. "One answer. Both."

Jeff nodded. "You got it, bro. It's the only answer there is. Get some sleep."

Erin lay back, closed his eyes, and let the darkness take him.

Until his phone rang. And rang. And rang. Erin came out of his drug-induced fog and answered it. "Hello?"

"You poor dear. Such an awful thing to happen. You need your mother to take care of you."

Erin closed his eyes. "What do you want, Felicity?"

"I want you to call me Mom. I want my men all back together. I want us all to be one happy family."

"It's not going to happen. Any of it."

Her tone became threatening. "I suggest you think again. Your niece's life, as well as your girlfriend's, might depend on it."

Erin opened his eyes and stared at the phone. "What are you talking about?"

"If you were nice to me, I might be able to help you get them back."

"Might? What do you mean?"

"I mean, if you give me what I want, I might be able to help you get what you want."

"Are you saying you know where Vy and Talitha are?"

"I might."

Erin's hands shook. "Don't play games, Felicity."

"Mom. You're supposed to call me Mom."

"Not until Vy and Talitha are back and safe."

"Yes, well, that's the issue, isn't it? You want them. I want you to be nice to me. You'll have to go first."

"Prove to me you know where they are."

"Prove to me you love me first."

Erin disconnected the call. *She's lying. She doesn't know anything about where they are. She's lying.*

The phone rang again. "What?"

"You need to be nicer to me if you want to see your niece again. I'll send you a picture. Will that satisfy you?"

Erin's insides went cold. "Of both of them."

The phone went silent. Ten minutes later, the phone buzzed with a photo coming through. Erin peered at it. A woman with a hood over her face. Her hands behind her back. And no way to tell whether this might be Vy or not.

A second notification. Another photo. A baby girl. Wrapped up in a snowsuit, her face barely visible. Again not visible enough to tell if it was Talitha or not.

Erin took the chance. "You don't have them. You don't have either one of them. This is all a joke. A sick joke."

"You're willing to take the chance?"

"I know where you live, Felicity. I know where to find you. Do you really think you can kidnap anyone, call me, threaten me, and get away with it? You don't have them. And I'm pretty sure the FBI won't think this is funny, either. You should look for a visit from them in the near future."

"I didn't say I—"

"You sent me a photo purporting to be them. You're done, Felicity. Done."

He hung up again. There would be no further conversation. *She's an idiot. Lord, forgive me, but she is. I'll pray for her, but not right now. I know. I know. Forgive as You forgave me. And I will. But not right this minute. Not until Vy and Talitha are back. And I'm sorry.*

FRIDAY MORNING

Vy's prison door opened. The gorilla-masked man came in. He pointed to the gag and blindfold hanging around her neck. "Put them on. Hurry." Vy shifted both into place. Her captor tied her hands behind her back. "Cooperate. Please." He tied her ankles in front of her, forcing her into a sitting position, leaning against the wall.

Carefully he propped Talitha on Vy's lap, pulling Vy's arms forward to keep the little girl sitting up. Talitha seemed to think this great fun and laughed. Vy's heart shattered. *Please, Lord. Save this little one. Please.*

Footsteps sounded. Someone lighter. Faster. The female voice carried triumph. "He wants proof. I'll give him all the proof he wants."

Vy heard more than saw a flash go off, followed by another. Two more were taken. "There. Those should settle it."

Gorilla-man croaked, "You want him to suffer. You have to give him time to think about it."

"I know! He'll have time. He'll have three days. Maybe four… I could even drag it out another week. I want to see his father twist and squirm."

The voice trailed off. Vy sensed the figure turning and leaving the room. Gorilla-man whispered, "When she's gone, I'll undo the ropes. And I'll bring you some food and water. Remember to act hungry and thirsty when she comes in."

Vy nodded. *Pictures. Proof. They've contacted our people.* Vy filed the information away. Her captor left, closing the door, leaving Talitha sitting on Vy's lap. Vy tried to corral the baby, spreading her knees to form a circle around the little one. She had to keep Talitha above the ground and away from the heat-sucking cold. Talitha laughed again and rocked her body against Vy's.

What do I know? It's personal against someone. Him. Jeff or Erin. But by grabbing Talitha and me, my guess would be Erin. But what did she mean about him being almost killed?

Defending Talitha. He fought. And got beaten harder than she wanted. Because she wants him to suffer. But for what? What does choosing between us do for her? Besides torture Erin?

Or is that the endgame? Making Erin suffer.

Except she can't see him. It won't feed her need for revenge if revenge is what she's after. Sadists want to see their victims in anguish, not just imagine it. Will she call him out? Think like the perp. What would she want? What theater would suit her? Vy scraped her bands against the wall. Yes, Gorilla-man said he would come back. But there were no guarantees. She would do what she could. Always.

What theater? Me, weak and dying of thirst on one side of the divide. Talitha, dirty and crying on the other. She will want him to see what 'he' has done to us. Then force him to choose. Maybe force him to actually kill one or the other? No. Not nearly as satisfying. Too much chance he would turn the gun on himself.

She had no intention of letting either of them go. Erin knew. The cops knew. It's how it always works. Kidnappers rarely live up to their end of the bargain. And she already said she'd kill both of us. Vy let the thought pass by without comment. She rested in the Father's hands. Nothing touched her except what He allowed. No safer place existed.

But what about 'see his father squirm.' Erin's father? Robert Winger? If she thinks doing anything to Erin will hurt his father, she's delusional. If I tell her…will she write us off as a lost cause and kill us? Or would she find some other use for us? Father, tell me what to do. Put doubt in her mind, or let her continue in her fantasy? Tell me, please.

And still, she scraped her bonds against the wall.

Time elapsed. How long Vy couldn't know. Long enough for Talitha to fall asleep and wake up hungry. Gorilla-man returned. He pulled Vy's gag and blindfold down and released her hands. Their captor brought a bottle for the little girl, a bottle of water, and some strips of chicken for Vy. He fed Vy while she fed the baby. Talitha smiled and wrinkled her nose at Vy.

Vy whispered, "No playing, little one. Not now. You need to drink it all gone. We can play when we get home again, okay? I promise you will go home again."

Vy took the chance to look straight at her captor. She held his eyes, even through the mask. "She is going home again, right? You will make sure she goes home. Right?"

The man dropped his eyes. "If I can."

Vy shook her head. She hardened her voice. "No. Not good enough. You have to promise me Talitha goes home safe, no matter what."

The man jumped to his feet. "I don't have to promise you anything!" No shielding his voice. Pure frustration.

Which Vy wanted. "No, you don't. But you don't like this arrangement any more than I do. This wasn't your idea, and you don't want to go along with it. But you have to, for now. That's what you said. 'For now.' So when the time comes, I want you to promise me you will do everything you can to make sure Talitha goes home to her mother and father. Will you give me your word?"

The man hesitated. He sat slowly, handed Vy more of the chicken. "I will. I'll do what I can to keep her safe and see she goes home. Father would want me to. He'd never agree with any of this."

Push now? Or wait? Wait. *I've upset him once already. I need him to keep talking to me. Each time he comes, I learn something. Wait.* Vy swallowed the chicken and the water he offered her. She finished feeding the baby. "Did you bring a clean diaper?"

"Another one? We changed her an hour ago."

"Yes, and she just ate. Which means she'll need a clean one about…" Vy waited.

And was rewarded with the unmistakable sound of a diaper needing to be changed again. "Now." She smiled, shrugged. "Babies."

Talitha giggled. Gorilla-man sighed, rose, disappeared, and returned with a clean-up kit. "Here. I can't do it right. Always get the diaper on the wrong way."

Vy cleaned and diapered the baby, then handed the dirty one to Gorilla-man. He took it with two fingers and laid it aside. Vy burped Talitha, rubbed the little one's back, and snuggled her close. Five minutes of rocking and humming, and Talitha fell asleep.

Gorilla-man whispered, "You'll make a good mom."

"If I get the chance. But that's sort of up to you, too."

The man lowered his head, tied Vy's hands again, placed the gag and blindfold back over her mouth and eyes, tied her hands and feet, and walked from the room. The door closed.

I'm doing what I can, Lord. I'm gathering all the information he gives me. If You want, help me get it to the good guys so we can get out of here. Please.

Vy leaned back against the wall and hummed praises.

* * *

The walls of the Garen Penitentiary needed painting. Jim knew the budget had been passed. His taxes reflected it. But no work had been started. Figured. Drab yellow, dirty white, olive greens...no light, no cheer. *It's a prison. What color should it be? Lime green with hot pink spots? Maybe there wouldn't be a recidivism problem.*

Two correctional officers brought a prisoner through the door. The man's hands were shackled. *Hmm. Can't stay out of trouble even here, can you?*

The officers seated the man. He picked up the phone. "Detective Russo. I thought you retired after you put me here."

The face on the other side of the glass had aged more than four years from being behind prison bars. Robert Winger looked old. Tired and old. Repentant and old? Probably not.

Jim nodded. "I did. Two years ago. I'm here on a personal matter."

"Personal? Can't help you."

"Maybe you can. It concerns your grandchildren. Or one of them."

Winger's eyes narrowed slightly. "So? Their parents put me here."

"'I' put you here. 'They' put you here. How about you put you here? Any chance you put you here?"

Winger shrugged. "Semantics. What's the problem I can make worse for them?"

"You can't. Nothing can." Winger's eye's sparked. A light of curiosity. *Good. Maybe he will help.* "Someone kidnapped your granddaughter. An infant. Four months old. Firebombed the house and snatched her from Erin after nearly killing him."

Winger shrugged, but Jim could see the curiosity lingered in the man's posture. He leaned forward, body cocked to listen out of the 'good ear.' "Lots of kidnappings. Doesn't mean it's personal. People with money—"

"It happened a few hours after Erin's fiancée was kidnapped. Erin got a text demanding he choose one. Presumably, one to live, one to die."

Winger's eyebrows rose. His mouth drew down into one of contemplation. "Hmm. Interesting dilemma. What did he say?"

"Immaterial to my question. Who would hate you so much they would punish your son?"

"Why hate me? I'm sure my 'son' has enough enemies of his own."

Jim shook his head. "No. This is personal. And I'm convinced directed at you. Humor me. Who would want to get back at you by using your children?"

Robert Winger sat back in his chair. Jim watched the man's eyes. They cast back and forth, looking up and down. He snorted. "I'd say look first at their aunts. Women scorned play vicious."

"Aunts. Multiple? I didn't know Rupert had married."

The convict chuckled. "He thought he hid it from all of us. He didn't want them 'tainted' by the Winger 'curse.' Look in the financials. Last name O'Beck. He paid her regularly."

Jim scribbled the name down in his notebook. "I'll look into that." He lifted his head. "Next?"

"Why do you care about this?"

"I'm godfather to Joshua, one of the triplets. So yeah, it's personal to me, too. Next?"

Winger shrugged. "I don't know. I had a lot of enemies. None who tried to kill me, though."

"Threatened?"

"I got those all the time. Threw them in the shredder. Business is business. I can't help you any further." He stood up. "Nice talking to you. Tell the kids I said good luck. I suspect they'll need it." His eyes sparked. "Let me know what he chooses. I'd like to see how the Chessmaster plays his way out of this one." Winger chuckled, turned, and had the correctional officers escort him away.

Jim shook his head. *Lord, forgive me for my thoughts about*

Robert Winger. He tossed his visitor badge on the table as he left the prison.

The drive back to Oakton gave him time to think. And consider a second avenue of information. One which might be less antagonistic. He'd let Agent Nicks know about it after he got back. Two friends having a conversation. That's all. He dialed his voice-activated Bluetooth phone. *Handier than finding a pay phone. Some of this technology isn't so bad.*

"Detective Russo. Hello. Is this a business call?" Patrick Winger's voice sounded inquisitive.

"I'm retired, so just Jim. And it's personal. Have you been in contact with Collin or Erin in the past week?"

"No. I saw the news." Patrick hesitated. "I…I don't know what to say to them. I wanted to call, but what do you say? 'I'm sorry your kid is missing'? I…I don't know what to say."

"Say you heard, you care, and that will be enough for them."

Patrick's voice became sad. "Yeah. I'll do that." He paused. "Is that what you called me about? To be my conscience?" Patrick's tone contradicted the sarcasm in the words.

"You know Erin's fiancée was kidnapped as well?"

"You mean the woman who got snatched in the parking garage? I didn't know she and Erin were engaged. Or if I did, I didn't make the connection. Is he still in the hospital?"

"No. He checked himself out."

"Doesn't surprise me. Stupid, but doesn't surprise me."

Jim chuckled. "Agreed. Patrick, I have a hunch these kidnappings are personal, and they're against Robert Winger. I can't prove it yet, but that's my gut feeling. Who would hate your father enough to get back at him this way?"

Patrick snorted. "How much time do you have? I could make you a list."

Jim grinned. "Yeah, I know. But narrow it down for me. I don't think this is about money. I think this is more personal."

Silence on the other end. After a few moments. "I'll send you some names. Dad may have shredded the threats he got, but I kept copies. We were a munitions company. We caught blame for making the guns, or the ammunition, or the explosives, whenever someone died. But there were a few who went beyond writing letters. Let me get to my files, and I'll send you what I have."

"Thanks, Patrick. I appreciate it. How are you doing?"

"I'm good. Working for myself is a new experience, but I like it. Much less stress than working for Dad. Listen, I have to go. I'll get in touch with Collin. I will. But tell her and Erin I'm praying for them."

"I'll let them know. It will mean a lot to them."

"Thanks, Jim."

Jim ended the call. *Garth? Gareth? Before we start investigating their mother? Why not?*

He punched up the number.

Very tentative, "Hello?"

"Hello, Garth. I need your help."

"Detective Russo? I didn't do it, whatever it might have been."

Jim smiled. "Guilty much? No, not anything you did." He stopped. "What did you do?"

"If you don't know, I'm not telling."

Jim laughed. "Fair enough. Have you heard about Collin and Jeff's daughter being kidnapped?"

"I received an Amber Alert about a baby. She's their daughter?"

"Yeah."

"Wow. I'm sorry. I didn't know. Wow. I need to call them."

"They'll appreciate it, I'm sure. Erin's fiancée was kidnapped the same morning."

Silence. Long silence. "I didn't know. We haven't been in close touch for a few months. My fault. I sort of dropped off the face of the earth. Needed some space, you know?"

Wish this could have been a video call. He'd love to see his face right now. "I understand. Anything in particular? Or life in general?"

"School or work. Social life or future. Been battling for a while and just wanted to get away from all the outside voices. Haven't even talked to Mom in a month. Guess I should drop back into life, huh?"

Jim shook his head. "I understand, Garth. You've had a lot happen in the past couple years. It can be hard. But yeah, some people need your help about now."

"What can I do?"

"Did your father ever mention something happening, someone dying, and Winger Inc. caught the blame for it?"

Silence. The voice tentative. "There were a couple of times."

Garth stopped. "Did it have to be from an accident or something? Not just regular work?"

Jim glanced in his rearview mirror, watched an idiot fly by him doing in excess of the speed limit. On a frozen road. Jim would see him in the ditch in a mile or two. Happened all the time. He looked back to the road in front of him. "It wouldn't have to be. What are you remembering?"

"Dad told us about this crazy woman who came barging into the offices one day. She was mad as...well, mad as a wet hornet. Madder, he said. Never seen anyone so out of control. She had a baseball bat and smashed glass as she walked through. Screaming about Winger killing her son, and she knew which Winger. She would get even if it was the last thing she did. Dad laughed about it because he wasn't the Winger the man worked for."

"What happened?"

"Security caught her. The police came, calmed her down, she apologized and said she had been overcome with grief. Her son had died... Heart attack from overwork. Too many long hours, so she said. Now she had to raise his children, his sons. Robert made the mistake of coming out of his office, and she went berserk again. Police had to haul her out in cuffs. Dad thought it the funniest thing ever."

"Do you remember the name?"

"No. Mom will. I'll get it from her and send it to you."

"Thanks. And if you think of anyone else who might have been serious about harming Robert Winger, let me know."

"I will. Jim?"

"Yeah?"

"Tell Collin and Erin I'm sorry. I'll call them later this week. After I call my mom. And my girlfriend. And my boss. I've got a few bridges to rebuild."

Jim raised his eyebrows. "I can understand. Thanks again, Garth."

He ended the call. "Lord, I hope some of this information pans out. We need a break. Please. Keep Vy and the baby safe. Please."

He drove past the idiot in the ditch and kept going.

FRIDAY AFTERNOON

Agent Duves stared at the projection on the wall. Even exploded to as large as they could, the photo only added to his frustration. What could they tell from the picture? Vy and Talitha lived. Talitha looked happy. Vy, less so. Yes, her eyes and mouth were covered. But he knew Vy, and the clothes were the ones he'd seen her in the day she disappeared. There were scrapes and bruises on her face. The dimensions of the room were tiny, the floors, dirt. Sunlight filtered in through cracks in the boards.

Given the time stamp and the direction of the sunbeams, they could narrow down the location of the building. But narrowing down to within a few miles still left too many to cover quickly. Drones were flying the area, searching for wooden structures which might fit the description. But that still left a whole lot of buildings to be searched. And no promise Vy hadn't been moved since then.

His search of Felicity's bank records yielded nothing. Well, nothing regarding this case. There would be plenty there to interest the IRS, should they choose to do an audit. Oscar and Felicity had been involved in plenty of less-than-honest deals and investments in their lives. Enough to impoverish them to living off their children's income. Sad.

Sad, but did it equal kidnapping? Felicity's medical records had been subpoenaed. Unstable, you bet. Obsessive? Well, yeah. Controlling? Above the norm, yes. But capable of this level of anger and hate?

Possibly. All the combined agencies had people watching and analyzing the family. Oscar faced multiple charges of insurance fraud, conspiracy to commit fraud, and various other crimes the prosecutors could think up. Felicity going to jail with him made her involvement in the kidnapping somewhat more likely.

Yet, at the same time, not. Agent Duves shook his head. It didn't make sense. Something or someone was missing.

His phone quacked. Not a business call. He started to ignore it, checked the number, and picked it up. "Detective Russo."

"Just Jim. I've got some information I'd like to share with you when you have a free moment. I can't vouch for the reliability of it. Unless the word of one crook against another counts for much."

"Jailhouse informants can usually be trusted. When can we meet?"

"I'm retired. I can meet anytime. What works for your schedule?"

Agent Duves looked at his calendar. "Two? Can you come downtown?"

"Cuppa's?"

"Right. I'll be there."

"Thanks."

Agent Duves drew in a deep breath, let it out, and stared at the projection on the wall. "Where are you, Vy? Stay safe, Agent. We're coming for you." He looked at his phone, placed the call. "Agent Nicks? You free at two?"

* * *

Erin stared at the picture on his phone. Unable to take his eyes off the image of Vy bound and gagged. Dirty and disheveled, utterly helpless, posed against a wall like a rag doll.

He acknowledged Talitha's presence. Celebrated she looked happy and well. His gut told him to comment, to allow Collin and Jeff to feel some sense of relief. Their pain had to be recognized. It wasn't all about him. Or Vy.

Erin tore his eyes away from the image of his beloved. He lifted his eyes to those of his sister. He forced his heart to feel the words, forced his voice to mean them. "Talitha looks good."

Collin fell on his shoulder, embracing him. He'd released her, he knew, to be happy about seeing the baby. While still hurting for Vy. She kissed his cheek. "We're bringing them both home, A-One. We are."

He nodded. *God, help me believe it! I'm losing it, Lord. I'm so scared. Help me!*

His phone alerted. The text read, *Five days. Choose. Only one.*

He motioned to Agent Pope. "Send this: 'No. Both live.'"

Then both die.

"Send: 'No. Both live. God has them.'"

The kidnapper went silent. *Do they fear You, Lord? Not love You, but* fear *You?* Erin showed the exchange to Collin and Jeff. Both nodded. Tears fell, but they nodded.

Jeff had to clear his throat. "What do you think will happen? How will the exchange go?"

Erin started to answer. He stopped. He looked at the text again. Looked up at Collin and Jeff. "It's not Felicity. This is proof it's not."

Collin's eyes grew wide, narrowed. "What makes you sure?"

"Any time I mentioned God, she came back with an insult. Always." He pointed to the text. "This person didn't. Not a word." He nodded to Jeff. "It's not Felicity." He felt some satisfaction in knowing he'd been right. And relief he hadn't played into her game.

"Then who is it?"

"Who hates us?"

Collin looked at the floor. "Family. The only ones not in prison are Aunt Sarah, Garth, Gareth, and Patrick. Why after all this time?"

"Revenge is best served cold. That's the saying, right?"

"Or waiting until the stakes were high enough." Jeff kicked the leg of the coffee table. "You both have someone you're equally invested in, and the choice puts a permanent wedge between you."

Collin's face hardened. "And we left them enough money to hire people to do the job."

Erin raised his hand, palm up. "But Garth and Gareth have been cool with me. I mean, we're good. I can't see them getting involved. And Patrick... Patrick accepted the Lord. Honestly. I don't see it being him."

Jeff looked at Erin sideways. "Have either of them contacted you about Vy being missing?"

Erin closed his eyes to think but couldn't make the timeframes fit. He handed his phone to Jeff. "You look. I can't."

Jeff took the phone and scrolled through the text and phone messages. It took several minutes, but finally, he looked up. "I don't see anything."

Erin reached for his phone. "Maybe I should contact them."

Collin held up her hand. "Wait, little brother. Let's call Jim. He said he wanted to dig into the family connection. Let's see what he came up with first. Or maybe we can add to what he already knows. Or suspects, anyhow."

Erin thought about it. Thinking still hurt. He closed his eyes. "Yeah. You're right. You call him."

Jeff lay his hand on Erin's arm. "You're hurting. Go lie down."

Erin pounded the arm of the wheelchair. "I will not take this lying down! Vy is out there. And Talitha. I am not invalid. I will see this through." The venom and steel in his veins melted as quickly as they came. He sagged.

Jeff squeezed his shoulder. "We know, bro. We do. No one is leaving you out. Build your strength while you can. You are going to need it. We all are."

Erin let Jeff roll him to his bedroom, transferred him to his bed, then stretched out. The image of Vy wouldn't leave his mind. *I'll find you, Vy. I will. We will. God, make it true. Make it so. Bring her home. Bring them both home.*

* * *

Jim and Agent Duves arrived at the same time to the shop across the street from the Federal Building. Fist bumps were exchanged. They ordered coffee, took it to a table in the back. FBI Agent Nicks slid in moments behind. He grabbed a canned power drink and sat down. Jim started the reporting.

"Talking to Robert Winger proved enlightening."

"How?"

"Turns out Rupert, the youngest brother, has a secret wife. Well, she's not secret anymore. Wife and sons. He hid them from the family so they wouldn't get caught up in the family drama. He hoped, anyhow."

"So?"

"So we now have two separate Winger women with motive to hate Collin and Erin." Jim swallowed a judicious amount of his drink. Too expensive not to enjoy all of it. The cost these days...

"Except I've seen the financials, and both families were left with sizeable fortunes and funds to live on. And their houses, cars, land. They all made out very well." Wyatt snorted. "I wish my enemies were this generous."

Jim swirled his cup. "Revenge is rarely about money."

"True. So you think it's one of them?"

"I don't know. Patrick and Garth gave me some interesting characters to look into. I've got friends in the city chasing the information down. If they can find me names, I'll go talk to them. Felicity still looks like the best bet, but I don't want to focus on her alone."

Jim's phone rang. He looked at the caller. "Collin." He put it on speaker. "What's up?"

"Erin thinks it's not Felicity. She didn't clap back at him about God. That's way out of character for her."

Jim looked at Wyatt, his eyebrows raised. "Interesting. I'm with Agents Duves and Nicks, and we're discussing a few new possibilities. According to your…to Robert Winger, Rupert had a wife and kids."

There came a long pause on the phone. "Oh, really? That's news to us."

"News to everyone. We're checking it out now. And we'll let you know what we find. But your Aunt Sarah isn't out of the running, either. I talked to Patrick and Garth, and they added some information we didn't have before. We're covering all the bases."

"This is hard. On everyone. We know you're all working with everything you have." The woman's voice shook ever so slightly.

"I understand. How is Erin?"

"Not good. But he is keeping his faith."

"It's all we have, Collin. I'm praying for you."

"Thanks. If we hear anything else, we'll let you know."

Jim pocketed his phone. He looked at Wyatt and Nicks. "What are we missing?"

"I wish I knew." Wyatt chugged the remains of his drink in two swallows.

Guess he thinks the way I do about the price of coffee. Jim finished the remains of his cup. "We've got five days to find it." He looked at his notes again. "If Erin is right and it's someone out for revenge on Robert Winger, who does that give us?"

Agent Nicks chugged half his can of power soda. "My people will go over the records, crosschecking the names Garth and Patrick gave you." He growled. "Still leaves too many, though. It's been nearly two weeks, and we still don't have a single good suspect."

"If there's one there, you'll find it." Jim tried to sound encouraging.

Nicks wasn't having it. "If. We're putting a lot of resources into chasing down one clue."

Wyatt asked, "You have a better idea?" There was a hint of fire in the tone.

Nicks swirled his can. "If I did, I'd be chasing it. I don't think I want to throw out any of our other suspects, though."

Wyatt smiled, and it wasn't from mirth. "Felicity looks very good for the church burning and the vandalism at the Farrell's and Johnson's houses. Motive and opportunity. We've got gas receipts showing she had been in the area at the time. The old, 'keep at least half a tank in the winter' is hard to break. Even when you're trashing someone else's property."

Jim frowned. "Anything showing up in the forensics on the incendiaries used in the kidnapping?"

"ATF is chasing them down. They have a partial signature match on one of the canisters. They're trying to make a positive ID before they say anything."

Nicks's eyes narrowed. "They know the time constraint, right? We don't need to convict. Not yet."

"They know. They promised me something, partial or not, by this afternoon."

Jim banged his fist on the table. "We're missing something. I know it. Something obvious. What aren't we seeing?" His eyes narrowed. "The baby…"

Jim looked at Agents Duves and Nicks. "That's it. The baby. Someone has to be buying formula and diapers."

Duves shook his head side to side. "Jim…"

"Hear me out. I know. It's a long shot. A very long shot. But with the photo, you narrowed the area down to a few miles. If we can find who is buying the items in that area…who shouldn't be…maybe, maybe we can isolate our kidnapper even closer." Jim felt his gut twisting. But with excitement. As if, for the first time, there might be hope. They had a chance. They had something.

Nicks's eyes narrowed, sparked. "Yeah. Maybe we can. I'll have my staff call the hospitals around the area and see what newborns were discharged recently. It will give us an idea of the location of who might legitimately be buying those supplies."

Jim nodded. "I can get a team of volunteers together to canvass door-to-door."

Agent Nicks held up a hand. "Wait. We can do better. I have an IT team that does this stuff for a living. They can cross hospital records with suppliers, orders, sales… we can narrow the field down even further." He smiled at Jim. "Then we'll take your volunteer team and hit the doors."

Jim grimaced. "Okay, you're right. That's faster than the old way."

Nicks shook his head. "Nothing wrong with the old way. It all comes down to the personal intuition in the end." He swallowed the rest of his power drink. "Let's go find a baby."

Jim slapped a twenty on the table, tapped knuckles with Nicks and Duves's fists, and headed out the door. Agent Duves followed one step behind him. Agent Nicks brought up the rear.

SATURDAY

Vy waited anxiously for one of her captors to come relieve the screaming of the unhappy infant. Talitha had been crying for hours now, utterly inconsolable. Gorilla-man hadn't returned to feed or change or otherwise care for the infant. It wasn't like him to be gone this long. Had 'she' found out he had helped her? Been sidelined for other work? Forgotten his promise?

He'd been in that morning, or what Vy believed to be morning. He'd bound and gagged her, saying 'she' might be coming to take more pictures. But no one had come, and Talitha suffered for it. Her screams tailed off into pathetic sup-supping before she would fall asleep from exhaustion. But she would wake as miserable as she had been, if not more so. Vy could do nothing beyond pray. For Talitha. For herself. For her captors. Erin. Collin and Jeff. Her parents. And she would start all over again.

The cold of January sucked the heat out of her as well. The fire went out, leaving the small shack to equalize to the outside temperature. Below freezing. Way below freezing. Though she tried to keep Talitha off the ground, nothing and no one warmed Vy. She rocked back and forth, hoping the motion would raise her heart rate and body temperature enough to sustain life. At least for a little longer. Just a little longer.

Hours of rocking left her exhausted. The siren-song of sleep grew louder in her ears. If she could be still for a minute…maybe two…she would be able to fight it. Even Talitha's screams couldn't provide incentive to keep rocking. She needed to quit. For a moment. Talitha's cries stopped. The baby must have nodded off. Maybe Vy could, too. For a moment. Just one moment…

The door banged open, startling Vy back to consciousness. She felt large hands massaging up and down her arms. "Wake up! You have to wake up. You're too cold. I've got to get you warm." Someone pulled the gag down, and warm liquid poured down her throat. "I'm sorry. I should never have trusted... I knew better. I knew better." Disgust and anger laced through the voice.

A rough blanket wrapped around her body. Her hands were cut free. "Hold the baby. She's as cold as you are. On your feet. Move around. Get the blood pumping. You can do this. You have to do this."

Vy didn't bother to pull at her blindfold. She recognized the voice of her Gorilla-man. He supported her as he made her walk around the inside of the building. "Come on, ma'am. You can do this. You're strong. I know you are."

More liquid warmed her insides. Vy nodded, trying to let him know she felt better. But he didn't stop walking her around. "I'll kill him for ignoring you. I will. I should never have expected him to help me out. I'm sorry." The walking slowed. "Is the baby okay? She's not crying."

Vy realized the truth at the same time. She jostled Talitha, jostled her hard. She grabbed the little girl's hands. They were ice cold. She shoved the baby to her captor. "Quick. Take off her clothes. Put her against your skin. I'm not warm enough. But she needs to get warmed up. Now."

The man grunted. "She's like an ice cube."

"Is she breathing? Is she?" Terror knifed through her. *NO! Not now! Not like this!*

"Yeah, yeah. She's still breathing. But she's so cold."

"Hold her close. Hold her tight. On your chest where it's warmest. Walk around with her." *Lord, don't let this child die. Please, please. Don't let her die.*

Vy heard the weakest of whimpers. "Keep it up. You're saving her. You are."

More sounds of walking, then of running, in place. "That'll get my blood going. And it'll warm her up. Come on, little girl. Come on. Cry for me. This time, I won't care. Cry loud. Please."

She could hear the desperation in the man's voice. Not from fear of punishment but from compassion for the child. He cared. He wanted her to live. Talitha had him, now.

Another whimper. A pitiful cry. Still so weak. "Come on, baby girl. Come on. You can do better. You're strong. You've got strong genes. I know you do. Come on."

"She needs food."

"He didn't feed her, either? I will kill him. I will. I only brought one bottle."

Vy chuckled. "She'll only take one. They don't double up like we do when we miss a meal."

"Oh. I thought…"

"It's fine."

Vy heard the sounds of Talitha beginning to suckle from the bottle. The man bumped her arm. "Here, you take her."

"No, you're doing great. You're still warmer than I am and she needs the warmth." *And you need to bond with her even more. Work your magic, little girl. Smile at him. Just once.*

Contented sounds of a baby eating filled the room. A few moments later, Vy heard, "Hey! She smiled at me."

"She likes you. She knows you made her warm. She trusts you." Vy sat down near the wall, wrapping the blanket around herself. A good, thick blanket. One that would keep out the cold.

She heard off-key humming. There could have been no more beautiful sound. She sat on the tarp and listened to the soft chatter. "Hey, you're not done eating. You've got some more in there. I know you've got to be hungry.

"Finish it up. There's a good baby. I'll make sure you get fed. I'll beat my brother to a pulp for neglecting you. I will. You don't mistreat a baby. Not a sweet little baby like you are. Yeah, that's right." The voice sounded deeply satisfied. "She's smiling again. She does like me."

"Of course she does. Babies have a good sense of who they can trust and who they can't. She knows you won't hurt her."

"That's right. And I'm not going to let anyone else hurt you, either." The voice stopped. Vy guessed he realized what he'd said. She held her breath. He continued, "Never. I won't let anyone hurt you ever. No matter who they are."

Vy felt a diaper being put in her hand. "I'm sorry, but I can't do this part. I can't."

She smiled. "It's okay. I'll handle it. Even with my eyes closed." She did, too, as her captor didn't pull down the blindfold. Vy decided not to push it. They were making progress, and she didn't want to jeopardize it.

While she diapered the baby, Gorilla-man relit the fire, piling it high with wood, stoking to make it burn faster, to heat the room quicker. Vy rolled around to sit with her feet behind her. She intended to curl up around Talitha when the man left and make a better effort of keeping the little girl warm and alive.

The door slammed open. The female's distorted voice demanded, "Why does she have a blanket? Why are her hands untied? What are you doing?"

The man met the demand with vehemence of his own. "They both nearly froze to death. The baby almost died. She told me how to save it. You would have let them both die, and where would your revenge be, huh? You're lucky I saved them for you."

"Don't you talk to me like—"

"I'll talk any way I want. What are you going to do, kill me too? Sure you will. Who'll do your dirty work? I do everything for you. And I saved them. So don't talk to me about whether her hands are tied or not."

The man hadn't finished. "She knows there's no way for her to walk out of here. It's ten miles to the nearest house. She'll freeze to death before she gets anywhere. But she needs to be able to move around, so she can stay warm. And so she can keep the baby warm too."

The masked voice hissed. "Are you getting attached to her and the baby? Getting soft on me?"

"Have I ever not done what you told me? Have I ever got attached to one of your victims?"

Vy's eyes would have widened in surprise if they weren't securely tied shut. *Victims? Plural?*

"They all had a part in Dad's death. I haven't forgotten that. And I always take care of things, don't I? So leave me alone. And get off my back."

Vy heard footsteps leave. The man sighed. "I swear, she gets harder and harder to stay with." The voice turned to face Vy. "I promised you I'd help you and the baby. I will. I just have to figure out a way. A way so no one gets hurt. I still got four days. It'll come to me by then. I promise. Stay warm. I'll be back and bring you some food."

Vy settled back against the wall, rocking Talitha to sleep. Tears fell despite the blindfold. *Lord, help us, please. I don't know this man. I don't know what he's done. I have my suspicions. I don't know I can shield him from the law if I'm right. But please, if there is any way, save him too.*

She prayed as she wept.

* * *

Erin's phone pinged. *Who do you choose?*

Erin motioned for his sister to pick up the phone. "Tell them both."

Collin typed in Erin's response. He flexed his fingers but still didn't have the dexterity to text his own answers.

The answer came back. *Choose one or both die.*

Erin looked at Collin. "Type, 'Why? What did I do to you?' They've got to tell me. No one does this and doesn't say why."

He cost me my son. Punishing you punishes him. He'll feel what I felt.

Erin's eyes widened. "'He'? Who do they mean?"

Collin glared at the phone. "Who else? Robert Winger. Has to be. Why else come against you?"

"Answer them. 'Robert Winger does not care what happens to me or anyone I love. He is in prison, and I helped put him there.'"

Lies. You're his son.

Erin waved to his sister. "Get the card with the prison contact information. Winger's prisoner number and the phone number of the penitentiary." Collin dug through the desk drawer and pulled out a three-by-five note card. She handed it to him.

"Type it. All of it."

Collin typed. *Prisoner number 55567. Garen Penitentiary Garen, Ohio. He hates me. He'll think you've done him the greatest favor ever.*

You're lying.

Call the prison.

Lies.

Read the court records. It's all public knowledge. Trial number 8877234, the People vs. Robert Winger. Read what he said about me. He hates me.

Collin read her responses to the queries as she typed them. Erin nodded. "Perfect. You could have put us, but since they think they're after me, I guess it's better that way."

He looked at Agent Pope. "Right call? Wrong approach?"

The agent pursed her lips. "With what we don't know, it's a good call. You're doing the best you can based on what we know."

"You're not exactly encouraging."

"It's the best I can give you. I'm sorry."

Erin nodded and waited.

Collin glanced from the phone to Erin. "You think they'll make the effort?"

"I can only hope." He held his hand out to his sister and touched her arm. "I know the calls go to Wyatt Duves. Call Jim, too, and see what he thinks. Maybe we get another breakthrough."

"I will." Collin squeezed his shoulder. "Think. I know the concussion makes it hard. But think. Who would hate Robert Winger this much? It's personal. They 'lost' their son over it. Do you remember anything at all about something like this?"

Erin shook his head, but very slowly. He needed all the brain cells to cooperate. "I'm trying, Cane."

"I know." He felt her hand tremble. He grabbed it. "We're getting them back, Cane. We will. Both of them. And alive. I know it. I know it."

Tears filled his sister's eyes. She sucked in her lip, bit it, nodded, and moved across the room to find her phone and call Jim Russo.

Erin looked at his phone. *God, please. Please. Please turn their heart. Please. Bring Vy back to me. Bring Talitha back to my sister. Make us whole again. God, I beg You. Please.*

So much to say, all of which He knew already. Erin cried it out anyhow. God would hear it. All of it. The hurt, the pain, the emptiness, the longing, the anger…yes, the anger. Anger at the kidnapper. Anger at Robert Winger. Anger at himself for losing Talitha. Anger at God for letting all this happen.

God already knew. Why hide it? Erin bowed his head. *God! Why? I know, I don't need to know why. But I want to know. I want to know there is a happy ending to this. Somehow, somewhere, there's a purpose and a reason. You are going to swoop in and make it all right. I want to want Your will. I don't, but I want to. Make it right, Lord. Me. Vy. Talitha. Cane. Make all of us right. In Your Name. Amen.*

* * *

Agent Nicks looked across the table at Sarah Winger. Mother to Garth and Gareth Winger. Ex-wife of Richard Winger. The woman presented herself well. Having a wife with excellent taste himself, he knew Mrs. Winger's outfit came from the uptown mall, the exclusive one-off shop his wife loved to peruse but never enter. Better sense. Lower budget.

The coat draped across the chair belonged to another designer line, meant to look good, but probably wouldn't provide a while lot of warmth. He couldn't see her boots, but he bet mud didn't stick. *She's the type who would manage that somehow.*

Nicks smiled his best. "Thank you for coming in so quickly, Mrs. Winger."

"Renfort. I've returned to my maiden name."

"Ms. Renfort, excuse me."

She shrugged. "It's not official yet, so I can forgive the error. How can I help the FBI? I thought you were done investigating my family. We were all cleared of any charges. The only decent thing he ever did for us." The sneer in the woman's tone told Nicks some wounds hadn't healed yet. If ever.

Nicks kept his expression even. "This isn't about your ex-husband, Ms. Renfort." *Let's see if it buys me any goodwill.* "This is about a baby who was kidnapped two weeks ago."

Sarah's face lost its combativeness. "Baby? The Amber alert? They still haven't found the little thing? That's terrible. So it isn't a custodial dispute?"

"No, it's not. The little girl is the daughter of Collin and Jeffrey Farrell."

Scott Nicks watched the woman's expression closely. Minutely. And unless she'd been a trained thespian once in her life, he would swear her reaction had to be genuine. "Collin's baby? Oh, no. How horrible! I had no idea! We live in Ft. Newton, and they didn't give those details. I'm so sorry." Her voice cracked. "How awful. I need to call them. I wish I'd known."

She dropped her head to cover her tears. After a moment, she looked up. "My son Garth keeps up with his cousin better than I do. But Garth dropped off the face of the earth last month, and I haven't heard from him."

She looked at her phone. "Speak of the devil. Someone must have talked to him. But an email? Couldn't think of calling me, could he? Especially with something like this?" Anger laced her voice again. "I will shred him when I see him. I will. He left a note saying he needed to 'find a place for himself.' Yeah, I'll find a place for him. Six feet under."

Sarah looked up. Horror filled her eyes. "I didn't mean it the way it sounded. I didn't."

Nicks laughed. "Don't worry. I have teenage boys. I understand. I do."

Sarah laughed, but Nicks could see she still felt shaken by her threat. She recovered and asked, "What do you want to know? How can I help?"

"We're investigating another kidnapping at the same time. A young woman, a Federal Agent, was snatched from her place of employment downtown."

Sarah appeared confused. "You think the two are related?"

"The woman is Erin Winger's fiancée."

Blood drained from Sarah's face. She dropped her head into her hands. "That poor family. What must they be going through? Those poor kids. I am so sorry." She looked up. "What can I do? How can I help?"

"Do you know anyone who might have held a particular grudge against Robert Winger?"

Again the fire lit her tone. "You mean, besides everyone he ever dealt with? No. Not a one."

Nicks let out a short breath. "I understand. Haven't had to deal with the man myself, but the people I talk to all tend to agree with you. Those who aren't in prison with him." He leaned forward. "What I'm looking for is someone who had a grudge more than the norm. Someone who might have threatened him directly or threatened the company, threatened to come after his family... Anything above and beyond the usual hate." *Which, in this guy's case, seems to be above and beyond everything anyhow.*

Sarah sat still for several moments. She looked off into space, glanced at the floor, focused on the table. After a moment, she nodded. "I remember one incident. A woman took after Robert with a baseball bat. Richard told us about it over dinner one night. He thought it was funny. I failed to see any humor in the situation. But it seems a woman who had recently lost her son—but due to a heart attack, not due to anything Robert Winger had done to him personally …"

She trailed off. "Let me remember." Sarah's eyes narrowed. "She blamed Robert for making her son work extra hours. Long hours, for long stretches of the time. Trying to make him into a protégé."

Sarah focused her eyes back on Nicks. "But the man died. His mother came in from the funeral with the bat and began making a shambles of the office, looking for Robert. I guess security tried to calm her down and get the bat away from her. Some of the office staff knew her and tried to get the cops to go easy on her."

She snorted a lady-like snort. "It might have worked if Robert hadn't come out of his office about then and totally ignored her. Maybe if he'd have said something nice, something sympathetic, it all could have ended there. But not Robert. Not him."

She shook her head in disgust. "Security asked what they should do about the man's mother, and Robert asked 'who'? As if he didn't know the man's name or even that he'd recently died. I guess the woman grabbed the bat and went after Robert. Got in a few licks before they dragged her out."

Sarah pursed her lips. "They should have let her have him. Might have avoided all this tragedy."

Nicks wanted to agree but kept it professional. "I see. Do you remember a name?"

"No. But I remember the year and about what month. Will it help? I mean, there can't be too many assaults on Robert Winger with a baseball bat, can there? By older women?"

Nicks smiled. "I would hope not." *But I don't put anything past the guy.* "Let me get a web tech in here who can help with the search, and we'll see what we can find." He extended his hand. "Thank you very much, Ms. Renfort. You've been more than helpful. You might help us break this case open."

"I hope so. Those kids deserve better than they got, believe me."
Oh, I do. I do.

SUNDAY

Vy heard gravel spinning and an engine straining to climb the hill. It didn't have the sound of her Gorilla-man's vehicle. Someone else was coming. Rescue? Vy's gut jumped. *Please, Lord. Can we go home now? Please?*

The truck skidded to a stop. The door opened and slammed shut. Vy heard the voice of the woman, still concealed but muttering angrily. "Lies. Lies. Winger's son. Winger will do anything to protect him. You watch. I'm right. He'll pay." The voice sneered. "Both ways."

Vy prayed. *Guide my words. Give me what to say and how to say it. Wisdom, Father. I need wisdom.*

The door banged against the wall. Vy felt someone pick up Talitha. The baby began to fuss. The woman shushed her. "It's going to be alright, little one. You're going to be just fine."

Vy put all the vitriol she could muster in her words. "Don't lie to her. Tell her the truth. Tell her that her grandfather paid you to kidnap and kill her. Tell her you made a deal with Robert Winger to torture her mother. How much is he paying you to murder the baby, hmm? What's the going rate for an innocent child? I'm sure he's delighted to pay it, whatever it is. Of course, it will be hard for him to come up with it in prison."

Vy stopped. "Oh, no, wait. You and he made the deal before he went to prison, right? His revenge for his children putting him behind bars for life. How much is he paying you to send him pictures of the dead baby? He'll hang it as a trophy in his cell, I'm sure of it."

The voice seethed. "You don't know anything about what I'm

doing."

"I know you're doing Robert Winger's dirty work for him. Getting his revenge for him on his son and daughter." She snorted and scoffed. "This is exactly what he would want. His kids took his beloved money from him. He's taking everything they love from them. Shrewd. Very shrewd. Worthy of him. How much is he paying you?"

The voice remained silent. Vy could hear the sounds of Talitha sucking on her bottle. *Eat slow, baby. Give me time to turn the screws. Please. Smile once. It'll help.*

Finally, the woman beside her spoke. "What do you mean?"

"Don't play games. Robert Winger hired you to get his revenge. He'll be dancing in his cell celebrating when he hears you killed his granddaughter. And his son's fiancée. His kids took his money, his power, his position, his freedom from him. He'll rot in prison. No chance of parole. But his revenge will be sweeter. What is worse than the death of a child? Especially the murder of a child? Of an infant? A triplet. Collin will never look at her sons without thinking about the one who isn't there. That's cruelty. And Robert Winger will love it. So I ask again, how much did he pay you?"

The woman seethed. "He hasn't paid me anything."

"Oh, I see. He's got something on you. Holding something over your head to make you do this for him. Must be something bad if he's got you getting revenge for him on both his daughter and his son. Killing the woman Erin loves? I can see Winger's eyes. He'll be hooting for joy. So sweet for him. He gets back at both of them at the same time. He's the mastermind, alright. Always working the angles."

Talitha giggled. The woman shushed her again. "You need to eat, little girl. Not play."

Vy needled one last time. "It still amazes me how he could arrange this so neatly. Did he hire you before he went to trial? While he waited to be sentenced? Or did he contact you after, when he went in the penitentiary? Which would make it even more likely he had something over your head, or you'd never go to see him. Right? What is it? A son in trouble? A daughter he swore he could bring back? How much did he promise you to destroy his children's lives for him?"

Sounds of the woman patting Talitha's back. A satisfied burp. A giggle. A full diaper. More giggling. Humming. Soft humming. "Took his money? All of it?"

"Yeah. Robert Winger's stepfather left all the inheritance to Collin, Talitha's mom. All of it. Winger tried to have her killed. That's when the police found out he and his brothers had killed their own father back years ago. Winger lost everything and will rot in prison. You didn't know? You really didn't know he was using you to get his revenge? That's rich. Like I said, he plays all the angles. And he never loses."

"Humph. Humph."

Vy's captor cut lose her hands and feet. The woman put Talitha in Vy's arms. "Hold her." She touched the blindfold, but Vy stopped her. "Please. Leave it in place. If I don't see you, I can convince myself Talitha and I might get out of this alive. But if you take the blindfold off and I see you, it means you'll have to kill me. Call it self-delusion, but I'd rather not see you."

"Humph." Vy heard the wood stove being loaded, the door open, then close. Heard the car slide in the gravel and fade from hearing in the distance.

Vy sighed and leaned back against the wall. "I'm trying, Lord. I'm doing all I can. We need your help. Somehow, we need your help. Please."

She rocked slowly back and forth. And she sang. "Jesus loves me, this I know…"

MONDAY

The FBI Agent Nicks gathered his team together in the situation room. Photos of Vy and Talitha were plastered on the bulletin boards. Maps were up, pushpins in various locations, strings connecting them. Five agents and Jim Russo huddled near the board, trying to get as good a look as possible.

Nicks pointed to the board. "We've narrowed the search area down to three stores." He indicated the three pins. "Each of you will take a partner, photos of our suspect, and go canvass the pharmacies."

He checked the eyes of the men and women in the room. *Are they listening? Paying attention? Taking this seriously? So far, yes. Good. It's why I chose you.* "Baby formula is kept under lock and key, so someone has seen who's buying it. We have the sales records, so we know what day and time the items are purchased. Any details we can get from the sales clerks is information we didn't have before."

He motioned to Agent Brooke Jors. The young woman sat sprawled on the corner of a desk. If she wanted to give the image of an experienced, "I can do this on my own" agent, she failed. "You will be partnering with Jim Russo. He's former City Police, is familiar with the area, and can assist you in the search."

Nicks saw the flare of Agent Jors's eyes. *Yes, I'm assigning you a civilian partner. Get over it. Get over yourself. You're young, you need the practice, and he's been around the block a few times. If I had more agents, I'd send you out with one of them. But I don't. Live with it.*

Jors glanced over at Jim. Jim nodded to her and left it there. The woman turned back and glared at Nicks. He swallowed the smirk. *Bad form. Be a pro. She'll learn.*

Agent Nicks handed out photos and files to each of the three teams. Jors looked at the papers, disdain in her eyes. "Wouldn't it be better if we'd gotten this electronically? I can carry it on my phone easier than I can in a folder."

Nicks nodded. "Easier for you. But we want to make sure the people we show the pictures to can see all the details without having to squint or put on glasses. We can also leave copies behind for future reference. Sometimes 'old school' works best."

Jors shrugged. As ever, her face said she did not like being contradicted. *And that's something else you need to get over. It's an occupational hazard here.* Nicks snuck a look at Jim Russo. Jim's eyes were bright as if anticipating the challenges ahead. And looking forward to them. *Good man. I knew I liked you for a reason.*

"Okay, you have your assignments. Get to it. And keep everyone in the loop. There're two people's lives depending on us. Make it count."

Teams partnered up, grabbed coats and gloves and scarves, and headed out. Nicks tapped fists with each agent as they left the briefing room. Jors glared at him as she left, Jim a step behind. Russo smiled and muttered, "Thanks, boss. This will fun."

Nicks shrugged in apology. "You can handle her."

"For Vy and Talitha, we'll make it work." Jim tapped fists and left.

* * *

Agent Jors tapped her foot, waiting. The freezing cold added to her chilled attitude. *A civilian. Why? I can handle this on my own. I don't need a supervisor. Especially a flat-foot ex-cop. I'm a trained agent. What training does he have? Oh, he walked a beat around the corners a few times. Wonderful. I am not taking orders from him on anything. My way or the highway.*

The man caught up with her in the parking lot. She pointed to a silver SUV. "My car. I'm driving."

Mr. Russo nodded. "Your call." He began clearing the snow and ice build-up off the windshield with his gloved hand. Brooke shook her head. "It has a heated windshield. Be clear in three minutes."

The former policeman clapped his hands together to knock off the snow. "I'm impressed. Beats the ice scraper." He slid into the passenger side and strapped in.

Brooke typed the address of the store into her GPS. She waited for the directions. Waited. Waited. She tapped the screen. Reentered the address. Frustration mounted. She googled the store address. Exactly what she'd been entering. She tried again. Still nothing. She glared at the screen. "What is the problem?"

Mr. Russo cleared his throat. "There aren't a lot of cell towers in the area. GPS doesn't always work there. It's remote."

"How are we supposed to get there?"

"I'm familiar with the area. I can give you directions."

Nicks! I'll kill you for this. Give me a civilian I have to take orders from. I swear... She smiled. Tight-lipped, but she smiled. "Great. We'll depend on your memory. This should be a joy a minute."

Brooke put the car in motion. "Is it okay if we use the freeway, or is there some secret backroad I should take?"

The quiet patience beside her said simply, "The freeway will be fine. And fastest. The roads will be clearer. This is about finding the hostages and getting them home safe."

Brooke growled, but only to herself. *Right. I hear you. Okay, I'll remember.*

They drove in silence for several miles. Mr. Russo broke the tableau. "What do you prefer to be called? Agent Jors? Ms. Jors?"

She noted he left off her first name. *Afraid I'll bite your head off for the familiarity? Still, you did ask.* "Brooke is fine. Since we're going to be working together. What about you? What was your rank when you left the force?"

"I retired from Homicide. Detective. But Jim works nowadays."

Okay, recalculating. Not a flat-foot. "While we're getting to know each other, what is your connection to this case?"

"I've been involved with the family for several years. The little girl who got kidnapped is a triplet. I'm the godfather to one of the boys in the set."

She glanced over at him, back to the road. "Doesn't that create a conflict of interest? Make it too personal?"

"I discussed it with Agent Nicks. He agreed I could separate my feelings from my professional duties. I'm here as a civilian and to add any insights I can. I want to find Vy and Talitha and bring them home. But, I know more than likely this isn't the first time these people have kidnapped and terrorized others. And while I know it's about bringing them in for justice, the prime objective is getting the hostages back alive. Capturing the kidnappers comes second."

Brooke nodded. "Agreed."

Jim pointed to the highway marker. "We'll want the Swathford exit."

Still ten miles out. Nice of him to give her plenty of warning. And not wait until she was right on it to say, 'Oh, by the way, there's the exit you want.' He did have some skills.

The older man's eyes were kind. "How long have you been with the FBI? And what got you into this line of work?"

"I've been with the firm about five years. This is my first year in the field, though." *Say it. Everyone else does. 'What took you so long?'*

Russo proved more diplomatic. "What did you do in the home office?"

"Forensics. I loved putting the clues together."

"Why'd you switch to the field?"

"There's no advancement in the office. Have to have the field experience to move up."

"I see. Not much different than in the City Department. Why we can't do what we're good at and still work up the ladder is beyond me."

Brooke smiled. Actually smiled. "Right." *Okay, he might not be so bad. We'll see.*

They took the exit, drove south several miles before turning northeast, then south again. Without her GPS, Brooke would have been lost after the second turn. But Russo did seem to know exactly where they were headed and how to get there. He had her turn on roads with no names, only numbers. Roads with names like "Whiskey Flats" and "Ernest." Roads with no designations at all. Yet Russo must have recognized some manner of landmark. With the ice on the pavement, Brooke needed to concentrate on keeping the wheels between the white lines rather than worrying about where to turn.

It took over an hour to reach the small "we have it all because there's no other place around" store. Brooke debated, decided. "Tell you what, if the manager is over thirty-five, you do the talking. If they're younger, I'll do the questioning."

Russo laughed. "Good call." They walked in together. Shelves stacked with merchandise blocked out most the sun. It gave the room a "closed-in" feeling. Brooke pointed to the sign which indicated the pharmacy. *In the back. Always in the back. Make you walk past all this junk first...and last. Buzzards. Well, I guess it makes it harder to rob and get away.*

The woman behind the counter looked to be younger. Maybe it was the purple hair which gave Brooke her first clue. She noted Jim stepping away, moving over to the baby goods area, scanning the shelves. *What is he looking at?*

The clerk asked, "Can I help you?"

"Are you the manager?"

The woman snorted. "I'm as close as this store will ever get. What do you need?"

Brooke checked the file, handed the photo to the woman. "We're wondering if you've seen this man in here before?" The woman had to reach over the cash register, the "Buy 2, Get One Free!" signs, and the assortment of chewing gum and candies on the counter to get the file.

To her credit, she gave the picture a long look. "He doesn't ring any bells." Her eyes narrowed. "Who are you, and why are you looking for him?"

Forgot the ID. Rats. "I'm Agent Brooke Jors, with the FBI." She held out her ID. "We're looking for him in connection to a break-in." *Don't want to give her too many clues. Not yet.*

"I see. Let me look again." The clerk studied the picture. "No. I don't know. I can't be sure."

"That's fine. All we ask is for you to look." The clerk handed her back the photo.

Jim wandered over to the counter. "Do you carry preemie-size diapers?"

"No, those are specialty items. You have to get those from the medical supply places or the hospitals. Most folks around here make do with newborn."

"Do you get a lot of sales of newborn sizes?"

What is he doing? He already knows they sold a case of them. Why is he...?

The clerk shook her head, then nodded. "Wait a minute. We

normally don't. I mean, would you want to raise a baby out this far away from everything? But a guy came in a few days ago and bought a case of them."

The woman nodded again. "Yeah. Matter of fact, there were two different people." She laughed. "One is old lady Jellings. She has this dog that has to be older than Moses, which she keeps in diapers. She needs to put him down, but she just can't bring herself to part with Mr. Wiggles. Dog hasn't wiggled in years, he's so crippled up."

Jim laughed, but his voice remained kind. "What about the other person? Do you know who the family is?"

"No. Not really." The clerk's eyes narrowed again. "Give me the picture back. Let me look at it again."

Brooke handed it to her. The clerk studied it. "That's him. He's the one who bought the diapers. Asked me about formula for newborns, too. If there's a special kind for preemies. I told him we didn't carry it, so he took the regular newborn formula." She scowled. "Bought the cheap stuff, too. I bet it gives the baby colic. Serve him right."

Jim phrased his questions with caution. "What about anyone else who bought formula? Especially for a newborn."

I get it. He doesn't want to lead her. He wants her to remember on her own. Good trick.

Again, the clerk stopped and thought hard. "I don't think so. I think... No, wait. There's a family over in Cooperton who comes in and buys newborn formula. And the Woman's Center keeps a supply on hand to give away."

Jim continued to lead the questioning. "The family over in Cooperton. Do they bring the baby in with them?"

The clerk grinned. "Do they ever. Along with three other rugrats. It can get real lively in here when they come in."

Russo smiled. "I imagine it does. What about the man? Did he bring the baby in with him? A wife or girlfriend or significant other?"

"No. I've only seen him the one time, and he was alone." She looked at the picture again. "I don't mean to be judgey, but he just didn't strike me as the kind to have a newborn anything. Rough. Real rough. And asking questions about things babies need any parent—new or old—would know. He asked what pacifiers are for and do babies really need one?"

She looked off into space. "Like he had to be reading from a list. That's it. He read from a list. And everything on it, after I'd explain it, he'd say, 'she doesn't need it.' Like he didn't care about the baby. Everything ended up being the cheapest and the least."

Jim prompted, "And he paid with cash?"

"Yeah. He gave me two fifties. I made sure they were real before I took them, you can believe me. The dude stuck the change in his pocket. I heard him saying something about 'more for me.' Not sure what he meant. I asked him if he wanted the receipt, but he said no. Added 'she doesn't need to know how much I spent.' Creepy."

Jim smiled at the woman. "Ms. Dolcie, we really appreciate your help."

Ms. Dolcie cocked her head. "This doesn't have to do with the Amber Alert, does it? The baby who went missing?"

Jim looked to Brooke. She addressed the clerk. "It does. If you should see this man again, or the next time someone comes in to buy diapers—except for Mr. Wiggles—if you would call us, we would be grateful for the information." She handed the woman a card with her information on it. *Old school, huh? Okay, so sometimes it's still appropriate.*

Brooke and Jim walked back to her car. She called in the information to Agent Nicks. Then came the burning question: "What do we do now? We can't exactly camp out here waiting for him to show up, can we?"

Jim's eyes twinkled. "I've done stakeouts in worse places. But I doubt it. If no one else gets a hit, I'm betting Agent Nicks will have the team regroup here." He smiled. "And he'll bring a camper trailer."

Brooke grumbled. "That'll be just peachy." She held up her hand before Jim could—or might—chastise her. "I know. It's for the hostages. We'll do whatever it takes." She looked around the parking lot. "What do you think will happen? I mean, we've got the guy nailed." The teammates climbed back into Brooke's car to keep warm. So to speak.

Jim nodded. "Yes. But. If this isn't their first rodeo, they might use more than one shop to keep the police off the trail. We don't know if there's ever been a baby involved before or if they are familiar with the surrounding area. We'll know by this evening."

Brooke turned to face Jim. "So what happens if we see him come in here while we're waiting for Nicks? Do we stop him? Tail him? Do nothing?"

Jim studied the picture of the suspect. "If—and it's a big if—he comes in, and we don't have guidance from Nicks, my suggestion would be to follow him. Find out where he's staying. My guess is the hostages aren't being kept with the kidnappers."

Brooke did a double take. "Why would you say that?"

"Kidnappers usually keep the hostages somewhere safe, so the bad guys can use them as bargaining chips if they get caught. They will usually say they're buried and only have so much oxygen. Or there's a time bomb or some other device that will kill the hostages if the kidnappers aren't let go."

Jim shook his head. "It's almost never true, but there's always one chance. So we have to tail the kidnappers to the hideout where the hostages are being kept. In this case, it's the small wooden shed in the photo with Vy and Talitha. That's what we need to find and why we need to wait."

Brooke gazed out the window. "Too bad we don't have a drone with night-vision."

Jim's eyebrows rose. "Don't you? I thought you had all the good toys."

"That's the CIA."

"I'm sure Agent Nicks will find someone to talk to about borrowing one or two."

Brooke grinned slightly. "While we're thinking wild toys, how about a heat-sensing, infrared, night-vision drone with stealth capabilities?"

Jim smiled. "That would just about do it." The ex-detective's eyes went far away. He pulled out his phone, checked the bars, punched in a number. "Psi. Jim Russo. Yeah, I know… Not since Turner. How's his wife doing? Good. Listen, I need to know if you have a heat-seeking, night-vision, stealth drone the military doesn't control…? Yeah? Really? Don't let anyone take it. I don't care how much they beg, got it? I may need to borrow it and a pilot who can fly it… Yeah. It's going to be a life or death thing, Psi... Not a joke."

Brooke's eyes widened. *No way. No way. He can't arrange that. He can't. He's a retired cop. Who does he know? More to the point, why does he know someone who has something like that??* She paid meticulous attention to the conversation, one-sided though it might be.

"Thing is, it's rough terrain. Trees and hills. How high can you fly and still get decent heat signatures? Really? No, it's perfect. You'll need a topographical map of Swathford County. You should be able to input it to your drone... Yes, I do know some things about technology, Psi. I've been going to school since I retired. Right. The wife wants me out of the house. It's her Euchre night."

Brooke rolled her eyes. *Does anyone in this state not play Euchre? Probably the same two people who aren't The Ohio State Buckeye fans. I need to get out of this place!*

Jim pulled the chat back to business. "Hang tight with me, Psi. I'll know if we need you by this evening. Thanks. Right." He hung up the phone. "If Agent Nicks can't find one, I know a guy."

She shook her head. "How? How do you know these people?"

Jim shrugged. "You stay in the field long enough you meet all manner of interesting characters. Psi helped us with the last case I worked on. I've kept in touch with him. He's a unique individual. With some unique talents."

"And a night-vision stealth drone."

"Right."

They waited another hour before Agent Nicks called Brooke. She put it on speaker.

The boss got straight to the point. "Okay, here's what we have. The store in Chelsey has sales records for diapers and formula, but the manager knows the customer. Young family, small child. Abbott has the diapers but no baby formula sales."

Brooke threw in, "I'll bet the diapers are for a dog."

"A what?"

"Never mind. Go on."

"Neither of them have seen our suspect or anyone who looks like him. I'm going to have the others muster at your location. I'll bring a camper down, and we can start watching the place."

What size house trailer are you bringing?

Jim leaned over to be heard. "Scott, you'll need two campers."

"Why?"

"In case someone snores. Like me."

Brooke could almost see the wheels turning at the office. "Um...okay, I get it."

"And I have the loan of a drone if we need it."

"A drone? What kind?"

Brooke threw in, "It has everything but heat-seeking missiles, trust me."

Jim cleared his throat. "Those are optional."

Again, there came silence on the other end of the call. "Um…okay, I think. Where is this drone?"

Jim said, "I can have the craft and the pilot meet you at your office, or he can come down separately. Your call."

"Um… I think I'd like to see this thing. And the pilot."

Jim smiled. Small smile. "It's a prototype, Scott. Keep it in mind. Not all the permissions and certifications have been acquired for it yet."

"But it's legal, right?"

"It's legal. I wouldn't suggest something which isn't."

"Gotcha. Okay. Send your man here. We'll load up and be at your location in about two hours. Can you hang tight where you are and not draw attention to yourselves?"

"There's a burger joint across the way. We can hang there and not be noticed. For a little while anyhow." Jim suddenly sat back and looked at Brooke. "I'm sorry. I shouldn't have offered. You're in charge. This is your call."

Brooke waved him off. "Don't worry. You're right. We'll be less noticeable across the street." She did take back the call, though. "We'll keep an eye out for our suspect. Or anyone coming out of the store with diapers. And we'll wait for your arrival."

She disconnected the call. "I'm going to run in and have Ms. Dolcie signal us if someone other than Ms. Jellings comes in for diapers."

"Good thinking." Jim settled in the seat. "This is a nice car."

"Thank you. I like it." Brooke got out. *He's a nice man. I can't believe he retired, though. Not and stayed this…nice. Stupid word, but it's the one that works. Wonder why he really wants two campers?*

Brooke pulled open the door and walked in.

* * *

Late in the afternoon, three cars pulled in, followed by a truck pulling a fifth-wheel camper-trailer. Brooke and Jim met Agents Scott Nicks and Wyatt Duves as they climbed out of their cars. Each had been accompanied by two other agents, men and women both. Brooke made the count five men, three women. A multi-colored van with "Not for Human Consumption" on its sides rounded out the troop.

A tall, round-faced younger man jumped out of the driver's side of the van. Brooke pursed her lips in amusement as the man's below-the-shoulder-length hair flew in all directions with the stinging wind. He gazed around the groups gathering, spotted Russo, and yelled, "Jim! Hey, Jim! We made it!"

Russo looked, then jogged across the parking lot to clutch the younger man in a strong hug. "Glad to see it, Psi. Hoped the bears didn't decide you were for their consumption."

Psi laughed. "Me, too. Could you get any further back in the sticks?"

"Matter of fact, that's where we need you. Got your pilot?"

The younger man motioned to the even younger female climbing out of the van. "Meet my niece, Tracer. Best video pilot I've ever seen."

Jim didn't seem at all fazed by the arrival of an early-teen female bundled in a silver parka with unicorns on the sleeves. Brooke shook her head as the retired detective greeted the newcomer. "Thanks for missing school and coming out here."

The girl grinned. "Thanks for needing me! Real-world experience beats the classroom any day. Psi says this is serious stuff, though. Like someone's life depends on it? You sure you want me?" She looked around carefully. "Not someone more…you know…with more spy experience?"

Jim laughed. "No. Psi says you're the best. That's what we need. The best pilot to fly in this terrain and find our missing people." He lay a hand on the youngster's shoulder. "But no pressure, okay? Do your best, and that's all we can ask. This is only a long shot. If it works, we save some tramping around in the woods. If it doesn't, we do it the old-fashioned way and beat down the doors."

Psi quipped, "And scare up a few bears in the process."

"Right. We'd like to leave the bears sleeping where they are." Jim laughed, his eyes sparkling.

Brooke shook her head, but only on the inside. Life or death, and he's joking about sleeping bears. By his own admission, this is personal. But he's laughing. *What does he know I don't?*

A second truck towing a trailer pulled in with the group. Brooke eyed it and recognized the cargo at the same time Tracer did. The pilot exclaimed, "Horses! You brought horses?"

Scott Nicks came over to join Jim. "You met our pilot. Good." He nodded to Brooke. "We don't want anyone driving by thinking we're a law enforcement strike team of any sort. So we're a horse and camper team, pulled over to let the horses get some rest from the mountain roads. We can set up for the night, and no one will think anything about it."

And that is why, Brooke Jors, he gets the big bucks. I would never have thought of bringing horses. Brilliant. More brilliant if I get to pet one of them. I love horses.

Tracer must have had the same thought. "Oh, can I pet one? Or are they like...working horses, and you can't touch them while they're on duty?"

Scott laughed. "As soon as they get them unloaded, you can pet them. No rides, though. I'm sorry."

Brooke suggested, "I'll stay with Tracer. Keep her out of trouble." *Sounds good anyhow.* Woman and teen walked to the back of the rig and watched as two horses and a mini-horse were unloaded. Tracer all but cooed. "They're so pretty. The little one looks so fluffy and soft!"

I'm glad you're here, girl. You're saying everything I'm thinking. Now I don't look like a twelve-year-old. You do. But you probably are.

Brooke did ask one of the handlers, "Why bring the mini?" *See, I know the difference between a mini-horse and a pony...*

"He keeps the mare calm. She doesn't load up well unless Little Punk gets in first. After him, she's fine."

For once, Brooke didn't wait for Tracer to voice her thought. "You call him 'Little Punk'? Why?" She laughed.

"Because among the other minis, he is."

Tracer held out her hand. "Can I pet him?"

"Of course. But stay away from the back end."

"Oh, I will. I know all about how horses kick."

Brooke pet the tall horses, and long before she wanted, she returned to duty and walked back to where Jim and Scott were talking with Psi.

Psi laid out his plans. "We'll put the drone up tonight. We'll get better heat signatures after dark. People turn their thermostats down, but their bodies still register a warm 98.6 degrees. Makes 'em easier to locate."

"Got it." Jim seemed to be looking around as if searching for something he wasn't seeing. He asked, "Where is the other trailer?"

Scott frowned. "I'm sorry, Jim. I couldn't get one. Psi and Tracer are driving back tonight, and the camper sleeps eight. With two on duty, that gives us plenty of room. Or so I'm told. Transportation wouldn't budge."

Jim took the news without comment. Brooke noted the man's face became drawn, and his eyes narrowed slightly. She watched him pull Psi aside, speak to the younger man quietly, nod, then come back over to the group. His face looked satisfied again. *Wonder what they're talking about?* She'd have to ask him.

Scott called everyone together. "There's an abandoned lot about half a mile south. We can set up there and not be in the flow of traffic."

Brooke looked around at the corner they occupied. *Traffic? What traffic?*

Scott continued, "And we won't discourage our suspects from returning to purchase more supplies. Which, if my sources are correct, they will need again any time now. So let's get mounted up and move, people."

The horses were loaded, the people climbed back in their respective vehicles. Jim slid back into Brooke's car and waited for her.

She got behind the steering wheel, looked at him. "What were you talking to Psi about after Nicks said there would only be one sleeper?" *Wait, does he have a problem with races sleeping together? I know Sims and Abbott. They don't deserve that kind of—*

Jim cut off her thought. "I'm married. When I went out in the field, my wife knew I would have to be out on stakeouts and undercover. I made a commitment I wouldn't take an assignment which would force me to 'sleep' with other women."

He smiled. A little. "I may be retired, but the commitment to my wife and the Lord still stands. Which is why I suggested two campers. When Agent Nicks couldn't provide a second one, I decided the best thing would be to ride home with Psi and Tracer. I'll come back in the morning early to catch up on things."

Brooke sat and stared at Jim for several moments. "You have any younger brothers who aren't married? Who have your ethics? I mean, Jim, that's unheard of."

He chuckled. "Not unheard of. Rare, I'll grant you. But no, no younger brothers who aren't already married."

Brooke put the car in gear. "Let's go catch a bad guy."

"And bring our people home."

"You got it."

TUESDAY

The task force reassembled the following morning. Brooke noticed Jim had arrived back at the command center, ready to accept any orders, or help wherever he got assigned. He looked a little more bleary-eyed than the crew which had remained behind. Must have been the late-night/early morning driving. He handed a sheaf of papers to Scott Nicks. Nicks took them, examined them, nodded, and handed them back. Words were exchanged. Jim dug something out of his trunk.

Two somethings. Silver shiny pump-top carafes full of coffee. Brooke heard several cheers from her fellow agents. Jim dug out a third carafe and explained, "Hot water for tea drinkers."

Two more cheers went up. Nicks called, "Water drinkers, melt snow! The rest of you can get in line behind me." Jim even brought insulated cups. *Does he sit up nights thinking how to please other people?*

Okay, not all night. He only brought two kinds of tea: oolong and green. And the coffee drinkers had to rough it with regular creamer. But she didn't notice too many declining the selections.

Only after everyone had a beverage of choice in hand did Scott call everyone back into the camper for the briefing. "Jim brought up the images from last night. If everyone can sit, we'll look at them."

The agents made quick work of sitting down with a view of the large-screen panel on the wall. Scott did the play-by-play. "This is what the thermographics showed last night." The screen showed a small galaxy of heat signatures on the hillsides. "These are the ones we're interested in."

He zoomed in on a single image. There were two heat signatures in the middle of a vast expanse of nothingness. One of the signatures had a solid box shape and seemed warmer than the other. *A heater? Fireplace?* The second had a rounder profile, looked longer, and its heat seemed concentrated at its core. Scott zoomed in even closer, and the second image separated into two clear signatures, with a barrier between them. A blanket?

Brooke turned to focus on Scott. He nodded. "Our two hostages. Or at least what we believe to be them. There's no other reason for two people to be out in the middle of nowhere like they are. We had the computer overlay the results on the surrounding countryside, and there are no houses in the vicinity."

He changed the display on the screen. "This is what digital night vision showed us." A non-descript hill had a falling-down shack on its top. The hill looked like all the others around it. The only thing different was the shack. And it only stood out because Scott pointed to it on the TV image.

"That's what we're looking for."

An agent Brooke didn't know asked, "We have the coordinates, right?"

"Sure. If we wanted to call in an airstrike, they might help us. We don't know if the suspects are in a bunker somewhere close and could get to the hostages and kill them if we tried to drop a helo team in. We're closer than we were last night, but we've still got work, people."

Agent Quincy raised his hand. "So, what do we do now?"

Scott pulled up another display. "These are the homes closest to the location we believe the hostages are at." He pointed around the room. "We *believe* the hostages are. We don't know for a fact. Remember it." He went back to the display. "We want to canvass these places. We're going to go in as FDA personnel. Baby formula sold in this area has been highly contaminated and will cause death if too much is consumed."

Scott handed out flyers. "We need to find the cans before anyone dies. We've got lot numbers to make it look like we really are from the FDA. Unless our information is wrong, no one in this vicinity has a child on formula, nor has purchased any. Anyone who produces a can will more than likely be our suspect."

He looked around again. "But remember, we're still trying to put the pieces together. Unless they come out shooting at you, don't assume we've found the bad guys."

Scott surveyed the assembled crew. "Any questions? If there are, keep 'em short. We've got a two-day blizzard forecast for this afternoon, and we need to get in, get out, and plan our next move."

If there were questions, no one wanted to raise them. "Good. Get out of here. Let's get home. This could be the 'big one' you know."

General laughter. Brooke scoffed. Agent Sims snorted. "Yeah, right. Meteorology. Only job you can be wrong one hundred percent of the time and still stay employed."

Someone—Brooke wasn't sure who—objected. "Hey, my brother's a meteorologist."

She didn't get to hear the end of the discussion as she found Jim and partnered up with him. "You have the addresses?"

"Such as they are, yeah. We're going into some areas where government employees of any kind aren't looked on too kindly. If you catch my drift."

"I do." Brooke checked her sidearm. She cocked her head. "You still have a permit to carry?"

"Yes. And I still carry."

That would have been my next question. Thank you for not making me ask it.

They climbed into the car and headed for the first stop.

* * *

By three, they had completed their survey of names and locations. No one admitted to having any formula, newborn or otherwise. Disappointment washed over Brooke, though she tried to hide it from her partner. It would have been nice to get the 'hit' on the suspect. But not this time. Oh, well. All that mattered would be for someone to get it. Then they could get on with finding and bringing home the hostages. And Jim could go back to his boring retirement. Or so it sounded to Brooke.

They were the last team to arrive at the parked camper. Scott waited for them. He looked anxious as Brooke handed in their report. "No hits. I guess someone else got lucky."

Scott's eyes darkened. "No. No one else reported anything, either."

Her eyes widened. "How can that be? Did we miss them?"

Scott shook his head. "I don't know. We're going back to look at all the data and see what we can find out. Maybe the search wasn't wide enough. Maybe the suspects are staying with someone who doesn't know what they're up to. It's hard to say. We'll fall back, regroup, and come up with another plan." He tapped Jim's arm. "Sorry, Jim."

Jim nodded, but he didn't lose his perpetual good humor. "That's life in law enforcement. We think we've got the bad guys outsmarted, and they come back smarter. We will catch them. And we will bring the hostages home. I know it."

"Keep the faith. And get home. You don't want to get snowed in on these roads." Pellets of snow had begun falling.

Brooke looked at Jim. "Pellets are bad."

"Pellets are bad. Let's get home."

"If I can find someone to drive my car, can I ride with you? You've probably got more experience on ice than I do."

Jim smiled. "I think we can make that work."

WEDNESDAY EVENING

Collin watched the snow come down the rest of Tuesday and into the afternoon Wednesday. But even six inches couldn't stop the Farrell/Winger/Johnson group from meeting for prayer and company. George and Martha spent the evening with the Farrell's. As did Grandparents Farrell, Harmon and Lacey. Seven adults made sure the two little boys had plenty of love and warmth and attention to last at least through the evening. Jeff kept the coffee flowing (with filters.) Lacey brought cake, one to eat, one to send home with George and Martha. Eating gave everyone something to do with their hands besides wring them.

Or pound them in frustration. Gnaw at the nails. Tap nervously on the chairs or table. Collin loved how Mom Lacey drew Martha and George into conversation about the rebuilding of the Calvary Church. Harmon and George talked about construction. Martha and Lacey talked about colors and patterns. If it weren't for the ache in her heart and the pain in her brother's eyes, you would have thought it like any other social visit.

Lacey asked Martha, "Do they have a bride's room in the church? I know not many of the newer churches are including them, as a matter of course. I like the tradition, myself."

Martha laughed. "I agree. How is a bride supposed to be ready to walk down the aisle if she hasn't got a room to prepare in?"

Collin watched to see if Erin would participate in the discussion. He'd been quiet most the evening. Whether from physical pain or from pain of heart, she didn't know.

He groused at Lacey and Martha. "What's the big deal with weddings, anyhow? Vy throws on a dress and comes out. Everyone oohs and awws and takes a million pictures. You two cry. Pastor Tim glares at me the whole time he talks. So do George and Vy's sisters. Vy and I promise never to fight, which is a lie, to always talk things out first, which is another lie, we get declared husband and wife. And I finally get to kiss Vy properly. Or as properly as I can in a church full of people watching."

Martha raised her brows at him. "Should I have Aunt Viola explain it to you?"

Erin shuddered and held up both hands. "No, ma'am. No, ma'am. I know better."

Collin smiled at her brother. "You'd never put up with anything less than what Vy wants anyhow."

Martha laughed. "If I know my daughter, she talked to you about eloping, right?"

Erin looked at the floor, looked at the ceiling, looked at the floor. "Maybe."

Lacey eyed Erin. "Why don't you?"

"Sisters. Hers." He motioned towards Collin. "Not mine. I've been threatened with death and destruction if we don't have a 'proper' wedding. Ellie and Blaise think this is the perfect time to get their men to 'dress up.' Wanting to see if they're marriage material."

Martha snorted. "I'll believe it when I see it."

Erin's phone pinged. Collin watched his eyes widen then close before he ever looked at the phone. He stared at it for several moments, handed it to Collin.

The room quieted instantly. All eyes focused on Collin as she read, *Ten million dollars. You'll be told where.*

Seven bodies drew in a single breath. Erin turned to the FBI agent. "Same phone number as before?"

The man shook his head. "Different last four. But same area."

Collin's hands shook as she keyed in, *For both?*

Both.

When? The phone wouldn't be still long enough for her to type anything else.

Instructions will follow.

Jeff took the phone. He texted with deliberate motions. *We will pay anything you ask. Bring them back unharmed.*

No police.

Erin motioned to Jeff. "Tell them, 'Bring them back unharmed. We'll do what we can to mitigate charges.' As long as they're safe."

A minute went by.

Two minutes.

Five minutes.

Jeff whispered, "Did we lose them?" Collin gripped his hand, afraid to breathe.

Ten minutes.

Seven adults sighed. George voiced everyone's thoughts. "It had to be offered." He nodded to Erin. "Good call, son."

Jeff's phone buzzed. "Agent Duves. I'll put it on speaker." Jeff answered. "We have Vy's parents and mine here."

"We saw it. Good call on your part. I know the FBI is tracking, but so are we. Keep the faith."

Seven people, one thought. Jeff spoke it. "The money doesn't matter. We'll lose it. But we get Vy and Talitha back safe."

"Totally understood. We'll be in touch."

Jeff lay his phone down. Collin turned to the FBI Agent Pope. "We're making progress, right?"

She nodded. "Yes, it is. We'll mark the money when we get the instructions."

Jeff spoke for all seven adults in the room. "We don't care about the money. We'll lose it so long as we get Talitha and Vy back."

Ireland Pope smiled. "In all my years, I've never once had a victim's family remind me to get the money back. Seems they all have their priorities straight."

Six people laughed. Erin didn't. Jeff prayed the grandparents (and parents) out. Collin walked over and kneeled beside the wheelchair. "What is it, A-One?"

Erin dropped his head. He touched the arm of his wheelchair. "Me. In this."

Collin hugged him. "She'll love you no matter what, Erin. She's told you before. She stood with you through the last relapse. This will be no different."

Erin nodded. The pain in his eyes remained. Tears welled up. "Did I make the right move? Did I? Did I screw it up?"

Collin threw her arms around her brother's neck. "Oh, A-One. You did it right. You did it perfect. They're coming home, bud. They are. Safe and happy and forever. Got it?"

He stared at her. "But what if they don't? What if—"

Collin shook him sharply. "Stop! It's not your fault, Erin. None of this has been. None of it. We're going to get them back. We will. That's all there is to it. We will." *God, restore his confidence. Not in himself, but in You. Lift him up. Lord.*

Erin drew in a deep breath, squared his shoulders, nodded. He smiled a small, crooked smile. "Did you have to rattle the brain cells? They're fragile as they are."

Collin kissed the top of his still-bandaged head. "And few and far between. Go to bed, Erin. You need to get your strength back."

"You're right. The kidnapper's going to want me to deliver the money. I need to be ready."

Collin started to object but stopped. There was no reason to start a fight now. Let him keep his delusion. It gave him hope. And they all needed hope right now.

* * *

Erin lay in bed staring at the ceiling. *Ten million dollars. Chump change. I could get it out tomorrow. If I contact them, if I initiate the contact on a different phone, no one else gets involved. The kidnapper and me. Straight-up swap. They get the money. I get Vy and Talitha. They'll do it. This isn't what they wanted to start with. They're trying to make a way out, that's all. Something worth the time.*

His gut turned. So did his soul. *Not the way, I know. I know. I'm supposed to be trusting You and waiting. But maybe this is You showing me how to get them back. Maybe?*

He knew better. If it was God, Erin would have no problem telling Cane and the others what he wanted to do. To do it in secret meant he lied to himself and to them.

And if something goes wrong, it will be my fault. God, show me. Tears filled his eyes again. *I want her back. I want both of them back. Help me. Show me. Stop me. Your way or none. It has to be. I want to run out and save her. I do.*

His soul and his mind both stomped his emotions. "Trust in the Lord...do not lean on your own understanding..."

I know. I know. But I want to save her! I want to show her I'm her Superman! He-man. Thor. Iron Man...all of them. Not some cripple in a wheelchair who can't even hold onto a baby.

STOP!

The command came from outside himself but inside his head.

Who formed you in your mother's womb? Who knows every hair on your head? Who has numbered all your days? Yours and Vy's and Talitha's and yes, Caleb and Joshua and the kidnappers as well? Who AM I?

Erin breathed out. And spoke aloud. "You are God. I am not." End of discussion. He closed his eyes and slept.

THURSDAY MORNING

Morning. Erin rose, and for the first time, transferred himself to his chair. He rolled into the kitchen. The coffee pot had been left half-full. Erin swirled the muddy liquid and, yep, grounds. Lots of them. Jeff had been up. So much for sleeping through the night.

He made a fresh pot and poured juice for Collin to drink. After the coffee. Healthy is one thing. Sanity is another. Erin emptied the dryer of its perpetual load of baby items—t-shirts and socks and receiving blankets—and folded them. He didn't try to match the socks. Collin, in her wisdom, only bought white one-size-fits-all booties. No fights.

The aroma of the coffee brought Collin up from the depths. He handed her a mug. She saluted him with it and sipped. Sighed. "Ahhhhhhh. You are too good to me in the mornings."

He forced a grin. "I'm too good to you always, but who's keeping track?" Erin blew on his cup. "Were both boys up?"

"Yeah. Multiple times. Could be a growth spurt."

"They could use all of them they can get. Especially Joshua. Caleb is going to be a chunk all on his own."

Collin smiled. "He's about as tall as he is round."

Ireland Pope came in from the guest room. "Thought I heard voices." She smiled. "Anyone get any sleep last night?"

Collin grumbled. "Not in this house."

Erin poured coffee for Agent Pope. He blew on his own still-hot brew. "Do you think the boys miss Talitha?"

Collin sighed, looked at the ceiling, the floor. She sucked in her lip, let it out. "How can they not? They were together for nearly seven months in the womb, and even in the NICU, they kept them together. And we've had them together since then. At some level, they have to know she's gone."

Erin glanced from his sister to the FBI agent, sipped at his mug. "I…uh…thought about going off on my own last night. Calling the kidnappers and offering them the money. No police. Hand over Vy and Talitha, take the money, and go."

Collin held his gaze. "Did you now? What stopped you?"

"God. And better sense. I wanted to, though. I really, really wanted to."

Collin set her mug down, walked over, and kissed the top of her brother's head. "I was right there with you, A-One. I tried to figure which accounts to take the money from so no one would know. Had my plan all made out."

"What stopped you?"

"God. And the fear I'd mess it up and get both of them killed."

"Family failing."

Erin noted Ireland didn't jump on either him or his sister. *Probably not an original thought.*

Jeff's voice entered the room before he did. "Family failing what?"

Collin stood behind the wheelchair with her arms clasped around Erin's neck. She directed her words to her husband. "Wanting to run out on our own and try to pay off the kidnappers so we could bring Vy and Talitha back."

Jeff poured a mug of go-juice and sat at the bar. His eyes moved from Erin to Collin to Ireland and back again. "So, what would your plan have been?"

Erin shrugged. "Take the money from the personal account. I know, I can't move that kind of money all at once. I didn't think that part through before the Lord squelched me."

Jeff eyed Collin. "You?"

"I figured I'd hit five different accounts. All of which I have access to at amounts which would raise an eyebrow but not get turned down outright. I'd pull the number off Erin's phone, call it, leave a message telling them where the money would be."

"Where?" Jeff seemed more than a little interested.

"I thought Walker Pond. It doesn't freeze over, so they wouldn't be walking through snow, leaving tracks to be followed. Not unusual to have people out there feeding the ducks and the geese."

Jeff nodded. "I see." He drank from his cup, set it down. "Morehead Park. There's an art exhibit. 'Snowflakes of the world.'" He looked at the floor. "And I planned on moving funds around so fast and furious no one would notice the ten million missing."

The three sat in silence for several moments. Erin cleared his throat. "Family failing. Merciful God."

Another silence. Which Collin broke. "My plan would have worked."

Jeff guffawed. "Really? Walker Pond? You know how far it is from the pond to the parking lot?"

Collin huffed. "Not as far as Morehead Park's exhibit center." She looked at Agent Pope. "Settle this. Whose plan is better, Jeff or mine?"

"What's wrong with my plan?" Erin protested.

She huffed again. "You didn't have one. You weren't prepared."

"But I know the number. Neither of you do."

"Details." Jeff decided to get into the game. "I'd have gotten the money faster."

"But it would be easier to track."

"Not the way I planned on doing it."

"It still wouldn't work."

"Well, neither would yours."

Erin held up a hand. "Fine. I'll leave my part out of it. Agent Pope?"

All eyes turned to the FBI agent in expectation.

The door opened. Jim Russo walked in. He had blue jeans, a Buckeye hoodie, and a Michigan toboggan. Gifts from children, Erin knew. Family feuds die hard. The retired detective looked around at Collin and Jeff's faces. "Did I interrupt something?"

Erin nodded. "Well, yes and no. Agent Pope is about to make a ruling on whose scheme to run off and deal with the kidnappers alone is the best."

Jim hung the hoodie and the hat by the door, poured himself a cup of coffee. "Um-hum. I see." He raised his eyebrows. "And the winner is?"

Erin sighed. "God. We all had the same thoughts last night, and God stopped all of us."

The retired detective nodded. "It wouldn't be the first time people in your position thought of it. Or tried it." He motioned to the hat. "My apologies."

Jeff grinned. "Forgiven."

Collin chewed her lip. She looked at Ireland. "How does it usually end up?"

"With someone being killed, the kidnappers taking the money, and the hostages never being found."

Jeff stared, wide-eyed. "That bad?"

She nodded. "Yeah."

Erin asked the next question on everyone's minds. "How does it go when the police are involved?"

"With the 'asking for ransom' kidnappings, ninety-seven percent are returned when handled by the professionals."

"Really?"

Jim swallowed some of his coffee. "Where kidnappings for ransom are common, almost a business, the professionals manage to get a release most often."

Collin shuddered. "Kidnapping as a business. What about the families? The loved ones who are torn up by the person going missing? Do they matter at all?"

"You already know the answer. No, they don't. It's a business, or, like with Vy and Talitha, it's personal. All about them."

Jeff poured another cup of coffee. "What do we need to do?"

"Besides not go crazy and try to do it yourselves? You're doing it. Live. Take it one day at a time. Let the professionals handle as much as possible." Jim motioned to Ireland.

Erin studied Jim. "If it were you? Your wife? Your child?"

It was a sad smile. "I'd be fighting with God about going rogue. Being a cop—ex-cop—doesn't mean I don't have feelings about it. But we have the Lord, and He's pretty good at keeping me from operating from my base nature."

Erin chuckled. "Ain't that the truth."

Ireland tossed her head sideways. "And I'd be right there with you all. This is hard. We know. I know. There are no wrong feelings. Wrong actions, maybe. But not wrong feelings."

Erin's phone pinged. *Five a.m. Instructions will be given. You alone. No police.*

Collin tapped her brother's arm. She looked at Ireland. "Tell them he's not mobile. From him. Someone else will make the exchange, or someone will be with him."

Ireland read aloud as she texted. "I'm in a wheelchair. The goons who beat me did a thorough job. Me and another person to help me, or someone else. Collin. Jeff. George."

George?

"Vy's father."

The texter fell silent. The group waited five minutes for the answer to come.

It came as a question. *Collin baby's mother?*

"Yes."

Robert Winger's daughter?

"Yes."

The one who put him behind bars?

"Yes."

Her. And you.

Ireland texted back. "Agreed. Five a.m. Where?"

Instructions will be sent. One address at a time.

"We will come. Give us time for bad roads. Roads may not be clear by then."

Russo nodded to Ireland. "Good thought."

Silence on the other end meant they were checking the weather, too. After a few moments, the answer came back. *Will send instructions in the morning. You and baby's mother. No police.*

Nothing else came.

Collin held out her hand for Erin's phone. Ireland handed it to her. She examined the exchange. "Does this mean the hand-off will *be* at five a.m., or they'll start giving directions at five?"

Erin breathed in and out carefully. "It doesn't matter. I'll be in a car and ready at midnight."

Ireland seemed to study both Collin and Erin. Erin noticed. "What?"

"I'm trying to figure which of you will be easier to impersonate at the end."

Collin's eyes narrowed. "Neither of us. We're not taking any chances something goes wrong."

Jim stepped in. "Neither are the police. You three have to remember, as much as you want your people back, this is a capital offender you're dealing with. Someone may have done this with others they were 'offended' by. You don't know their history. But I can bet this isn't their first time doing something like this."

Jim swirled the remains of his coffee around. "They were too slick, too well-planned. First-timers screw up with regularity and are busted in days, if not hours. This took planning and timing and a knowledge of who to hire and how to find them."

He drained his cup. "The DEA, the FBI, and city and state police have been looking for this crew. And there is not one shred of hard evidence leading us to anyone. So no, this isn't the group's first rodeo. And why it's imperative we catch them now."

Collin's eyes flared. "Does that mean they're searching for pictures of what we look like?"

Ireland nodded. "Probably. Erin, I'm sorry. But with all the bandages and bruises, you're going to be easiest to copy."

Erin's gut twisted. Anger surged through him. To be replaced by the thought, *This is for Vy. Not your ego. Listen to the experts. Suck it up, nod, say, "You're right." Let it go.*

Erin nodded. "You're right." He looked at the floor. "I hate it. But you're right."

Jim placed his hand on Erin's shoulder. "We all know you'd be the first one out there, Erin. You made the hard choice. But the wise one."

Erin ground his teeth. "I'll believe it when we get them back. Both of them."

A full-fledged cry of anger and frustration bellowed from the nursery. Collin sighed. "Feeding time at the zoo. I'll be right back."

Erin held up his hand. "Take me with you, and they can ride back with me. Easier than you carrying them both."

Collin grinned. "You got it. Let's go."

Collin wheeled Erin to the nursery. Caleb and Joshua both were expressing their displeasure with life in general at the top of their lungs. Collin shifted Joshua to Erin's lap, changed Caleb, swapped babies with Erin, changed Joshua, nestled Joshua next to his brother, and wheeled the threesome to the living room.

Jeff asked Jim, "I know you didn't just stop by for the coffee, though you're always welcome. And one of us is almost always up."

Collin called, "And if we're not, make a pot, and we will be."

Jim chuckled. "I hear you. No, I came by to give you a heads-up on some research we've been doing. Formula and diapers."

Erin looked towards the kitchen. "How does that help? Looking in the trash for some which shouldn't be there?"

Jim called out, "We've looked through trash for lesser things, believe me. No, we were looking for someone buying newborn diapers, where there was no newborn in the vicinity. It seemed like a long shot, yeah, but we did get an area to focus on. And it matched the general vicinity of the wooden building from the first picture they sent."

Erin and Collin reached the living room. Erin noted Collin grow quiet. Still, even. Her eyes focused on nothing. Her voice sounded measured. "Really. You have a lead?"

"We have leads, Collin."

Ireland's voice remained gentle. "We're all working each and every one we get."

Jim nodded. "This is just another one of them we're looking at. But…" Jim's voice softened. "It's one we didn't have before. It gives us somewhere to look. Somewhere we didn't have before."

Erin reached out and touched his sister's hand. "Cane. Come back." She looked at him. He nodded. "I know. I know. I'd go with you door-to-door if I could."

Collin lowered her head. He squeezed her hand. "We're going to do this the right way, Cane. We're not going to be stupid and try to solve this on our own. We've done it in the past and it might have worked out, but maybe it would have worked out easier if we'd done it the Lord's way first. We have to do this right, no matter how wrong it feels."

Collin chewed her lip. "When did you get to be the smart one?"

"I've always been the smart one. I'm finally catching up with you on the maturity level. Maybe."

She smiled. Sadly. "When this is all over, we'll compare notes."

"Deal." They tapped knuckles.

Jim added, "And if it helps, we've already done the door-to-door stuff. Now we're working on narrowing it down." He reached out and gripped Collin's shoulder. "We're going to bring them home. Both of them. You have to believe me."

Erin saw the tears fill his sister's eyes. Her voice cracked. "What did the man tell Jesus? 'I believe. Help my unbelief?' Yeah. That."

Jeff walked over and hugged his wife.

FRIDAY MORNING

The first instruction came at 5 a.m. *Drive north on Rey-New Albany Rd. to Morse Rd. Pull over. Stop five minutes.*

Collin drove. "Erin" sat on the briefcase with the money. Tension lay like a blanket of snow after a three-day blizzard.

North on 605. West Dub-Gran Rd. South on Main. Fox in Snow Café. Order coffee.

The café stood empty with only the drive-thru open. Collin ordered her usual, "Black. As large as it comes."

Erin's order followed. "Creamer. Two sugars. Large."

They could see no one, and no other cars were in evidence. Collin looked at the cup. "You think they were testing us to see if we'd follow orders?"

"Maybe. They'd have to know your standard order, though."

"How could they? I've never been here before."

"I don't know."

"You don't think they poisoned it, do you?"

"Not and take a chance you'd get sick, crash, and the money would burn up."

"Truth." Collin snorted. "I'm going to drink it. I don't waste coffee. Unless Jeff makes it. Then it's questionable."

Why am I making jokes?

Because I'm scared and I want my baby back, and I don't know what else to do.

Understood.

North 605. West Walnut St. North on Schleppi. East Fancher. North 605.

"Why didn't we just stay on 605?"

"I don't know, Ms. Farrell. It's the scenic route, perhaps. I suggest you follow it."

"What do you think I'm doing?" She paused. "Sorry I snapped at you." She tried to smile. "They do know I'm the one driving, right? And North-South-East-West is problematic for me?"

"That's why I'm navigating." "Erin" smiled at her.

West on 37. West on 36. North on 34.

"Erin" tried to shift his weight from one hip to the other. Collin glanced at him. "You want to let me sit on it for a while?"

"I'd love to, but I don't think we should stop."

"Yeah. I get it."

West on 521. North on 10.

They'd been driving for forty minutes.

"How far out do you think they are?"

"With this route, I have no clue. My maps don't show anything out here. Empty fields."

"Empty fields you can't see for all the snow. You could hide anything, and no one would ever know."

"Until the snow melts. We're going to get them back, Ms. Farrell. We're doing everything they say."

"I know." The muscles in the back of Collin's neck knotted and twisted and contorted. Deep breaths were her only comfort. Deep breaths and the reminder from the Lord He was there. It still hurt. It still felt terrifying. But He rode with them. He knew.

West on Leonardsburg.

Fifteen miles down the road, Leonardsburg dead-ended into Cackler. Collin looked both ways. "Which way?"

"The instructions don't say."

"What do we do now?"

"Wait for further instructions."

"How long?"

"They'll contact us. We have their money. It shouldn't be long."

Five minutes.

Ten minutes.

Fifteen minutes.

Twenty minutes.

Collin's guts twisted and turned and danced and roiled. "Something's wrong. Something's happened."

"We'll wait an hour."

Thirty minutes.

Forty-five.

Fifty-eight.

Drive the money to Winchester Point. Leave the bag under the Welcome sign. Behind the rock mound. You'll be given instructions on where to find the hostages.

The agent typed. *You were bringing the hostages to the drop site. We see them, you get the bag.*

Drop bag as ordered or no hostages.

Agent Wiley keyed. *Prove they're alive. Let me talk to Vy.*

No. Drop the bag.

Not without video from Vy.

Sending picture.

Collin forced herself to breathe. In. Out. In. Out.

The phone pinged.

Collin grabbed the phone and looked at the picture.

It was the same photo as before.

She closed her eyes. Lifted her chin. "Oh God oh God oh God. Please. Please."

Agent typed. *Send video.*

No answer.

No answer.

An hour passed.

No answ—

"What happened? What went wrong? We did everything they said!" Collin's voice climbed an octave. Her heart banged in her chest. Her whole body shook. Desperation threatened to melt her body into a heap on the floorboard. Her soul wailed. *God! My baby!*

Agent Wiley touched Collin's shoulder. "We should go back. I'll drive."

Collin's body shook with sobs. But… "No. I'll drive. We told them you couldn't. If this is some cruel test, I don't want them to see anything."

She breathed in and out and in and out and finally found her control. "I'm fine. I am." She steeled herself. "I can do this. I have to do this." Her soul, dead. Her spirit, empty. "I'm fine."

* * *

Collin sat on the couch, unmoving, unthinking, unfeeling. Lacey held Jacob, walking and dancing and humming to the boy. Martha came in from the nursery carrying Caleb. She smiled at Lacey. "This one grows fatter every minute."

Lacey grinned. "I swear he gains a pound looking at a bottle."

Martha sat beside Collin. She handed Caleb to Collin. "Hold your son. He needs his mama." She touched Collin's cheek. Collin glanced at her, her eyes blank. Martha nodded. "His mama needs him, too."

Collin took the baby, her eyes still unseeing. Martha put her arm around Collin's shoulder. "Listen to me, young woman. Listen good." Collin brought her eyes into focus on the older woman. Martha's tone stayed gentle but firm. "I've been where you are, girl. First time Iris disappeared. Thought my heart would never beat again. Lay on the floor and screamed at the Lord. Called Him anything and everything except God."

Collin lowered her eyes to the floor. Martha nodded. "She's my baby, my firstborn."

Martha's voice trembled. "Was she cold? Hurt? Hungry? Dying somewhere alone, calling for me? Would I ever see her again? Yes, I thought all those things, too." Collin lay her head on Martha's shoulder.

Martha continued. "Only thing kept me from dying too…I knew the Lord had her. Didn't make the pain go away. Didn't heal the hurt. But I knew that I knew He had her. I didn't know where she might be. But He did. And where could she ever be safer than in His hands?"

The older woman lay her head on top of Collin's. "Wherever she might have been, she wasn't missing to Him."

Tears burned. Collin's lip trembled. "But I want her."

"I know you do, honey. I want my Vy with me, too. You think you got it settled, and this happens, and you have to settle it all over again. God is good, or He isn't. He loves us, or He doesn't. Every time something happens, we have to make the choice. Is He God, or isn't He? And if He is, we have to trust Him. Hurt or not, the answer we want or not, He is, or He isn't."

Martha rubbed Caleb's back. "But let me give you a secret. There is only one choice. If He's not God, we have no hope. Things happen by chance, we're lucky, or we're not, and the world just *is*. But if He is God, there is a reason. And one day, maybe only in

Heaven, we will understand the why of it all. Until then, we trust Him, we love Him, we bring Him all our hurts and tears and pain and fear. And we get up in the morning, and we keep moving because He gives us another day."

Caleb swatted at Collin's cheeks, caught her tears, and put his mouth on her nose. Collin laughed, her heart breaking. "Oh, Caleb. Sweetness. Mama loves you."

Caleb grabbed two chubby handfuls of hair and pulled her head down. Martha nodded. "You got to suck it up for these two. They need you. You have to find all the love you got in you and give it to them, too."

Collin closed her eyes and dropped her head to her son's forehead. "I will. I will, I promise. All the love I have."

Martha smiled and kissed Collin on the cheek. "I know you will, honey. I know you will."

* * *

Jeff sat in the kitchen. Harmon, his father, sat across from him. Jeff stared at the can of beer on the table. Harmon pointed to it. "The choice is yours. It always has been. You can numb it. The pain. The anger. The rage. But it comes back in the morning. You can keep numbing it day after day after day…and it keeps coming back."

Jeff stared at the can, his eyes unseeing and unfocused. Harmon's voice penetrated the fog of anguish surrounding Jeff. "Push Him away. Lash out at Him. Tell Him He's not God. Not *your* God. *Your* God would never hurt you like this. Your God would never take your child away. A kind, loving God wouldn't do this. Never. A cruel and capricious god, yes. But not One Who says He loves His children."

Jeff turned his eyes to look at his father. Harmon nodded. "That's right. Can't be God's will for this. Can't be. I mean, look at all you've suffered in your life already. Nearly losing Collin? Wasn't that test enough? Didn't that prove you trust Him? Why again? Why this way?"

Jeff's eyes burned, but he refused to cry. Harmon lay a hand on his son's shoulder. "Maybe it's not about proving anything to God. Maybe it's about proving something to yourself. One more time. Just one more time. He is God. He is Good. He is Love. Every day, every time you breathe. One more time."

Jeff lay his head on the table as the tears rained down. Harmon rubbed his son's head. "I know, Jeff. I know."

* * *

George sat with Erin in the family room, wheelchair and sofa together. George lay his hand on Erin's shoulder. "God, this man doesn't need my wisdom, my 'I know how you feel' or 'I been there' words. He needs You. Needs You to wrap Your arms around him, hold him, comfort him, and give him Your assurance You have this. Nothing else matters. It's all You, Lord. In the Name of our Lord Jesus. Amen."

The two men sat. Erin lowered his head, closed his eyes. Peace didn't come like a flood. It seeped in, filling the empty places. Comfort followed, finding all the cracks and crevices peace had missed. Strength washed in on the rising tide of knowledge nothing escaped God's notice. Security rested in God's unfailing promise of love.

Erin lifted his head. He breathed out, nodded once to George. The older man nodded once in return. Tears dripped down both men's faces. But they had work to do. Life called.

FRIDAY MORNING

Bitter cold seeped into Vy's bones. The fire had died late in the early morning hours. Gorilla-man hadn't been the one to build it the night before. The woman had. She'd tried, anyhow. Now, however, Vy and Talitha would suffer for it. Unless someone came early. *Please, Lord.*

Gravel spun. Snow crunched. Rocks slapped against the building. Someone was trying to get the truck up the hill and doing a poor job of it. Unless there had been more snow than Vy estimated from last night's fall. It had ended early, or so she thought. She'd worked the blindfold off after the woman left. She could slide it back on if she had to. Depending on who got out of the truck.

Maybe she should look and see who was coming. Maybe she shouldn't. She didn't want to take a chance and get hit by flying rocks. Not this close to going home.

And they were going home. She'd heard Gorilla-man and the woman talking the night before. Talking about dumping the hostages and getting out of town. Never to be seen again. Vy and Talitha would find their way from where they were dropped. No one saw anyone, so no one the wiser, and Gorilla-man, his brother, and the woman would be long gone before anyone could mount a search. On to hopefully greener pastures.

There had been some back and forth about the brother being upset or angry or disappointed. But the woman had assured Gorilla-man, "Leave him to me." He'd do what she said and be glad of it. He'd better.

Gorilla-man walked into the shack. He carried a bottle for Talitha and a thermos for Vy. She looked at it. "What's this?"

"Coffee. To keep you warm." He gave her a cup. When she finished it, he stuffed the thermos in his coat pocket. He hummed as he held Talitha. Vy could just make out the tune. She sucked in a breath.

He hummed, "Humm loves me..."

Vy asked, "You know 'Jesus loves me?'"

"Is that what that is? I've been hearing you sing it to her. Yeah, I may have heard it a long time ago. When I was a kid, maybe."

He didn't mention where, and Vy hesitated to push. Not now. Not so close to freedom. She listened to the man babble and coo at the baby. Talitha giggled back, choked on her milk.

Instantly he had her on his shoulder. "No, don't do that! No choking!" Talitha self-corrected. He set her back in his lap. "No more funny business. You need to eat. You're going home today."

Vy swallowed the impulse to grab him and shake him for more assurance. She stayed calm. "I thought I heard you talking last night. I'm afraid to get my hopes too high..."

He nodded to her. "When she found out there wouldn't be any revenge to be had, she decided to cut her losses and leave. No sense killing you. You never saw us. You don't know where we were staying, where we come from. I think she couldn't bring herself to kill a baby. I know I couldn't."

Vy had to ask it. "Could you kill me?"

He looked at her, dropped his head back down. "If I had to."

"If she told you to?"

"If I had to." He shrugged. "Not like you'll believe me."

Vy put a hand on his arm. "Give me something to call you. Anything. I'm tired of not having some kind of name for you. Doesn't have to be your real name. Just a name."

He thought about it for a moment. "Wendell."

Vy laughed. "Wendell? That's what you're going with?"

"Why not?"

"Do you even know anyone named Wendell?"

"No." He laughed through the mask.

Vy laughed back. "Okay, Wendell." She grew sober. "I want to believe you wouldn't kill anyone. You've been so tender with Talitha. And you've protected me. I want to believe there's a human under the mask. Under both masks. Is there?"

Wendell looked at the floor. "Does it really matter?"

"I think it does. God thinks it does."

He barely lifted his eyes. "What does He care?"

"He cares, Wendell. Isn't that what the song says? He loves you?"

"Maybe you, not me. Not now."

"Even now, Wendell. He never stops loving us."

"What would it matter now? You don't know what I've done."

"No. I don't. But I know what you're about to do, and that's let us go. Which means you can change. You don't have to stay the way you are. You can change. Choose a different way. God's way."

He laughed. Harsh laughter. "His way was never my way, lady. I may have known about him as a little kid, but not since then. I can't change anything I've done."

"You don't have to change the past. Just the present. Now. You stop being a liar when you stop lying and start telling the truth. You stop being a thief when you stop stealing and start working."

He shrugged. "We've gotta get on the road. I'm supposed to drop you off in a couple of hours. She's giving the directions out piecemeal so the cops can't track us. She'll give them the last one as soon as we get clear of the area. You'll be safe."

Wendell gave Vy the diaper for changing and handed her a clean blanket. "Here. Wrap her in this. I don't want her folks thinking no one cared about her."

What about my folks? Do they get the same courtesy? Except I'm not a baby. Vy let the thoughts drift on by.

Once Talitha had been fed, burped, changed, and wrapped up, Gorilla-man took Vy's elbow and led her out of the shed to a dilapidated truck. Vy couldn't see it clearly until they were right on it. Rusted black, missing tailgate, trashcan, and garbage bags stuffed in the back. Their captor didn't open the door for her; Vy had to push hard on the handle to get it to release the mechanism. The hinges creaked and groaned but opened.

Vy slid in. Wendell handed Talitha to her. Vy didn't bother with the seatbelt. Neither did Wendell. There were no shoulder belts. Lap belts only. Which meant the truck had to be older than mid-seventies, the year when shoulder belts were mandated on all new vehicles. Vy looked at the radio. Eight-track in the dash. So no earlier than sixty-five. All these were clues, details she could use to identify the man should she need to. When the authorities asked her.

And she had to be the professional law enforcement agent she'd sworn to be.

Wendell drove down a steep hill, carefully and cautiously. He slid sideways twice, finally reached a paved street. The truck hit a deep pothole. And another. And another. Obviously, the street wasn't *that* paved. Maybe not maintained by the city. The truck bounced hard.

Vy hissed, "Watch it! I almost bounced my head off the roof." Talitha voiced her displeasure as well. Vy hummed and cooed and did all she could to calm the baby.

Wendell glanced over. "I'm sorry. If I slow down, we'll be late. Maybe I can make up some time when we hit the highway. These back roads…"

Vy let out a breath. "I'm sorry, too. She's got a full tummy. I could end up wearing her breakfast."

Wendell slowed the truck and crawled over the next few potholes. "Better?"

"Much. Thank you."

She listened to the engine hum. No miss. No knock. No obvious lack-of-muffler roar. It drove well. And had to be street legal. You don't drive something that isn't if you want to stay under the police radar.

Vy decided to break the silence. "What year is this?"

"Seventy."

"Sounds good for something that old."

Vy couldn't see the man's expression, but there was pride in the tone of voice. "I've been working on it when I get the chance."

"Restoration or remodel?"

"Restoration." He glanced over at her. "What do you know about cars?"

Expressions. I'm missing all the expressions. "My dad had a sixty-four Ford Mustang he wanted to rebuild. Restore. Mom convinced him if he hadn't found all the parts by the time the last one of us girls graduated college, he'd never find them. She was right. Ended up selling her about six years ago."

"Pity. It'd be worth a mint now." The tone sounded sympathetic.

"Yeah, but he needed the money to pay off some debts of my sister's."

"Why's he paying off your sister's debts? She out of work?"

Vy lowered her head. "In rehab. The debts were part of restitution. The folks didn't want her going to prison, so Dad sold the Mustang. Broke his heart."

They rode in silence for several miles. Wendell glanced over at her. "Your sister stay clean?"

"How many addicts do you know?"

His voice became defensive. "I know some got their lives straight. It happens."

"I'm sure it does. And I'm like you, I know some do. Iris wasn't one of them." *Isn't one.*

"Where is she now?"

"Last I heard, she's living up in Canada."

"Why Canada?" Wendell's head jerked around to look at Vy.

"I don't know. It's where her boyfriend wanted to go, so she went with him."

"Gotta be hard on your folks." He turned back to focus on the road.

"Parenting is hard on any folks."

The conversation died as they came to a straight stretch of road. The snow lightened up. Vy could see tree lines, the occasional fallow field, more trees, but no markers of any kind. She began counting field/tree combinations. Maybe she could identify the road that way. *I am who I am. Lord, You'll have to tell me how to separate Law and Grace, my job versus mercy. After we get released. Right?*

She hummed again.

She reckoned they'd been on the main road about thirty minutes when Wendell's phone began "The Eyes of Texas" theme. Wendell snorted. "Him." He keyed the phone. "What?"

"Change of plan. Take the hostages to Riker's Pond. Drop them there. 'She' will pick them up after you leave."

Wendell cast a glance at Vy, shook his head. No, the caller couldn't see, Vy knew. But force of habit. "No. I don't like it. Why didn't she call me?"

"I don't know. I don't question her orders. Just do it."

Wendell stared at his phone. The caller had disconnected, but Wendell continued to stare at it. "I don't like it. And don't trust you." He made a call. Vy could hear a phone ringing but no answer.

No answer.

No answer.

He called another number. "She's not answering her phone."

"Maybe she stepped out of the car. Went to use the bathroom. How'm I supposed to know? Just do what she says and take them to Riker's Pond."

Wendell disconnected the call and threw the phone in the dash. "No. I don't like it. I don't trust you as far as I can spit. I'm not doing it."

He made a U-turn in the center of the highway, sped around three corners, stopped. He looked at Vy. "I don't know what game he's playing, but I don't like it."

Vy raised her eyebrows. "I got that impression."

"I don't like what I'm going to do, either, but I'm going to put you and the baby out."

The snow had stopped falling except for the lightest of flakes. The air remained white with the shimmer and dust. It made visibility difficult.

Wendell pointed to a fence line next to the trees. "You follow the fence line. Stay on the tree side, but follow the fence line. It'll go back aways...maybe quite aways. But stay on the fence line. It'll dead-end into another fence. Take the south T. It'll go another quarter mile or so. There's houses back there. You'll get help for you and the baby."

Wendell shrugged out of his jacket. "Put this on. Wrap it around you and her. It'll keep you warm. I'm sorry. I wanted to see you get all the way back to your people. That's what she and I were planning. Seeing your people pick you up. But I got a really bad feeling right now, and I'm not taking chances with you two. Get her and yourself safe. That's what counts."

Vy pulled the jacket on, shifted Talitha to the inside, and nodded to Wendell. "Thank you. For everything. You kept us alive. I can't...I can't...say..."

Wendell looked away. "Don't. Just go. Tell the baby to live a long, happy life."

"I won't forget this, Wendell. Ever. She'll know about you growing up. And she won't forget either."

Vy started to open the door. Wendell called, "Wait." Vy hesitated. "Let me see her one more time." Vy passed Talitha to him. Wendell reached up and pulled the Gorilla mask away from his face. He bent down and kissed the baby, turned to face Vy, letting her see him. She reached over, hugged him, kissed his cheek, grabbed Talitha, and slid out of the vehicle.

The truck waited. Vy struggled down the embankment, up the small rise to the treeline. She grappled with the barbed-wire fence, prying the strands far enough apart to give her room to writhe her wriggling parcel and herself through the opening. It took time, but she managed to make it with minimal blood loss to her hands. No fabric trail remained to betray her escape, either.

Vy looked back and saw Wendell spinning snow to cover her tracks, spinning snow on the opposite side as well. The scene would resemble little more than a vehicle leaving the road, overcorrecting, hitting the opposite side, straightening out, and moving on down the road. *He's a pro. He's done this before. Ex-law enforcement? Or career criminal?* Either way, Vy was grateful for his diligence in hiding her.

Less snow had fallen under the trees. The pines were too close together to be a natural forest. Bushy. Straight rows. Maybe a Christmas tree farm that had been abandoned? Through a clearing, Vy could see the remains of an old barn. Left to fall down on its own, rather than pay to have it removed.

Boards attached with one fastener, hanging over a broken window. Shingles, rotted with age, scattered along the side of the building. She could see the roof had caved in. The weight of the last winter storm had been too much for the aging timbers. Paint peeled away from the siding, revealing the sun-whitened boards underneath. The smell of pine seeped through her consciousness. Weak sunlight cast weaker shadows on the building's skeletal remains.

Vy focused her attention on the fence line. She shifted Talitha to her left arm and began a brisk walk forward. She could hear the highway though it had disappeared from view. For a brief moment, she considered going back and flagging down any passing motorist. But she had no clue what the second kidnapper looked like, if he would come after Wendell, or if getting in a car with a stranger would be better than walking her way out.

The thought of facing another stranger set Vy's nerves shaking. No. No more strangers. Except in a house. With a phone. And a heater. Vy trudged along under the trees.

She stopped once to lean against a tree trunk and catch her

breath. Carrying Talitha close to her kept the baby warm but made Vy too warm. She debated taking the plaid coat off but decided against it. Yes, it would cool her down. Yes, it would make her susceptible to hypothermia. No, she wouldn't take it off.

The fence line continued past the trees. Now she slogged through knee-deep fluffy snow. The kind you had to fight every inch. Like walking against an ocean current. Her hands were ice. Her legs burned. She reached the T. *What did he say? North? South? But which way is which?* There was no sun to help guide her. Clouds obscured the sky, threatening more snow to some. Light, heavy, it didn't matter.

Think, Vy. Think. He said south. Take the south T. She examined the fence. *South. South. Why is this so hard?* After several moments of no inspiration, she prayed. "God! Help us. Please. Which way is help? Which way do I go? I'm so tired. I can't think. Please. Help me."

She studied the wires again. To go right meant climbing through the barbed wire again. Tired as she felt, the choice became easy. Go left. Follow the fence line. Go left.

Vy shifted Talitha again. In doing so, she knocked against the object in the pocket. Vy pulled it out. The thermos. The thermos with the warm coffee. Vy rested Talitha against a tree, balanced her with a knee, unscrewed the cap, and drank straight from the container. The precious heat saturated her core. She could go on.

Vy finished the beverage, put the container back in her pocket. She wrapped both arms around Talitha and pushed off down the line. Follow the line. Always walk the line.

She had to slow her pace to pick safe and stable ground to walk on. Harder than it looked, as ice could be hidden under innocent snowdrifts. Her feet and pants were soaked and cold and freezing. She hugged Talitha as tightly to her chest as she could, enclosed between the folds of Wendell's plaid overcoat. Her breath came in spurts. This would be a race against freezing to death for both her and the baby.

The coat heated her. Overheated. Vy started sweating. *Not good. Not good. I should take it off.*

Talitha needs the warmth. Suck it up.

She couldn't feel her feet. Every step seemed like walking in lead boots. Exhaustion crept up her limbs. Talitha felt heavier and heavier. Deadweight. *Dead? No. No.* Vy jostled the little girl. Talitha stretched, grumbled, went back to sleep.

Sleep sounds good. Maybe a little rest? Five minutes? Just to catch my breath?

Vy could no longer lift her head. All she could do was keep moving. Keep walking. Keep dragging one foot ahead. Then the other foot. Then the other foot. Then the other foot…

All the while watching the fence posts. She couldn't see the wire. All she could see were the posts sticking out of the snow. Follow the fence line.

Vy went down on one knee, pulled herself back to her feet. She would not stop. She would not stop. To stop meant death. Talitha needed her. She had to push on. *Lord, help me. Cold. So cold. Five minutes. That's all. Five minutes to rest. You won't mind, will You, Lord?*

I have to move. I have to move. I have to move.

Vy stumbled over a rock, going down on one knee. It would be so easy to go down on both, to sit, to lie... One moment.

No! Get up! Keep going. She struggled to her feet. Fence posts. Follow the fence…

There weren't any. She'd lost the last one. Panic surged in her, giving her energy she didn't know she had. Vy lifted her head and looked up.

A house. Still many yards away. But a house. Smoke coming through the chimney. Steam coming from the kitchen vent. A house. People.

But she had to get through the snowdrifts. She had to reach the porch.

Children's toys littered the backyard. A toy riding horse rose out of a mound. Its faded head spoke of age and misuse. The spines of a child-size rocking chair stuck up through the icy coating. A giant ball shed its snowy cover, too round to hold the gentle flakes.

Vy stumbled again, barely managing to keep Talitha out of the snow. *Talitha. I have to move for Talitha.*

A voice yelled. "Hey! What are you doing?"

A woman's voice. For one moment, Vy nearly panicked. *Not her! Not after all this. Oh, please, Father. Not her.*

Vy staggered forward. Whether a plea or a prayer, it was all she had. "Help me."

Someone swooped in beside her. "What are you doing out here in this snow? How did you get here? What is that... Is that a baby? You have a baby in your coat? Are you crazy, out walking with a baby like this?"

Vy sank to her knees. She repeated, "Help me. Please." It came out as a whisper. Or a whimper.

The figure lifted Vy to her feet. "Lean on me. Come on. You can do it. We're going to get you inside. Herb! Come out here!" Vy closed her eyes. She needed everything in her to move, to lift her feet and lurch forward.

She heard a door open. A man's voice. Not one she'd heard before. Not her Gorilla-man. Not his brother. Someone new. "What's going on, Carol?"

"This woman has a baby with her. Come help me get them inside."

Someone lifted her elbow, supporting her, half-carrying her. Encouraging her. "Come on, Mama. You can do it. You can. We're almost there. Almost there. Keep moving. That's right."

The man joined them. His voice sounded kind. "Here. Let me take the baby."

It was the one goad which could still move her. Terror surged through Vy. She struggled. She shrieked, "No! No, you can't take the baby! No!"

The man caught Vy's arm and soothed her. "It's okay, it's okay. No one is going to steal the baby. I promise. It's okay. You hold her."

Stairs. Swept clean of snow. Salted. One. Two. A wooden door. White and cracked with age. A doorjamb. Worn of lacquer. Well-traveled. A warm room. A flowered couch. Crocheted afghans. Pillows. A blanket covering the back of the sofa. "Sit. We'll get you some blankets."

Vy began to shake. Her whole body shuddered. Her teeth chattered. "Police. Please. Call the police." A whisper. All she had.

The woman gave the orders. "Call the sheriff's office, Herb. Tell them we have a mama and a baby who came in from the field out of the snow."

Someone wrapped a blanket around her. Held a cup to her lips. "Here. Drink this."

Warm fluid filled her mouth, drained down her throat, warmed her insides. Vy gazed at her rescuer. "Thank you." She closed her eyes.

Vy heard the smile in the woman's voice. Carol. He'd called her Carol. Carol kneeled beside Vy, pulled off Vy's soggy wet shoes and socks, slid a pair of slippers on her. Vy opened her eyed and looked down. She laughed. Her teeth chattered. "Al…li…gators?"

Carol nodded. "My kids have an intense love of the absurd. Every year we try to find the worst pair of slippers to give each other. These aren't even a contender for the award."

The man—Herb. She'd called him Herb—walked into the living room. Vy lay Talitha down on the couch. The little girl looked around, stretched, let out a tentative cry. Vy grasped the baby's hands. Cold. So cold. Tears spilled from Vy's eyes. She leaned back on the couch. "She's cold. I'm cold. Can you warm her up?"

Carol picked up Talitha and cradled her in her arms. The little girl snuggled against Carol's chest. Whimpers and cries and protests were offered.

But Talitha was alive and safe and going home. Vy began to sniff and leaned against Carol. The woman put an arm around Vy. "Whatever happened, it's over now. You're safe. The baby's safe. It's over."

Vy lost it. She began to cry. The ordeal, the fear, the violence, the not knowing, all washed through her. Hard sobs wracked her body. Carol wrapped her up in a motherly hug. "I got you. I got you, Mama." She instructed Herb. "Get the first aid kit."

The hysteria slowed. Sobs were replaced by breaths. Deep breaths. Calm breaths. Well…calmer breaths. At least ones which didn't rock her body. Vy lifted her head and closed her eyes. "Thank you. Thank you. I…I…"

Talitha decided she wanted to say a few words, too, and began to wail with all her might. Carol let go of Vy and put Talitha down on the couch beside Vy. "Let me guess. Hungry?"

"Yes. And wet, I'm sure."

"You're in so much luck. I have a grandson about her size. And he leaves his things all over the house. I'll get her a bottle and a dry outfit."

Herb handed Vy another warm cup of tea. "Here. Drink this, too. It should help." He smiled. Grandfatherly. Safe. Silver hair. Kind eyes. Gentle eyes.

Vy took the cup and sipped at the life-giving fluid. "Thank you. Thank you. I'm Vy Johnson." She picked Talitha up and bounced her on her shoulder. "This little one is Talitha Farrell. We were both kidnapped."

The words were hard. They made her shake. Vy raised her gaze to the ceiling to calm herself. "I have no idea what day it is. I don't know how long we were held." She looked into Herb's eyes. She had to crush her lip to keep it from trembling. "We both want to go home."

Herb's face drew down. "Kidnapped? From this town? Are they following you?"

Vy admitted. "No. No one knows we got away. All my tracks were covered until I got into the field. We were grabbed from Oakton. I don't know where we are now."

Carol returned to the room with a bottle and the necessary niceties to give Talitha a dry bottom and every other part of her body as well. She eyed Vy closely. "May I?"

Vy nodded. "I'm sorry. I…"

Carol shook her head as she changed and diapered the unhappy baby. "Don't apologize. If I'd been held by kidnappers, I wouldn't be letting anyone take my baby away from me, either."

With a grandmother's expertise, Carol propped Talitha with one arm and fed her with the other. She smiled into the infant's face. "Oh, you are a pretty little one, aren't you? I bet your daddy is frantic to get you two back."

Vy leaned back against the couch. "I'm not her mother. I'm the aunt-to-be. It's a very long story, and I'd like to wait until the sheriff gets here before I try to tell it all."

Herb pushed the valanced lace curtains away from the picture window and looked down the street. "Here he comes now."

Carol raised her head from concentrating on feeding Talitha. "They got here fast."

Herb shrugged. "Maybe they've been out looking for these two. On alert."

He went to the front door and opened it. Vy could hear the voices. "They're in here, Sheriff. Carol's feeding the baby. Unless you need the diaper for evidence, it's the only thing we've touched."

The sheriff walked into the room. Tall, darker than Vy herself. Maybe a few years older, which meant he'd made sheriff in record time. Small county, maybe? Since she had no idea what county they were in, she'd give him the benefit of the doubt.

The man walked into the room and smiled first at Carol. "Hello, Mrs. Weathers. Bill sends his regards. Third grade already. Where does the time go? He can't wait for school to start again next week." The man's eyes twinkled. "His mom and I can't wait, either."

Carol laughed. "We get that a lot this time of year. Have a seat, Sheriff."

The man sat down across from Vy in the gold rocker-recliner. His eyes studied Vy closely. Vy sensed it. *Social time is over. Everything from here on out is all business.* She noticed his gaze lingering on the cuts on her wrists, the scrapes along her cheeks and chin. He met her eyes, and his gaze was even. "When you feel up to it, tell me what you can."

Vy nodded. "My name is Vy Johnson. I work for Drug Enforcement in Oakton. The baby is Talitha Farrell, daughter of Collin and Jeff Farrell. Their address is 122 Walden Lane. His phone is 614-555-4578. Hers is 614-555-8754."

Vy closed her eyes. "My father's name is George Johnson. My mother is Martha. Their number is 614-555-5378. They all need to be told we're safe."

She drew in a breath. "We were kidnapped—separately—from Oakton. Um…I…"

Sheriff Logan nodded his head. "We'll make sure they get contacted. Do you want me to call an ambulance for you before we go any further?"

"No. I don't need medical attention right now." She stopped again. *I'm a professional. I can do this. I should be able to do this. Pull it together.* "I know I'll have to go after this for the sake of the evidence. So will Talitha."

Vy stopped. Her mind raced. "I'm not sure which will be harder on them….being told she's safe now, but they have to wait to see her, or still thinking she's with the kidnappers."

Her mind went blank. "I…I…can't think. I can't. Do whatever you know is right." She took in some deep breaths and tried to marshal her nerves. "I'm sure you have protocols for this."

He smiled. "We do. But we like to assess each situation. Tell me what you can, stop when you can't go any further, and we'll take it from there." He looked at Carol and Herb. "Are we interrupting anything you had planned? Can we stay here and do this, or do you want us to move out?"

Carol waved her hand. "No, no. Right here is fine. The less excitement, the better." She smiled at Vy. "And I can keep the tea flowing."

Gratitude washed over Vy, and tears welled in her eyes once again. "You don't know…thank you. Thank you."

Carol finished feeding Talitha. "Good burp, please." Talitha obliged. Carol bumped Vy's shoulder. "You're welcome." She cuddled Talitha as the infant slipped off to sleep. "I'll keep her out here where you can see her." She lay the sleeping baby beside Vy and moved to the matching rocker. "She'll be right here beside you on the couch. You can keep your eyes on her the whole time."

Herb pulled up a kitchen chair and sat to listen as well. Vy closed her eyes, nodded, and opened them again. Carol jumped up, handed Vy a box of tissues. "Just in case."

Vy laughed. "Yeah, maybe." She bit her lip, turned to the sheriff. "What day is it?"

"It's Thursday the seventeenth.

Vy's eyes widened. "That long? We were gone over two weeks? Poor Collin and Jeff. And Erin. And Mom and Dad." She dropped her head back, lifting her chin to the ceiling. "I went to work. I got a call at the office; someone had crashed into my car." She met Sheriff Logan's eyes. "The loaner car because mine had been vandalized a few days before."

Vy realized the sheriff hadn't taken out a recorder or a notepad. So this wasn't the "taking it all down for evidence's sake" interview. Logan wanted to try to decide what had happened and what to do next. *Like we do. Assess the situation. Listen. Gather information. Then go for the minutiae.*

She kept the telling short. "Thugs in the van who hit mine grabbed me, stuffed me into the back, and drove off. They tied, gagged, blindfolded me. I don't know where they took me. An old shed. Dirt floor. I'd been there a few hours, maybe, when someone, a woman, brought Talitha in. They shoved her at me, threatened me, and left us there."

The shaking began again. Whether fear or rage, Vy didn't know. "From then on, they came in to feed the baby, and not much else." *How do I tell about Wendell? His help? What do I say? Lord?*

She sipped some of the still-warm tea to settle her muscles. "A man…yes, he was one of them. He helped us. He always wore a gorilla mask, so I couldn't see his face. He untied me so I could hold Talitha. I think he bonded with her… He hated what was going on but seemed indebted or connected to the woman. He brought me food and water when he could." She wouldn't tell about the being frozen part. Not yet.

Vy held the sheriff's eyes. "We had a lot of back and forth between him and me and the woman. There was another man, too, but I never talked with him. I heard him talking to the man in the mask but never saw him. I believe he was brother to the man in the mask."

She drew in a deep breath. "The woman planned to kill us. I know. Except no one knew when. She wanted revenge against a man, Robert Winger. When she found out he'd already been put in prison, she gave up the idea and decided to let us go."

Sheriff Logan's eyes narrowed. "No ransom? Just let you go?"

"Yes. She…she…the idea of killing the baby didn't set well with her in the end." Vy closed her eyes to remember the sequence. "The man in the gorilla mask got us up early. He fed Talitha, wrapped her in the blanket, took us, and started to drive us to a meeting spot. We were going to be left there, and our people would pick us up. But something went wrong, or something changed."

Vy had to look away. Out the window. In the air. Anywhere but at someone's eyes. "He got a call from the other male kidnapper. The guy told him plans had changed. The man who had us—he told me to call him Wendell—didn't believe his brother. Wendell tried to call the woman, but she didn't answer her phone. That's when Wendell let us go. He drove us to the field by the trees."

Vy looked at her hands. She twisted them. Interlocked her fingers. Unlocked them. "He told me to follow the fence line to where it Td. Then to follow it south. I'd find a house and be safe. He…he pulled off his…his…mask. He wanted me to see him." Vy sucked on her lip until the trembling stopped. "He gave me his coat, hid our footprints, then left. I have no idea where he went or what happened to him after that."

Carol's eyes glistened. She stood up, crossed the room, and hugged Vy again. "You poor thing. How awful. I'm so sorry."

Vy sucked on her lower lip. She nodded, knowing her voice

wouldn't hold. Sheriff Logan's tone remained even but filled with compassion. "I'm sure there's a lot more to the story. And after you've been checked out by the doctor in the ER, I'll get it from you. Since we're about an hour and a half from Oakton, I think we should call all your people and have them come down and meet you at the hospital. By the time they get here, the doctor should be ready to release you."

He spoke into his phone. "Neville, I need a squad and an ambulance to transport a woman and child to the ER to be checked out. This address. Soon as you can, but don't need the sirens." He smiled at Talitha. "Don't want to wake the baby."

Vy grinned. It turned to tears. "Thank you." *You are a professional. Stop with all the blubbering. This is ridiculous. Handle it.*

You've just spent the last two weeks protecting someone else's child from death. Allow yourself to acknowledge the stress.

Before the argument could continue, sounds of three gunshots rang out. They were distant, but not so distant Vy didn't recognize the sound. Her head jerked up. She stared out the direction of the back door. *Lord? Lord, please?*

Sheriff Logan made another call. "Shots fired. Sounded like behind the old tree farm on Cackler. I'm out here with the kidnap victims. Get someone out right away. Yeah. Good."

Talitha woke, stretched, and rolled, breaking up the silence. She sucked her fist, smacking loud enough to cause Carol to laugh and pick the little girl up. "You just ate. You can't be hungry." She carried the baby over to Sheriff Logan's side. "Isn't she beautiful?"

His eyes twinkled. "Which side of the family do I say she resembles? I don't want to get into any trouble with the grandparents."

Vy grinned. "Her father's. There aren't any grandparents on the mom's side." Vy stopped. "At least not who are interested in claiming her as family."

Carol looked up. "Really? That's sad."

"Yes. That's a family with a lot of history, and not all of it is good. But the Lord has turned some of it around. There's always redemption."

"We can hope."

A siren far in the distance wailed. Sheriff Logan watched out the back window. Herb drew his attention to the front. "The squad and an ambulance are here."

FRIDAY AFTERNOON

Paramedics came in, followed by ambulance attendants. Both Vy and Talitha were checked out, strapped to the gurney, rolled out, and placed in the ambulance. Talitha was not happy about the situation and let her feelings be known. A sterile pacifier didn't pacify her. The force of the restraints were not Vy's idea of fun, either. Too much reminder of the past weeks.

She could, however, talk herself through it mentally. Talitha went way past being consoled. She screamed and cried and warbled. Only as the motion of the ambulance rocked her did she settle down and eventually give up the fight. By the time the ambulance reached the hospital, she had fallen asleep again.

And Vy nearly had her second anxiety attack. Having Talitha rolled out of her line of sight created panic in Vy's gut which made her want to scream. She swallowed it, however. *You're safe. They're helping. She's fine. Everything will be okay. Trust the Lord.*

She did ask the paramedic who accompanied them, "Please. When they're done examining her, bring her back to stay with me in the ER. We've…we've been through a lot together. I'm not ready to let go of her yet."

He nodded. "Will do."

Vy relaxed on the gurney. She behaved for the doctors and nurses, giving them the information they needed, height, weight, blood type, immunizations, surgeries… All the things doctors needed to know to assess her general health.

The scrapes and ligature marks on her wrists and ankles were photographed before they were treated and bandaged. The scratches on her face were also documented, washed, and covered. Any and all other bruises, cuts, scars were categorized. IVs were started, fluids pumped in, and recommendations made.

Half an hour in, Vy began to shudder again. She tried to pass it off, but her nerves had been ignored long enough. They were headed for a major breakdown. Over her feeble protests, they gave her an injection of a muscle relaxant/anti-anxiety medication. It didn't put her to sleep but stilled the tremors. The heated blankets took care of any lingering trembles.

She was about to nod off when the curtains flew open, and her parents were let into the room. Vy held her mother's eyes. Martha moved directly to Vy's side and caught hold of her. She wrapped her arms around Vy, buried her head in her daughter's shoulder, and wept soundlessly.

George came in from the opposite flank and caught Vy as well. Again, the raw emotion of the ordeal welled in Vy, and she felt the trembling start again. The three Johnson's held each other and cried until there were no tears left…and then they found some they didn't know were still around and cried those, too. The only words they spoke were the repeated phrases: "I love you" and "Thank You, Lord."

* * *

Collin and Jeff were only moments behind the Johnsons as they pulled into the hospital parking lot. They raced hand-in-hand to the front desk. Jeff spoke. Collin didn't trust herself to say anything except, "Give me my baby!" *Not the most diplomatic way to…*

Hang diplomacy! I want Talitha back!

Jeff's voice sounded as shaky as Collin's felt. "We're the Farrells. Our baby daughter is here. They said she's here…"

A sheriff's deputy stepped out from behind the desk. The uniformed woman said, "Yes. We need to make a positive identification. Did you bring the birth certificate?"

Collin wanted to shove the paper into the deputy's face but kept her composure. "Yes. And all her baby photos. She's ours, I know she is. She was with Vy Johnson, and they were both kidnapped at the same time." Her composure disappeared into pleading. "Please, can we see her now? Please?"

The deputy took the papers and the photos. "Please. I know this is hard. Have a seat." She motioned to the benches against the window. She smiled, her eyes gentle. "Or wait on your feet. I understand. I'll be right back." She disappeared down the corridor.

Every fiber of Collin's being wanted to race down the corridor and beat the deputy to whatever room she entered, snatch up Talitha, and run back outside the hospital again. *Not. Not. Not the way to do this. You have to hang on. You have to.*

Collin buried her head into Jeff's chest. "This is torture! She's so close. She's right there. I know she is. I want her so bad…"

Jeff didn't try to calm her. Smart man. He simply held her.

Ten minutes.

Fifteen minutes.

A tall, dark-skinned man in a sheriff's uniform came out of the back. "Mr. and Mrs. Farrell?"

Collin scanned his eyes for some sign of anything which would say they had Talitha in the back, waiting for them. He smiled. "I'll take you to your daughter."

Collin's knees buckled. Jeff held her up. She closed her eyes. "Thank You, God. Thank You. Thank You, Lord. Thank You."

The man motioned down the corridor. "This way. I'm Sheriff Logan. Vy Johnson carried the baby in from the woods. We've confirmed Ms. Johnson's identification, and she confirmed Talitha's." He smiled. "You're lucky Ms. Johnson's a Federal Agent and can make that call. Otherwise, you might have had to wait for a footprint match."

Collin nailed the man with all the rage in her. "And you would have had to build another hospital."

His eyes twinkled. "I can understand." He indicated a room on his left. "In here."

Collin and Jeff crossed the room to the infant bed. Collin sank to her knees as she touched the curls on her daughter's head. Talitha lay on her back, kicking and grinning at the world. Jeff scooped her up, kissed her, sank to the floor beside Collin. They held the baby, kissed the baby, touched her hands and feet and wrists and toes…kissed her from top to bottom and back to the top. One-size-fits-all tears rained down and drenched Collin's and Jeff's faces. They leaned against the crib, held each other, held Talitha, rested against each other, and the only words were the repeated phrases, "I love you," and, "Thank You, Lord. Thank You."

* * *

Eventually, the attending physician came into Vy's room. He cleared his throat as he came in. George looked up. "Can we help you?"

The man had on a medical gown and cap, so George could only guess his age from the lines in his face. Maybe as old as George himself. The doctor kept a kind face. "I'm sorry, but she needs to get some rest. She needs to sleep."

He smiled at George and Martha. "I know you want to stay with her. We have a pull-out couch and a sleeper-recliner. You may not be comfortable, but you'll be here."

George clasped the man's hands. "You are an insightful man, sir. How'd you know we weren't leaving?"

The man shrugged. "If it had been my daughter, I wouldn't leave, either."

George nodded to Martha. "You stay here. I'll go check on the Farrells. I want to make sure their reunion was as happy as ours." George exited the room with the doctor.

Vy held her mother's hand. "Did Erin come up with Jeff and Collin?"

Martha shook her head, and her eyes shone bright. "No. He insisted he didn't want to interrupt anyone's joy. Jim Russo is bringing him up tomorrow."

Vy's soul caught. "He didn't want to be here?" She stared at the floor, unable to process the why of it all.

Martha shook Vy's hand. "That man loves you, Vy. Don't even go thinking he didn't want to be here. He didn't want you to have to choose who to see first. He made a tremendous sacrifice to wait until tomorrow."

Vy stared at the foot of her bed. She whispered, "Are you sure that's all it is?"

Her mom fairly exploded. "Viola Johnson! Don't you ever doubt him. You haven't seen him these past two weeks you've been gone. It nearly tore him to pieces. I wasn't sure he would make it out of the hospital. He's been eaten up by guilt over you and Talitha being taken."

Vy stared at her mother, trying to make sense of it. "Why didn't he come up to see Talitha, then?"

"The self-same reason. He wanted to let Collin and Jeff have all the time they needed with their baby girl." Martha stroked Vy's cheek. "The man is suffering, honey. And he's going to continue suffering until he sees you. Do not for one moment doubt he loves you and misses you. Not for one moment. You hear me?"

Vy bowed her head. "I'm sorry. My emotions are all jumbled."

"I'm sure they are. And I'm sure they'll still be jumbled tomorrow. But a good night's sleep will help some. We're going to be right here."

"You don't have to—" Vy tried to protest.

Martha wasn't having it. "Maybe you don't need us, but we need to be here for ourselves. So hush. We're staying."

Vy's lip trembled. She rested her head in her mother's hand, kissed it. "Thank you, Mama. I love you."

"I love you too, girl."

George walked in after about ten minutes. "Yes, they have their baby back. The nurses may not get to put her in the cradle tonight. I think Jeff and Collin are going to set up shop on the floor beside the crib. No one is going to touch their baby without a fight."

He looked at his wife. "You tell her where Erin is?"

"I explained it to her."

George sat beside Vy and stroked her cheek as her mother had. His tone sounded as strong as his words. "I don't know many men who would have made the kind of sacrifice to stay behind and let us come instead." His eyes bored into Vy's. "Takes a godly man to put others first."

Wendell put us first. Lord, what did it cost him? Please...make it okay, Lord. Somehow, someway, make it right. Vy could only nod at her father. She closed her eyes and let the weariness take her.

FRIDAY EVENING

Harmon and Lacey sat with Erin and the boys while Collin and Jeff went to retrieve Talitha. FBI Agent Ireland Pope remained at the house as well, pending capture of all kidnappers.

Erin lay on the floor with the boys, letting them use him as speedbumps to their rolling escapades. Being surrounded by babies took the sting out of sending George and Martha up to see Vy rather than going himself. *I know, Lord. I knew it would hurt. I'm trying to be happy about it. Honest. I am. I'm not there yet. Let's say I'm happy I was obedient to You, okay? You said it would be best. I bowed to Your will and suggested it. I'm glad they went. I am. But it still hurts. Waiting...waiting one more day to see her.*

But tomorrow I get her all to myself, right? Okay, I hadn't really thought about that. That will make it alright. Better, even. Thank You!

Erin rolled over to look up at Harmon. "Can I get a hand up from here?"

Harmon smiled. "Happy to help." He locked arms with Erin and eased him to his feet and back to the couch with the other adults.

Lacey handed Erin his coffee. "I kept it warm for you. I figured you might want it."

"Thanks, Mom Lacey." He drank from the cup, sighed. "I can't stop smiling. I'm so happy they're back. They're alive, they're safe, and they're back."

Lacey laughed, a deep belly laugh. "I almost thought I'd never laugh again."

Harmon clasped his wife's hand. "It takes a very long time to get joy back, I know. After your stroke—during your recovery—I thought I might never have any kind of joy again. It comes back. But not for a long, long time."

Erin's phone pinged. He looked at it as it sat on the coffee table beside him. No longer the focus of attention, the central feature of life and hope.

The text chilled him. *Ten million dollars. You bring it to Winchester Pike. Place it in the dumpster of the Able's Chicken Hut. By 9 p.m. I'm watching.*

Erin's soul collapsed. Everything in him died. "No. No. They're safe. They're free. This can't be…" He looked up at Ireland. Life emptied from his very being. There were no words possible. Erin pointed to the phone.

Ireland scooped it up. She read it. Read as she typed, "We will comply." Then made a phone call and left it on speaker. "Agent Curry, do you have eyes on the victims?"

The answer came back. "I can have. We've been outside their rooms since we got here at noon."

"One visual check, please. We just received a ransom demand."

"On it." The urgency in the voice chilled Erin. He closed his eyes. Wait. Wait. They could do nothing else. Wait.

The answer came back. "Yes, we have eyes on the subjects. Ms. Johnson is speaking to her parents. Ms. Farrell is in the arms of her father at present. Being teased by her mother. They are safe. Your caller is bogus."

Erin heard the audible sighs from Lacey and Harmon. And his own. All three began breathing again.

Ireland finished. "Thank you. You restored life here. And we'll deal with the ransom demand."

Harmon asked first. "You think it's someone else? Someone playing a cruel trick?"

"Or someone who doesn't know Vy and Talitha have been rescued. Whoever it is, we're going to nail them." She looked at Erin. "By demanding you come, it shows they weren't involved with the texter this morning. We clearly told the person this morning you weren't able to 'come alone' anywhere. This is someone different. Someone who wants to change the game."

She stared at the phone. She looked up. "The person who texted first never said anything about bringing money. That came later. Like there were two texters. And one didn't know what the other had in mind to do. Or…" She trailed off. Ireland placed another call. "Scott, we've got a new ransom demand."

Scott's voice. "We see it. We're analyzing it now. The source looks like the same numbers from before. Same phone. Different caller?"

"That would be my deduction."

"Verify the subjects are safe."

"Eyes on them. All is well."

"Good job. We'll handle this from here."

"They wanted Erin. No acknowledgment he's in a wheelchair."

"We'll add it to the information pile. Appreciate the insight. Tell the Farrells and Mr. Winger they can relax. We're on this."

Ireland's eyes smiled as she looked at Erin and the Farrells. "They already have. Thanks, boss."

She disconnected the call. "This should prove enlightening to the bad guy, whoever he is."

Erin spoke for the room's occupants. "Thank you, Ireland. I wouldn't make it through tonight, thinking somehow Vy or Talitha were back with the kidnappers. I wouldn't."

Ireland smiled. "That's why I do what I do." She waved the back of her hand. "Carry on, people. Carry on."

And they did.

SATURDAY

Morning sunshine brought three Johnsons and three Farrells together in the atrium for a reunion. Vy eagerly held Talitha, laughing and cooing at the tiny girl. Talitha smiled and talked back, her innocent spirit not touched at all by the ordeal. Martha laughed as well. "Full tummy, dry butt, warm arms, and all is right with their world."

George kissed the small head. "As it should be."

Sheriff Logan stepped into the room. "Good morning, all." He looked to Vy first. "How are you this morning? Up to some questions?"

Vy nodded. Martha sighed. "Back to work, girl. You got one night off. Should be plenty, right?" Sarcasm drenched her mom's words.

George cautioned, "Martha…"

Vy lay her hand on her mother's arm. "It's fine, Mom. They need to get on this while the clues and information are still fresh." She addressed Sheriff Logan. "This wasn't the first time they've done this."

"I suspected as much. The FBI will be here in about an hour to take your statement. I thought I'd give you a head's up." He gazed around the room and smiled. "This is the ending we like to see. People alive and back together again."

Vy spoke for everyone. "Thank you, Sheriff. You've been more than kind. I appreciate all you've done for Talitha and me." She made Talitha wave her tiny hand.

Sheriff Logan touched the tip of his brim. "I'm happy we were able to help. And glad we could be of assistance for all of you."

Vy sighed. "Thanks again." He walked out. Vy turned to her mother. "What time are Erin and Jim Russo coming up?"

"Early. They should be here any time now."

Vy glanced at Collin. She almost reluctantly passed the little girl back to her mother. "Did the doctor say when they would release Talitha?"

"He said she could go home this morning." Collin's eyes twinkled. "The FBI may want to question her, but I'm not sure she'll be much help to them."

Vy laughed. It felt good. It felt right. "I'm sure she'll be willing to give them an earful of information. Whether they can interpret it or not is something else."

The sliding front doors whooshed open, and Jim Russo came in, pushing Erin in his wheelchair. Vy took one look at his bandaged head, the bruises on his face now yellow and green, faded from what must have been angry purple and black, his hands still wrapped from who knew what injury… She slipped to meet him, sank to the floor beside him. "Oh, Erin. Oh, my love…what did you do to yourself?" She kissed him as tenderly and gently as she could.

He wrapped his arms around her shoulders. "Vy…my sweet Vy. Did they hurt you? I am so sorry…"

Jim cleared his throat. "Excuse me, you two, but it's thirty-one degrees out. I think they'd like to close the front door."

Vy laughed, tears spilling over her face. Erin grumbled, "Spoilsport." Tears were wet on his face as well. Jim helped Vy to her feet and moved the party away from the entrance to a more convenient spot where the Farrells and Johnsons waited. Erin kissed Talitha, hugged her, and returned her to her mother. Jim made quick work of saying hi to the others and went to find a cup of coffee of his own.

Vy and Erin moved to an area less "peopley." Vy sat. Erin rolled as close as he could to be beside her. Another kiss, another hug. Vy held his hand. "What happened, Erin? What did they do to you?"

He half-grinned. "That's my line." His eyes held hers. "You look beautiful." Before she could object, he raised a hand. "Yes, you look like you've been through a war. And I know you have. But seeing your face again…you're beautiful." Tears choked him. "I thought I'd never see you again. Thought God had other plans for us. I was so scared you'd never come back."

Vy's spirit hitched. *Where's his faith? Where's his strength in God? Why...*

Erin lifted his head. "I knew the Lord had you, Vy. I knew He would be taking care of you. He would always take care of you. I didn't know if He would bring you back. And I hurt. It nearly crushed me."

Again, her spirit hitched. *Nearly? Only nearly? Why not totally? You didn't love me enough to be wholly crushed by losing me?*

That her spirit argued both sides against the middle occurred to her. And she hated it. Erin continued. "I felt like I would lose my mind. But God wrapped His arms around me, and I could bear it. He gave me the strength to keep moving. It wasn't me. He did it all."

He touched her face. "I'm not brave, Vy. I'm not clever or wise or spiritually mature or anything you are. I'm me. Just me. All the good parts belong to God."

Vy studied Erin's face, his eyes, tried to look in his mind and soul. "Are you breaking up with me, Erin Winger?"

"No." He shook his head. "Never. I love you. Nothing will change that. Ever." He lowered his head. "I'm giving you an out. They told me last night how brave you'd been. How strong. You saved Talitha and yourself. You never doubted for one minute." He looked back into her eyes. "I wanted to swoop in and save you, and I couldn't. I couldn't even be the bag man." Tears fell in a torrent down his cheeks. "You deserve better."

Anger screamed in her head. *You're right, I deserve better! I needed you, and you weren't there. Wendell saved us, not you. Even he was better than you are. You're nothing compared to him. He cared. He maybe died to save us. And you...you didn't even come up last night to see me! I don't need you.*

But Love. Love looked to the soul. Her soul. His soul. Love remembered her father's words the night before. *"Takes a godly man to put others first."* Erin had put aside his ego for her. Her father told her about Erin giving up the "bag man" spot, again for her. She suffered to stay alive. He suffered for love. Who'd been the stronger?

Vy curved her fingers around Erin's. Her lip trembled. "I love you, Erin Winger. Daddy told me what happened to you. I don't deserve a man willing to humble himself for me. I want to marry you if you'll still have me."

She lowered her head against his. She clasped his hands in hers. They sat.

Time passed. A throat cleared. "If you two are finished, the FBI have arrived." Vy looked up. Her parents, Jeff and Collin, and half the staff were missing. Sheriff Logan smiled at her. "I'm sorry to disturb you two. But it's been over an hour, and they really do need to talk to you."

Vy blushed. Erin looked over his shoulder at the officer. "So soon? Could they give us another day or two? Maybe three? We were just getting started with our reunion."

Vy squeezed his fingers. "Nut case." She stood. "I'll get dressed and come down…"

Logan shook his head. "That's not necessary. The doctor hasn't released you to go home yet, so they're going to do the interview here. Anything they need after that, they can contact you in Oakton. Same goes for here."

Vy stood. Erin and Sheriff Logan accompanied her back to her room. She glanced around. "Where did my folks go?"

"Out to eat. Talitha has been released, so the five of them—six with Mr. Russo— went to the Pancake Hut. Not sure the baby will eat much, but she'll keep them all company."

Erin grinned. "That she will. I'm certain she'll be passed from one to the other the whole time she's there. She'll be one spoiled baby before she gets back to Oakton."

Vy looked at him askance. "You can't spoil a baby by holding them."

"Tell her brothers. She's going to be in the nursery like, 'watch this.' And she'll barely make a sound, and someone will come running. Caleb and Joshua will scream their heads off, and all they'll get is a, 'not time, boys.' Don't tell me she won't be spoiled."

"You're rotten."

"I know babies."

Vy debated sitting in a chair but decided to get back into bed. It more closely resembled her position during the days of captivity. Maybe it would bring back memories she needed to help catch the kidnappers.

A knock. Two men entered the room. One tall, one stocky, both Anglo something. Agent Curry and Agent Freitas. They took seats across the room from Vy, put a recorder on the table, and began.

Agent Curry's first question came standard. "Do you feel up to answering some questions?"

"Of course."

"Do you have any objections to this man being here?" He pointed to Erin.

Vy shook her head. "No. I want him to stay."

"Just making sure." He settled back in the chair. "Walk us through what happened."

* * *

Vy relived two weeks of horror. Erin held her hand. She watched tears stream down his face. She watched anger burn in his eyes. She saw sadness, pain, love, agony…all the emotions she wanted to feel but needed to bury so she could relay the details.

Three hours passed. Vy stared into space, recalling the last moments before she and Talitha were set free. "He took off his mask. He wanted me to see his face. To be able to recognize him. He had tattoos on his cheeks. A dragon on the left. A Masonic pyramid on the right."

Agent Freitas pulled out a photo from his pocket. "Like these?"

Vy stared at the picture. The face had been blurred from the eyes up. But the tattoos were visible. She closed her eyes, bowed her head. "He killed him, didn't he?"

Freitas kept his tone soft. "Someone did."

"I heard the shots."

"Sheriff Logan told us. His people found the truck you described. 'Wendell' had been shot three times. I'm sorry."

Vy nodded. Empty. Nothing left but one plea. *Father, please.*

Curry handed Vy another photo. "He had an envelope in his hand. With a note to you in it. We've kept the original as evidence, but I had them make a copy. Maybe it will mean something to you."

A handwritten note. *"Vy, 'Jesus loves me, this I know. For the Bible tells me so. Little ones to Him belong. They are weak, but He is strong.' 'Jesus loves me, if it's true, here's what I hope He will do. Take my life and make it new, and…' I don't know how to end it. It's not very original, but maybe He'll hear it anyway. You said He cares. I hope so. Wendell."*

Tears flooded anew. She shook her head. "I didn't know a body could produce this much water and still function. I'm sorry. I'm a professional. I should be able—"

Three sharp voices cut her off.

"Stop!"

"Hold on there."

"Not true."

The men exchanged glances. Erin pointed to Freitas, who pointed to Curry. Agent Curry shook his head. "Professional or not, your emotions are real and valid and need to be expressed." He held her glance. "Especially in our line of work. If you don't express them, they will come out sideways and hurt the people you care about. We see it happen far too often. So don't apologize."

Vy lowered her head. "Thank you." She took a deep breath, let it out. "Okay. Do you have an ID on 'Wendell'? Priors?"

"We're still waiting on the system for any match. Ballistics on the bullets. Registration on the truck."

"He loved the truck. Said it was a seventy. He wanted to rebuild it. Restore it." Vy looked up. "I'm rambling. I'm sorry."

"Ms. Johnson, everything you tell us gives us a clue as to who he might have been. Knowing he wanted to restore the truck means we can contact the parts dealers in the area who would carry what he needs. Yeah, a lot of stuff gets bought online. But some of it has to be scrounged from junkyards. Maybe someone will recognize the truck. All of it helps."

Vy nodded. She dried her eyes on a tissue Erin handed her. And put it with the mountain she'd already used. "That's all I can tell you. I never saw anyone else. I heard the woman's voice, and Wendell referenced the other man as his brother. Beyond that, I can't help you."

"You've been a tremendous help, Ms. Johnson. If you think of anything else, you have our number."

The men stood. Freitas and Curry moved towards the door. Freitas turned back. "You don't remember what brand of diaper they gave you, do you?"

Vy crinkled her nose. "Brand of diaper?" She lowered her eyes and stared at the floor. "I...I think...a drugstore brand. Not the big box store." She laughed. "Who would have thought of diapers as a clue?"

He smiled at her. "Someone who buys a lot of diapers. Thank you, Ms. Johnson. I am thrilled this has a happy ending."

Vy smiled, but her heart hurt. "So am I. Thank you." The men left.

Erin waited for Vy to speak. She knew he wanted to see the note she'd been given but didn't want to ask. Could he be jealous of Wendell? Or her feelings of gratitude towards him? He would need to resolve those himself. She needed to sleep. About three days' worth of sleep.

Vy slid down under the sheets. Erin tucked a blanket up around her shoulders. "Do you want another blanket? I'll get one for you."

She shook her head. He reached out, stroked her cheek with the back of his hand. "Sleep, Vy. Sleep and heal, and I'll be here when you wake up."

"You don't need…" *Maybe you do. Alright, then.* "Thanks. I'll see you when I wake up." Vy closed her eyes. Exhaustion, physical, mental, emotional, poured over her in equal measures. She breathed deep and slept.

SIX WEEKS LATER

Mom was waiting when Vy came in from work. The expression on her mother's face said they were about to have "the talk." Vy had been avoiding it. Two weeks had passed since she returned to work after the kidnapping ordeal. Six weeks ago. Six long, lonely, confusing weeks…

Mom sat in the dining room, a cup of coffee in her hand, another cup waiting opposite her. Vy dropped her shoulder bag on the floor, kissed her mom's head. She poured coffee into the cup and slid into a chair. "What's up, Mom?"

Mom held her gaze steady. Her quiet eyes sparked. "That's what I need to know from you, Vy. What is going on in that heart of yours?"

"In my heart?"

"Of course. I know what goes on in your head. All rational and professional. You've got all the answers down pat about trauma and stress and needing time. Which your father and I gave you."

Her mother leaned closer. "But that's not what concerns me. What worries me is what's going on inside your heart." Mom held up her hand. "And don't say, 'Nothing.' I know better. Time you got it out. Time you sorted it out, girl."

Vy studied a leg of the table. There were teeth marks in the wood. Human or animal, it would be hard to say without a forensic examination. Either could be possible. She met her mother's gaze. *Maybe it is time. Maybe. If I knew.* "I don't know what is going on, Mom. I don't."

She dropped her eyes to the table leg and its toothmarks. "My head knows Erin did everything he could—everything he should—

when Talitha and I were being held. I appreciate what he suffered. I appreciate *that* he suffered."

She looked into her mother's waiting eyes. "But somehow, Wendell's sacrifice…"

"Seems more noble, more caring, more loving, right? And he accepted the Lord at the end, which makes his death more tragic. Am I right?"

Vy lifted her chin and held her mother's gaze. And its disapproval. "Yes."

"He was a criminal. We know he participated in countless other kidnappings. Some didn't end as well as yours."

"I know, Mom. I know." Vy stood to her feet. She paced around the dining room. "It doesn't make sense. I never claimed it did. I know I shouldn't be feeling this way and still say I love Erin. The two don't fit together."

Her mother studied her. Vy read the thought, the deliberation, the conjecture—the accusations?— in her mom's glance. Mom asked, "If Erin had been the one to meet you at the hospital, would it have made a difference? If it'd been his face and not mine and your father's…would you still be torn up about it?"

Vy shrugged. "I don't know." *I'll never know, will I?*

"Think about it. Think hard about it. There's a man who loves you deeply and wants more than anything to spend his life with you. You've been nothing but cool to him since we came home. You need to figure out what changed, girl."

"Wendell changed it, Mom."

"A kidnapper and a murderer. If he'd lived, he'd be on death row with his mother and brother. Would you still see him as a romantic hero?"

Vy didn't snarl, but it came close. "I never said I thought of him as a romantic hero."

"But you're treating him like one. What did he do Erin didn't? Or couldn't?" Vy stared at her mother. Mom nodded her head. "What did you expect Erin to do he didn't? Run in and rescue you? Die for you? You need to settle those things in your head, child. Because I suspect those are the real issues."

Vy scowled at her mother. "I didn't want Erin to die for me. I didn't expect him to swoop in and rescue me, either."

"What is it he did—or didn't do— you wanted him to? Because

before you got kidnapped, you measured Erin Winger against all other comers and said, "This is the one. He's the one I'm going to marry." Now, he's lacking something. What is it?"

Vy stared off at the floor but didn't see it. Her mom was right, of course. Something changed. Something changed in Vy. But what? She brought her eyes to match her mother's. "I don't know."

"I suspect you better figure it out. You owe Erin an explanation. He won't ask you for one, I know. But he deserves an answer to why you're putting him off. And today, not down the road, or tomorrow, or as soon as you feel like looking at yourself. You need to decide if you still love him and want to marry him. Give him that much respect."

Tears stung Vy's eyes. "You think this is easy? You think I wanted this to happen?"

Her mom's voice stayed even. "No one says that. No one denies you went through a horrible ordeal. It changes you. We know. We understand. We've given you time to work through it. And we'll give you all the time you need. I'm sure Erin has told you the same thing. There's a difference, though, Vy."

"What?" Her voice choked on the tears.

"You haven't said your feelings for us have changed. You still say you love us, and you mean it. You can't say it about Erin, can you? Be honest. Totally honest."

Vy chewed her lip. "No. I can't."

"He deserves an answer why. And you're the only one who can give it to him."

Vy nodded. She couldn't answer any other way. He deserved an explanation.

As soon as she could explain it to herself.

* * *

Vy walked to her bedroom. She'd moved back to the house after the kidnapping. Temporarily, of course. Until Wendell's brother's trial and conviction. The authorities had found the woman—Wendell's mother—shot to death as well. Wendell's brother had been picked up at the drop site the night he demanded the ransom. His defense had been he had no part in any of the kidnappings. He was just a homeless guy looking through the trash and found the bag with the money. The authorities were having him held without bond.

Until there could be a conviction in the case, Vy felt safer at her parent's house.

She closed the door behind her, threw her bag on the floor, and sank onto the bed. Quietly she mocked her mom's words. "Figure it out,' she says. 'He deserves an answer.' Well, so do I. But do you think anyone is giving *me* an answer? Nooooo."

She buried her head in her hands. "Lord! What is this? What is wrong with me? I don't understand."

Vy refused to cry. She had finished crying. Done. Maybe she needed counseling. Her parents had suggested it, but Vy had refused. Maybe she should reconsider.

Vy dialed the number for the church. Closed, of course, but she could at least leave a message for the office.

She got the recording and also an emergency number to call if she needed one. Is this an emergency? Is a life in danger? *A love-life, maybe, but not a real life.*

The question hit her: *What about Erin's life? Is his a real life?*

She shook it off. *His life isn't in danger.*

Isn't it, though? He can't move forward until I do. He's stuck in limbo, waiting for me to make a decision. He's been nothing but patient and understanding.

He can wait a little longer…

Her inner conscience chided her. But *why should he have to? Are you being fair to him? Or are you trying to punish him for something? Like your mom said…something he did or didn't do…you expected him to do. How can he be or do it if he doesn't even know what it is? When you don't know what it is? Call the number.*

Vy listened to the recording again and recognized the number as belonging to Pastor Tim. Great. Fantastic. This should be a hoot to explain.

Before she could dial, however, her phone rang. Aunt Ruth. Vy debated letting it go to voicemail but answered anyhow.

"Hello, Aunt Ruth."

"How are you doing, little girl? You feeling better?"

"I'm doing fine, Aunt Ruth. I am. I've been back to work for two weeks now. Almost back in my normal routine. Moving on."

"I hope so, Vy. I hope so." Ruth paused. She cleared her throat. *Here it comes. The real reason she's calling.* "Dear, Aunt Esther told me you've postponed your wedding. Is that true?"

Vy rolled her eyes. "Yes, it's true. Just for a little while. I needed to get adjusted, that's all."

"I heard all about how that man didn't even go see you in the hospital. What kind of husband—"

"He did come, Aunt Ruth. He came the next day. He wanted Mom and Dad to have all the time with me."

"How very noble." Sarcasm dripped from her aunt's tone. "A real man would have been there no matter what. He'd have been, 'she's my wife-to-be, and no one will get between us.' I'm sure your parents would have understood."

Vy's eyes narrowed. Hearing the attack from someone on the outside sounded different than from her own voice. "My father said it took a godly man to make that kind of sacrifice for others."

"Your father is a wonderful man, and I taught him most everything he knows. But I never taught him he could neglect his wife and call himself 'godly' for it. Never."

"Aunt Ruth, Erin—"

"Don't tell me what Erin did. I heard all about it. Didn't even have the guts to face the kidnappers himself. Sent his sister instead. How is that for godly, huh?"

Vy sat up straighter. "Now, wait a minute. Erin did what the FBI told him to do."

"Oh, sure he did. A real man would have been out there looking for you himself. Not waiting for the FBI or anyone else to find you. He'd have arranged—"

"Aunt Ruth!" Vy made her protest as strong as she could without being insulting to the woman. That might come later, but not yet.

"Don't you yell at me, little girl!"

"I'm sorry. Let me finish. Erin did exactly what the professionals told him to do. Like I would. They know their jobs like I know mine. I would never tell anyone to run out by themselves to bring in a criminal. Never. That's how hostages get killed. Erin did what he could to protect us."

"I'm sure that's what they all told you. Seeing as how they had his niece, too. I'm sure they made every effort to keep the baby safe. You just happened to be with her at the time. That's why they saved you."

Vy's eyes narrowed. "What are you saying, Aunt Ruth?"

"If the baby hadn't been kidnapped, would they have been putting out that kind of ransom? I doubt it very much. People don't put out that kind of money for us."

"'Us'?"

"Persons of color, Vy. Man thought he'd bought him a nice bride. Already paid for her once. Then—"

"What are you talking about? Erin didn't 'buy' me!"

"What do you think the repairs on the church were, little girl? The price he paid for getting you. Your daddy knew people in the congregation wouldn't be in favor of you marrying a white man. Especially not in our church. So guess what? The church catches fire. And who comes in to fix it all? Mr. Rich Man with all the money. Suddenly all the people supposed to bow down and be grateful to him? Let him marry one of our own? We got more pride than that, I tell you."

Vy drew in a deep breath and let it out very, very slowly. "Aunt Ruth, I love you. You are my Aunt. My Great Aunt. I respect you. I always will. But you are wrong. Erin is an honorable man. A godly man. He offered to help where he could, finding us a place to meet and getting transportation for those that needed it. He wanted to do it anonymously, but Brother Tim wouldn't let him. And Erin did everything he could to protect me and keep me safe while I was held by the kidnappers."

Her anger knew no limits. "If the Farrells and Erin had only been interested in the baby, they would have told the kidnappers they chose the baby. It's what the kidnappers wanted in the beginning: for Erin to choose between us. And he refused. He did exactly what I would have done. Don't tell me what kind of man Erin is."

She stopped to take a breath. Ruth went back on the attack. "It sounds all nice and pretty telling it that way. But none of this would have happened if it wasn't for the kidnappers wanting to get at him, right? His whole family is trouble. You have no business being involved with someone who brings on that kind of heartache. You'd do much better marrying someone else. And I think you know it too. Otherwise, why did you postpone? You're seeing it for what it is, aren't you?"

Vy swallowed her ire. "Aunt Ruth, I love Erin Winger. I'm going to marry Erin Winger. I postponed so I could recover from the kidnapping, get my head back where it needs to be, and return to work. Now I've done all that, he and I will be setting a date in the fall. Thank you for your concern about my welfare. Goodbye."

Vy threw the phone on the bed and stared at it. What just happened? *I knew Aunt Ruth had strong opinions but never like that.*

She thought about what she had said. And what she hadn't. *Wendell didn't enter the conversation, did he? Why?*

Because this is about Erin, not Wendell. Erin suffered and served right along with me. Wendell died for his choices. Erin has to live with his. Whose is the greater sacrifice?

Vy picked up her phone. She speed dialed. Erin answered. "Hello, Vy." His voice sounded so uncertain. *Lord, forgive me for what I put this man through.*

"Erin, would you put on a pot of coffee? I'll be over in half an hour. If that's okay with the household?"

"The house won't mind." He paused. "It will be good to see you, Vy."

"I'm looking forward to seeing you, my love. Be there in thirty."

Vy changed into something baby proof, grabbed her bag, and went in search of her mother. She found her in the kitchen. Vy caught her in a hard hug. "I love you, Mama. Thank you."

"What'd I do now?"

"Gave me back the man I love. I'm going over to the Farrell's. Don't wait on me for dinner."

"Hadn't planned on it, girl." Her mother smiled ear-to-ear. "Hug him for us, too."

"Right after I hug him for myself."

Vy marched out the door.

* * *

Erin stared at his phone. Collin walked past him, stopped, backed up. "Why are you staring at your phone?" She had a basket of laundry in her hands.

Erin looked up. "She called me 'my love.' She hasn't called me 'my love' since she left the hospital."

Collin grinned her Cheshire smile. "Oh, really now?"

"Yeah. She's coming over. She'll be here in half an hour."

"Go put on some clean clothes, slacker. Comb your hair. Brush your teeth. Pretend you have something to live for."

Erin sneered at his sister. But she had a point. He had been letting things slide since… Since Vy had said those fearful words, "I need time."

Nothing good ever comes after those words. Except she called me her love. Those words mean something. Maybe? Maybe she still loves me? Maybe? God?

He walked slowly to his bedroom. Using the dual-arm crutches still proved awkward, but it got him up and moving. *And falling, but hey. It's progress. The triplets and I may learn to walk at the same time.*

He performed some self-maintenance, changed clothes, made himself presentable, and tottered back to the kitchen. He made the pot of coffee Vy wanted, leaned against the wall to wait for her to arrive. Easier to stand and lean than sit and have to stand again. Much less time-consuming.

Coffee dripped. Minutes ticked. The coffee pot sent out one final poof of hot air and finished. The clock ticked. Twenty minutes.

Twenty-five.

Twenty-seven.

Jeff walked in from the garage. "Vy just pulled up. Are you expectin…" He examined Erin's appearance. "I guess you are. I'll disappear."

"No. Hang around. In case we need a chaperone." *She called me her love. Lord, please. Please. I know You know. Please.*

He breathed slow. In. Out. In. Out. Calm. He would be calm. He positioned the arm crutches so he could stand without leaning. *The condemned man will meet his fate standing. Or something like that.*

The door opened. Vy came in. She saw Jeff first and nodded to him. "Mr. Farrell, good to see you."

"Ms. Johnson, good to see you as well. You're looking fine this evening."

Vy turned to Erin. Her eyes watered. Erin watched her swallow, lift her head. "Good evening, Mr. Winger. You're on your feet."

He smiled. Tentative. Waiting. "I'm in rehab again. I think they can't do without me."

Vy stepped close, stood in front of him. "I can't do without you, either." She wrapped her arms around him. Erin leaned into her, wrapped both arms and crutches around her. She kissed him. A long, proper, "I love you" kiss. Erin poured all of his soul into the return.

They broke, stood, kissed again. Broke and simply held one

another. Erin went in for another kiss. Jeff interrupted. "Okay, enough, children. We have rules, you know."

Vy laughed. She stepped back from Erin. Erin blew a raspberry at Jeff. "You know how to spoil a moment, don't you? We weren't done talking."

"Yes, you were. Go sit. I'll bring the coffee."

Vy hooked her arm inside Erin's, and they moved to the family room. Vy plopped down on the couch, kicked off her shoes, and curled her feet under her. "Throw me a baby."

Collin grinned. "One baby coming right up." She handed Caleb to her. "Take the chunk."

Vy groaned, lifting the boy. "Chunk is right! What are you feeding him the other two aren't getting?"

"Nothing."

Erin laughed. "I'm convinced she can't tell the boys apart and keeps feeding Caleb twice."

Vy smiled. "That would do it." She put the boy on her shoulder, turned, and faced Erin. "It's always easier to talk to you when I'm holding a baby. Why?"

"They add a certain levity to the proceedings, I think. Keeps it from getting heavy. Except for Caleb. He adds weight to every conversation."

Her eyes sparkled. "It's a good thing I'm holding him. Erin, I want to apologize."

"No. You don't owe me or anyone else an—"

"Let me finish. I do. I think I do, anyhow." Erin let her put her thoughts in order. "Yes, I was under stress and stressed out. The kidnapping threw me. I accept I needed to get my head together. But I didn't need to take it out on you. I realized it wasn't you I needed to step away from. It was myself. When I did, when I seriously looked at what I was thinking and doing, I saw myself." She lowered her eyes. "I didn't like what I saw." She lifted her glance and held his eyes. "I don't blame you if you don't like me either."

Erin leaned in and kissed Vy gently. "I love you, Vy Johnson."

Caleb joined the conversation by grabbing Erin's ear and pulling on his head. Erin pulled back. "Listen, boy, you find your own woman. This one is spoken for."

Vy met his gaze. "Do you still want me?"

He smiled. Little smile. "I never stopped." He caught hold of

Caleb's arm, moved it out of harm's reach, and kissed Vy again.

Collin coughed. "Um…is this how the rest of the night is going to go?"

Vy laughed. Jeff handed her a cup of coffee, took Caleb from her. "Safer. He's grabbing everything now."

Erin accepted a cup as well. He sneered at his sister. "No, it's not. I promise."

Erin sat back on the couch and sipped the hot brew. He waited until Vy had downed some of hers. "I have something I need your opinion on."

"Oh?" Vy looked at him, curiosity in her glance.

"No one has claimed Wendell's body or his mother." Erin semi-shrugged. "I don't think the police really expected someone to come forward, but still, they have to wait and give next of kin the chance."

"Right. I understand."

Erin picked up her hand. "Whatever and whoever else they were, in the end, they saved you and Talitha. And Wendell accepted Christ. That makes him our brother in the Lord. I'm forever grateful to him for what he did. I want to pay to have him interred. Both of them, actually. If you have no objections. They did hold you captive." Erin held her eyes. "It's up to you."

Vy started to speak, stopped. She looked down, back at Erin. "I think that would be a good thing to do. Talitha should understand someone cared for her."

Erin turned to Collin and Jeff. "Any objections? Seriously, any objections?"

Jeff and Collin exchanged glances. Collin nodded. Jeff gave the opinion. "No objections. We'll help."

Erin breathed out. One down, one to go. He turned back to Vy. "Get your calendar." Vy didn't ask why but pulled out her phone and swiped up. Erin pointed to Collin and Jeff. "You two as well. Let's get this all straight."

He waited until everyone had arrived on the same page, so to speak. "Vy, what month? Least plans or conflicts."

She studied her schedule. "August."

Erin pointed to Collin. "You?"

"I take care of babies all day. What conflict do I have? Especially on weekends. August is good."

"Jeff?"

"Nothing that can't be moved."

"Like what? I don't want anything jumping up at the last minute."

"No, bro. August is good."

Erin looked back at Vy. "Tenth?"

She looked. "Better the week after. Seventeenth."

"Done. We get married the seventeenth of August." He stopped. "Um…call your folks. Make sure the day is good with them."

Vy leaned in and kissed him on the cheek. "You always think about others, don't you?"

"I don't want to get on your dad's bad side. Or your mom's. Call them."

Vy made the call, and they confirmed the date. Erin grinned at her. "My job is done. The groom's job is to show up when he's told. We already know the wedding will be at Calvary Church, so you tell me when to be there, and I will. Everything else, you get to decide."

Collin protested. "That's not fair! It's supposed to be your wedding…you as a couple."

"Tell that to all the bridezillas I've known. 'It's my day…it's all about me.' Not that you would ever be that way, I know, my love. But I'll allow you to have it so if you want."

Vy crinkled her nose. "I'll pass. We can make this a joint effort. A simple affair is fine. Family. Close friends."

Jeff held up a hand. "Don't forget all the relatives who will be forever offended if they don't get an invitation."

Vy's eyes burned. "Let them be offended. Some of them will be, no matter what. Let them work it out."

Erin eyes widened. "Um…are we talking about someone in particular?"

"Not naming names, but yes. And I'll deal with it."

Erin nodded once. "Ooookay, then." He thought, nodded again. "Yeah, there will be a few of those. But they don't get to have the final say about our relationship or happiness."

Vy swallowed more of her coffee. "Midday or evening?"

"Midday."

Collin suggested, "Naps are at one. Three-thirty would be great."

Vy laughed. "If you think they'll still be napping, okay."

"I meant my nap." Collin's eyes twinkled.

Vy laughed. "I think it would be darling if the three of them were the ring bearers and the flower girl. They could all ride in a wagon together."

Erin shook his head. "I have the feeling in eight months, the only thing Talitha will throw out of the wagon will be her brothers."

"You don't want them in the wedding?"

"Never said that. I want them, and I think riding in a wagon will be adorable. As long as it has high sides with air holes."

Vy laughed. "Oh, let 'em loose. It will keep the ceremony from getting boring."

Jeff scowled. "Are you using my children for half-time entertainment?"

"More like the warm-up."

"They will expect to be paid, and handsomely, I'm sure." Jeff steepled his fingers together and rolled them back and forth.

Vy cocked her head. "And what is the going rate for three children, sir?"

Jeff looked at the ceiling. "Half a day of babysitting. Each."

Erin jumped in the game. "Preposterous! Four hours, maximum."

Jeff placed his hand on his heart. "Sir, you wound me. Four hours for these magnificent specimens of humanity? This display of cuteness?" He waved a hand at his children. "I think not. Half a day, and you are fortunate I am willing to discount their services to such a paltry sum."

Vy looked over Erin's head to Collin. "Can I take the babies and leave these two?"

Collin grinned. "Oh, no. This is a package deal. You want the babies, you gotta take the comedians, too."

Vy shrugged. "Okay, I'll take the one on the couch. You can have the tall one."

Collin's eyes sparkled. "Deal." Collin leaned over and kissed Jeff.

Erin stared at Vy. "Madam, you—"

Anything else he wanted to say disappeared in a full, proper kiss.

AUGUST 17ᵀᴴ

Erin paced in the choir room, waiting for his cue to come out. Jeff perched on top of the first pew, his feet on the seat, staying out of Erin's path. Every two minutes, Erin would ask, "Is it time yet?"

To which the answer would be, "Not yet, bud."

Erin dropped his head back on his shoulders. "Arrgghh! This is killing me!"

Jeff laughed. "Relax, dude. You won't remember any of this in about an hour. Drags in the beginning, then flies by. Do some deep breathing."

Erin took Jeff's advice, stopped circling the room, drew in several long deep breaths (letting them out in between,) and finally dropped his shoulders. "Thanks."

"Better?"

"Yeah. Except now I want to run out on the whole affair." He motioned to his arm crutches. "Totter out on the whole affair."

Jeff smiled. "Sounds about right. I had the same thoughts. Funny thing, when I told Collin, she admitted she had the same idea. At about the same time."

Erin chuckled. "Must be why they make us wait in separate rooms. Don't want us collaborating and taking off."

Patrick stuck his head in the door. "Pastor says five more minutes. And Erin, you've got a friend wanting to see you for a moment. Briefly, they promise."

Erin rolled his eyes. "Sure. Why not? I haven't got anything important going on right now."

Jeff put a firm hand on his shoulder. "You want me to talk to whoever it is?"

Erin shook his head. "No. I'll do it." He motioned to Patrick. "Lead on."

Patrick led Erin out into the foyer. Erin glanced at the door and saw Felicity waiting, a dangerous look in her eyes. Erin bumped Patrick's arm. He lowered his voice so Felicity wouldn't hear. "Do me a favor. Get Pastor Tim to come up here. In case there's trouble."

Patrick's eyes widened. "Bro, I'm sorry. I didn't realize—"

"It's fine. Just get Pastor Tim, please."

Patrick disappeared into the sanctuary. Erin approached Felicity. "Hello."

"Mom. You're supposed to call me Mom, remember?"

Erin breathed carefully. "In our last conversation, you threatened me and my family."

Felicity shrugged. "Water under the bridge. Are you really going to hold a grudge? I thought you Christians were all about forgiveness."

Erin put a stranglehold on all he wanted to say. Instead, he asked. "What do you want?" The black pantsuit she wore spoke more of funeral than it did wedding. She'd colored her hair a strawberry tone since last he saw her. What the overabundance of gold jewelry meant, he had no clue.

Felicity tossed her head. "My invitation must have been lost in the mail. I want to see my son get married. Why should that surprise you?"

"Because you wanted nothing to do with my family. I had no reason to believe you changed your mind." *Do not say it. Do not say it. Doesn't matter what* it *is. Don't say it.*

She waved her hand. "If this is the only way I can see my sons, I'll endure the inconvenience."

Lord, help me. Help me.

Brother Tim walked into the foyer, and the temperature around Felicity dropped ten degrees. His very presence filled half the space. He clapped a beefy hand on Erin's shoulder. "You aren't running away, are you, Brother Erin?"

"Never. I've waited too long for this day. Brother Tim, this is Felicity Bennett."

Tim extended his hand. "Ms. Bennett. A pleasure to meet you at last. We have been praying for you for many months."

Every emotion except love, joy, peace, patience, gentleness, goodness, kindness, and self-control passed across Felicity's face. She ignored Tim's hand. "You've wasted your breath. I came to see my sons. I don't need your prayers."

Tim continued smiling. "I must insist you wait until the ceremony is over to speak to them. They are busy assisting Erin's wedding guests at present. If you would like to wait in my office until then, I'll be happy to escort you."

Felicity's eyes narrowed. A cobra, about to strike. "Are you saying I can't go in and see my boys?"

Tim never lost his smile. "Yes, I am."

The woman's face turned shades of red Erin had never seen in a crayon box. "You can't—"

"I assure you, ma'am, I can. Erin has guests from the FBI, the DEA, and the City Police force. I'm sure they would be happy to explain why we can forbid you from entering this building and disrupting the proceedings. Who would you like to speak to first?"

Daggers didn't describe the glare Felicity threw Tim and Erin. Samurai swords, maybe. Spears. Scimitars. Whatever. She turned and walked out of the building.

Tim keyed his earpiece. "I need Geoff and Lyman to keep an eye on the doors for me. Right away."

Erin breathed out. "Thank you."

Two burly, mahogany-skinned, buff gentlemen stepped into the foyer. Geoff lowered his bass voice even lower. "You rang?"

"Reddish-blonde. Fifty-something. Black pantsuit. Gold chain with a cross, Star of David, Crescent, and Pentagram."

Lyman chuckled. "No rabbit's foot?"

Tim chuckled but shook his head. "She's probably on the phone with her lawyer seeing if we can keep her out. Please make sure she doesn't gain access to the building."

Geoff smiled. "Can I rebuke the demon?"

Erin laughed. Probably louder than appropriate, but it felt good. "That I'd love to see. Go for it!" He grinned at Brother Tim. "Let's do this."

Tim chuckled. "About time. Your bride is waiting for you to get in place."

Erin worked his way back down the hall, canes and feet moving in one accord. He slipped into the office, motioned to Jeff. "Let's go."

Jeff raised his eyebrows as they crossed the hallway to the sanctuary. "Friend?"

"Felicity."

"Figures. I'm sorry."

"So will she be if she tries to get in here." Erin tugged at his jacket, pulled his sleeves down, adjusted his arms in the arm crutches, and walked into the packed room. He noted the sea of color in the room. Not the fabrics, the attendees. People of every tongue, tribe, and nation. As it should be.

Aunt Ruth sat beside Ren Farrell (Jeff's oldest brother) and his wife. Erin saw the two women were engaged in happy and animated conversation. *Thank You, Lord.*

The piano broke into the preparatory chords meaning the bride was ready. People stood. The wagon with the triplets came down the aisle, pulled by Rob, Collin's adopted (adult) son. True to form, Jacob tried to climb out, Caleb pulled him back in and sat on him, and Talitha waved at everyone she saw. No rose petals left the wagon. Par for the course.

Erin handed his canes to Jeff. George and Vy stepped into the doorway.

Time froze. Erin's existence scattered, shifted, became laser-focused. His life—his present, his future, his forever—walked down the aisle to join hands with him. "Until death takes one of us, or Jesus takes both of us."

In the Name of the Father, the Son, and the Holy Spirit. Amen and amen.

If you enjoyed *Despair* sign up for Colleen Snyder's Newsletter to stay up with new books and new projects. It will also give you a place to talk to the author directly!

Emails will NOT be sold, shared, or used for any other purpose. Promise!

Go to: colleensnyderauthor.com and leave your email to sign up.

Did you miss the first book in the Collin Walker series?

Verdict at the River's Edge

What terrifies you?

In the dark recess of your soul, what is it that you've managed to avoid, to hide, to bury deep, never to be faced? And what if the Lord asked you to face that fear for no other reason than, "Because I'm asking?" What would you do?

Welcome to Collin Walker's world.

Collin Walker, a social worker from the inner city of Oakton, Ohio comes to Camp Grace for what is billed as "an extreme sports camp." Her single purpose: to show her ward, Rob Sider, that there is more to life than the streets "…show you can be strong and still love, win without cheating, and succeed in life without all the bells and whistles…" Collin has no way of knowing that God has other plans for her week: facing a lifelong terror of rushing rivers, and perhaps her greatest fear of all, the possibility of real love.

Available now on Amazon: *Verdict at the River's Edge*

Also available, Book two in the Collin Walker Series:

Inheritance

Three hundred MILLION dollars. Your inheritance. Buy anything you want, go anywhere you want, do anything you want. All yours. Except…

You're a social worker. How do you maintain "street cred" with the kids you've devoted your life to?

How will that kind of money affect the man you love?

And then there's your birth family. The ones that abandoned you to die at fourteen. The ones you suspect even now are trying to have you killed over the money. How do you share with them? Or do you?

What would Jesus do? What would He want you to do? Would you do it?

Welcome back to Collin Walker's world

Collin's life has been both turned upside down and inside out. With her grandfather's passing, Collin has been forced into a position she never wanted. Her inheritance of millions comes with baggage. Her father and his brothers have been fighting for it since before she was born. It is the very heart of the reason she's been estranged from her family the past twelve years.

But now, with the will coming into effect, Collin must revisit all the old relationships and all the old traumas. She thought she had made peace with her past through the Lord. But when the past becomes the present, will she still forgive? Even if it's her family that wants her dead? Join her and find out.

Inheritance

Also available: Book Three in the Collin Walker/Farrell Series

Accusations

When was the last time you lied?
Do you lie to keep a secret?
Or do you keep a secret to hide a lie?
Collin Farrell has a secret, and she can't wait to tell her husband.
Jeff Farrell has a secret, too, one he's been hiding from Collin since before they married.
Collin's brother, Erin, has a girlfriend with a secret she won't tell.
Vy Johnson is a DEA agent who knows all about lies and secrets.
What happens when Secrets and Lies collide?
Cars get crushed (with the drivers inside.)
Homes explode.
Marriages implode.
Careers—and lives—are jeopardized.
Can God work even this together for the good of all involved and still get the glory from it?

Accusations

And coming in the spring, the fifth book in the series:

Collin Farrell carried the basket of clothes from the laundry room to the kitchen. "Third load of laundry today. Three loads. That's one per child. And they don't change clothes but once a day." An old joke swirled in her mind. Okay, Caleb changes with Joshua, Joshua changes with Talitha, and Talitha changes with Caleb. Yeah, no.

The hallway minefield challenged her. Step left around the multi-colored popcorn-popper-sweeper. Two steps forward. Right around the two-foot-long plastic firetruck ("with authentic siren sounds"—if you put in the batteries—which they didn't.) Another step right to clear the swirly-yellow-colored ball. Three steps forward. Almost there. Almost there…

The finish line came in view. Only one more obstacle…high step over the cardboard building blocks…

Made it! Collin set the basket and its load of "sort and fold" articles on the table. She took a breath…

A scream of anger, frustration, pain, and fear, amplified through the baby monitor, echoed from the playroom. Another equally amplified scream of, "Mama!" followed. Collin dropped her head, closed her eyes, and muttered, "I'm coming. I'm coming." She checked her watch. Ten minutes. A new record.

Collin walked to the scene of the murder, judging by the sound of the caterwauling. As she suspected, not-yet-three-year-old Joshua lay on his back on the floor. He kicked his feet, flailed his arms, and generally expressed his dissatisfaction with the world.

Joshua's brother, not-yet-three-year-old Caleb, stood behind a rocking chair, grasping the spindles and repeating, "Joshua fawd down."

Their not-yet-three-year-old sister, Talitha, sat on the floor beside her brother. She ducked his wayward limbs, patted his chest, and repeated, "You 'kay, bubby? You 'kay?"

Collin picked up her hyperventilating son, hugged him to her shoulder, and rocked back and forth. She held his head and soothed, "You're fine, buddy." She felt the back of his skull for lumps. Not possible. This carpet has Olympic-grade padding under it. Safest room in the house.

She waited until he stopped crying, held him back to look him in the eyes. "What happened, Joshua?"

"I cwimb a mountain. Mountain move. I faw down."

Collin closed one eye and stared at Caleb. "Did you make the mountain move?"

Caleb shook his head very emphatically. "No, Mommy."

Collin gazed at Joshua. "How did the mountain move?"

"I step foot on a mountain. I say, 'Cayeb, hol han Cayeb hol han. I step udder foot on a mountain. Mountain move. I faw down."

"Uh-huh." Collin kept from smiling. Her fearless pack leader. "Joshua, I love that you want to climb mountains. But this chair is not a mountain. It's a chair. It is for sitting in, not climbing on. Right?"

Joshua hung his head. "Yes, Mommy."

Talitha's sweetness poured into the conversation. "Bubby be 'kay, Mommy? He 'kay?"

Now Collin smiled. "Yes, Talitha. Joshua is okay." She set the still-a-toddler down, brushed his strawberry blond curls back. "No more climbing, Joshua." She looked at Caleb, her linebacker. "Thank you for calling me to tell me Joshua had fallen." *Thank you that you weren't the one who shook the chair. I'm not ready for fratricide yet.* She pointed to the beanbag chair in the corner. "Talitha, would you read your brothers a story while Mommy finishes folding the laundry?"

Talitha's eyes ignited a million-candle-watt light. "Yes, Mommy!" She ran to the book pile, pulled out the only book she could "read," and ran back to the child's school chair. She sat in front of her brothers, who got comfortable laying back in the beanbag. Talitha opened the first page. "Sam. I am Sam."

Collin smiled, turned up the volume on the monitor, and went back to the kitchen. Of course, Talitha couldn't read the book. But she'd memorized enough of the story that with the pictures, she could entertain her brothers. Enough for one or two read-throughs, anyhow.

Jeff sat at the coffee bar, reading a piece of paper, a puzzled look on his face. Collin kissed her husband as she passed him. It amused her to see him still in suit and tie. He'd had 'business' that morning and had an image to protect. Being home before four in the afternoon didn't serve that image. "What are you doing here?"

"Hiding so I can get some work done." He held up the page. "What is this? Ice breaker for tonight? Kind of macabre, isn't it?"

Collin narrowed her eyes. "What are you talking about?"

"This." He waved the paper at her. "I found it on top of the laundry basket."

Collin held her hand out. "Give me that." She cast him a sideways glance, pursed her lips, looked at the letter.

You have a killer in your Thursday Night Study group. Confession must be made. Post the guilty person's name on the One Way Builder Facebook page tomorrow. Judgment waits.

Collin's eyes widened. She stared at Jeff. "What? Where did this come from?"

"This isn't yours?"

"No! I'd never joke about something like that. Where'd you find it?"

"On top the laundry. That's why I thought…"

"There was nothing on the laundry when I brought it up here."

"Well, that's where I found it."

Collin went catatonic. A voice screamed in her head. *NO! Talitha! No! Not my baby! She's gone! No!* Collin's eyes widened but saw nothing. Nothing of the here and now. An empty baby bed. A hole in her heart. Emptiness. Despair.

An animal scream tore from her innermost being. "No!" Terror poured adrenalin to her limbs. She raced to the playroom. Unseeing, she caught all three of her children to her chest. She collapsed to the floor, hugging the triplets tight. Tighter. Tighter. *No one will ever take them away from me again. No one.*

The babies were crying. She could hear them. "Mommy!" "Mommy! Stop, Mommy!" "Mommy, u hur-ted me. Stop!"

Someone is hurting my babies! I have to hold them! I can't let them go…I have to hold them tighter…

"Mommy!" "Mommy!"

Jeff's voice. Strong. Calm. "Collin. Lady, it's okay. It's okay. No one is trying to get the babies. Collin. Hear me."

His hands, massaging her arms. "Come back, Collin. Listen to me."

The babies were still crying. *Why are they crying? Jeff is right here. Why are they crying?*

"Let go of the babies, Collin. Let your arms relax. Just a little."

Stronger massaging. "Let go, Collin. Let go. I've got them. I've got the babies."

Collin obeyed. Jeff would never let anyone hurt the babies. If he said let go, she could let go.

Her arms emptied. Her sight returned. Jeff sat in front of her, all three children in his arms. All still snuffling. All heads buried in his chest and shoulders. None of them looking at her.

Jeff caught Collin's eyes, held them. "Are you with me, lady? Are you here?"

Collin leaned back. Awareness seeped over the edges, then slammed into her consciousness. She'd been the one scaring the babies. She'd hurt them.

Collin lifted her chin and closed her eyes. Tears cascaded down her cheeks, poured off her chin, puddled on her shirt. "I'm sorry. Oh, Lord, forgive me. I'm sorry. I'm so sorry."

She didn't try to touch any of the triplets. She waited until she mastered her own tears, wiped her face with her shirt. She bit her lip, nodded to Jeff.

Jeff didn't release the toddlers but turned them to face her while still maintaining his protective hold. Collin read the fear in their eyes, and it sliced to the core of her being. She kept her voice soft and even. "Babies, Mommy is very, very sorry she scared you and hurt you. Mommy went to a bad, dark place."

Collin had to swallow hard. "I never want to hurt you, and I'm sorry I did. I love each of you. Caleb and Joshua, and Talitha. Mommy is very, very sorry. She would like you to forgive her, but she understands if you can't right now." Her soul shattered, the pieces remaining linked by a whisper. "I love you."

Jeff did not pressure the toddlers. He sat and held them. Collin sat in front of them. Jeff looked at Caleb. "Do you think you can forgive Mommy?" Caleb held Collin's eyes. He nodded very slowly. "Will you give Mommy a hug?"

Collin assured him, "I won't hug you unless you want me to. I'll put my hands behind my back." She did, sitting on her hands. *Lord, this is killing me. My babies. I hurt my babies.*

Caleb stepped away from his father's protection, crossed over, and hugged Collin. She whispered, "I love you, buddy."

He kissed her on the cheek. "I wub you, Mommy."

Her soul would make one attempt. If it failed, she would shatter irreparably. "May I hug you? I won't squeeze you. I'll only put my arms out this wide."

She showed him the size of a circle larger than he was around. Caleb eyed her arms then nodded. Collin kept her arms the specified circumference. Caleb walked inside her arms, turned around, closed them himself, and sat in her lap. He reached up, looped his arms around her neck, and smiled. "I wub you, Mommy."

"I love you, Caleb. I love you so much, buddy."

Joshua came over to join his brother. He wiggled his bottom next to Caleb until he could sit in Collin's lap, too. He reached up, kissed her as Caleb had, and smiled. "I wub you, Mommy."

"I love you, Joshua. I'm sorry I held you so tight."

"It 'kay. I o-kay."

Collin looked at Talitha. The little girl's eyes were deep and round and solemn. She did not move from her father's sheltering arms. She looked down, then back at Collin. "Mommy go bad place?"

"Mommy went to a bad place in my head. I'm sorry."

"Why, Mommy?"

"Mommy remembered when"—*careful...very, very careful*—"when someone took...a baby from me. My mind played a trick on me and made me remember and be afraid."

Talitha's eyes deepened. "Some took you baby?"

"Uh-huh. It made me very sad and very scared."

Caleb cocked his head. "You have 'nuther baby?"

"I had a very, very tiny baby. Much littler than you are. Teeny tiny baby."

Jeff watched her eyes. She knew his thought. *Almost six years of marriage. We should know some of what each other is thinking.* Collin kept her voice quiet. "The people who took the baby brought her back. She's very safe and very loved."

Talitha stood up, crossed over to Collin, and kissed her cheek. She did not sit in her mother's lap, however. She stood beside Collin. Collin bit her lip. "May I put my arm around you?"

Talitha stood for a heartache of moments, then nodded. "Yes, Mommy."

Tears fountained down Collin's cheeks, baptizing the triplets in her tears. "I love you. I love all of you."

Jeff stood and joined the group hug. Collin lay her head on his shoulder and whispered, "I am so sorry. I am. I'll call Dr. Sujit in the morning. And talk with the group tonight. I'm so sorry."

"It's going to be okay, Collin. We're here, we're together, and we'll make it through."

Also by Colleen Snyder:
Finding Freedom a novella.

FINDING FREEDOM

The stakes couldn't be higher.

Thirty-six years of marriage. Two children. Two granddaughters, the lights of her life.

Her home. Her friends. Her church. Her God?

Will she throw it all away for freedom? Freedom from abuse? From neglect? Subjection?

And what if he comes after her?

For Sheridan (Dash) Warren, the options have never been more clear. Stay, keep the status quo and watch her life descend further and further into the soul-stealing denial of all that is Dash Warren, all that is life and light and joy and peace…

Or abandon it all in a desperate flight to save what little of her true self she has left. If God is for her, who can be against her? But is God for her? Is He leading her out, or is it her own voice she's listening to?

And what will her husband, Roy, do if she does run? He's been violent before. Will he come after her? What if he catches her? What will her future look like? Will she even have a future?

Dash must make the decision of her life. Can she make the right one?

Finding Freedom available in paperback and Kindle

ABOUT THE AUTHOR

Colleen K. Snyder has always had a passion for writing. She authored two previously published books: *Journey to Amanah: The Beginning* and *Return to Tebel-Ayr: The Journey Continues* (B&H Publishing). She lives on a "ranchette" in California and is the juniorest ranch hand. She serves on her church prayer team, writes the weekly prayer letter, and exercises a ministry of intercessory prayer. She has worked as a factory line worker, pharmacy technician, USAF missile systems analyst, janitor, nanny, teacher, accounting manager and anything else the Lord required. Her son, Bear, and his wife Krystal, their two daughters, Mara and Kaylynn, and her daughter, Katie, all live in Ohio.

Colleen's story is for His glory, always.

Connect with her on Facebook at Colleen K. Snyder, Author and on her website colleensnyderauthor.com